Bog Warriors

Bog Warriors

JOHN GALVIN

TOWN HOUSE, DUBLIN

First published in paperback in 2000
by
Town House and Country House Ltd
Trinity House, Charleston Rd
Ranelagh, Dublin 6

ISBN 1-86059-113-2

Typeset by Tower Books, Ballincollig, Co. Cork

Printed and bound in Great Britain by
Cox & Wyman Ltd, Reading, Berks.

Cover Design by Jason Ellams
Cover Photo: Tony Stone Images

To

Deirdre, Dave, Chris & Anna

CHAPTER ONE

Jim Quilter dragged himself to the edge of the bed and sat there, rubbing his face vigorously. He groaned and stretched his hands above his head, squinting at the rusting alarm clock on the bedroom dresser.

Eleven-thirty.

Then it dawned on him. It was Thursday. Suddenly he jumped to his feet, and in a matter of minutes he was washed, dressed and seated at his kitchen table, a Gold Flake cigarette smoking gently in one hand, a mug of strong unsweetened tea in the other.

Dole day had that effect on Jim.

Forty-eight years of age and living alone, he had

few pleasures in life. After a few years of hard work on the buildings in England, he had returned home to help his ageing father with their small farm. The money he had sweated for was gone in a matter of months.

When the old man died, he had left Jim with the thirty or so acres, land which seemed to consist more of rock than of earth. He had soon grown tired of the work that had sent his father to an early grave, and so little by little, he had sold off the farm until he was down to the last acre, on which stood his run-down cottage.

'Anyone who works for a living is only an eejit!' he would shout loudly in Conroy's bar after an evening of heavy drinking.

He would continue to voice his opinion until Big Madge behind the counter would grow tired of him, warning him to hold his tongue unless he wanted 'his arse put through the door'.

Now, he threw the cigarette butt on the stone floor, stamped heavily on it with his boot and gulped down the last mouthful of tea. Then he followed his regular Thursday-morning ritual: standing in front of the small, cracked mirror which hung beside the door, hunching his back to look into it, he licked his hand and pressed down on his mop of wild red hair. But no matter how hard he tried, it would always spring back up to its original position.

'Ah . . . shite on you,' he cursed, and he took his dirty tweed coat off the nail which he had driven into the side of the kitchen dresser. He examined it before putting it on. He had bought it at the local fair while under the influence, and it was an uncomfortable garment. Though it fitted him perfectly across the shoulders, the sleeves were about two inches too short, and the front appeared to be much longer than the back. His friend, Myles Hickey, who had been with him when he had bought it, joked that it must have belonged to a circus strong man with short arms and a humped back.

Giving his appearance one final check in the mirror and again cursing loudly, he stepped outside and slammed the door behind him. Then in a panic he thumped at his pockets for the key. He sighed with relief as he located it. Glancing at his watch he calculated how long it would take him to reach the village, collect his dole and be seated on one of the high stools in Conroy's. But then, there was no point in rushing things. He looked up with one eye to the sun, whose heat was just starting to get the better of the cool of the morning. He wondered if the tweed coat would be necessary on such a fine day, but he remembered an evening when he had walked home in his shirtsleeves from Conroy's, right into the teeth of a west wind, so he stuck with the coat.

He ambled along the boreen at a casual pace, until he reached the main road, but then he straightened his back and removed his hands from his pockets, swinging his arms in time with his stride. The reason for this sudden change of walking style was two-fold. First, Jim believed that a man should maintain his dignity no matter what his financial circumstances, but what was more important was that when he straightened his back, it helped to balance out the length of the tweed coat.

Deciding to take a short cut across the old iron footbridge, he turned off the main road and walked through a recently cut hay field, raising flies as he went. At the end of the field he came to a river, where he and Myles had often stroke-hauled salmon when funds were low. The local hotelier was only too glad to buy the fish at the ridiculously low price they demanded. The largest of the catch would be dressed and displayed on a large silver platter in the dining room of the hotel, injury side down of course.

He stopped for a while to look at the river. A pint delayed, he believed, tasted all the nicer. Resting his arms on the iron crossbar of the footbridge, Jim gazed at the water sparkling below him. Looking more closely, he spotted three salmon hovering on the riverbed.

Twenty yards away, in the middle of the river with waders to his hips, stood a local businessman, John Burns, a passionate fly-fisherman.

Jim called out, raising his arm in salute, 'Morning, Mr Burns.'

Burns turned his head, a look of anger on his face. He glared up at Jim, who had broken his concentration. He raised his index finger and pointed to the water in front of him.

Realising his mistake, Jim quickly covered his mouth, then, removing his hand, mouthed 'Sorry' to the man below. Burns resumed his fishing.

Jim lit a cigarette and flicked the match away as he spat the tobacco from his bottom lip. 'I hope a shark bites your leg off, ya ignorant bollocks,' he said in a low voice as he turned and walked away.

As he neared the village, he considered calling to his sister's house. She was, to be fair to her, always good for a feed. However, the advantage of getting a good meal was counteracted by the lecture he would receive from her, on the effect of alcohol on living brain cells. He would, as usual, end up swearing on the graves of their dead parents that he would make a serious effort to give up the drink. Afterwards, in the peace of Conroy's bar, he would privately pray that taking such an oath would have no real effect on the afterlife of the persons concerned. For if it had, then his father and mother must be huddled somewhere in hell holding an empty fire extinguisher.

He decided to postpone the visit to his sister until the weekend. She always had roast beef on Sunday and so the lecture would be worth while.

On his arrival at the post office, he found his friend and drinking partner, Myles Hickey, standing at the door, leafing through a few bank notes. Myles didn't notice Jim until he walked up and slapped him hard on the back.

'All for the black babies I suppose,' Jim laughed.

Myles grinned widely and shoved the notes into his pocket. 'I'll see ya below,' he said moving away.

It was their private joke. On a drinking binge one evening, they had been stopped and admonished by the local curate who had lectured them on the evils of drink, their absence from mass, and how they were a source of embarrassment to the village in general. Sobered up and dressed in their best, they had called to him the following day, apologised profusely for their behaviour, and promised that from that day on, they would donate at least fifty per cent of their dole money to the 'black babies'. The curate was so impressed that not alone did he give them his forgiveness, but also his blessing. They had celebrated their absolution in Conroy's, the call of the evening being for, 'Two black babies and two half ones.' This was met with two frothy pints of porter and two small whiskeys.

Jim collected his money in the post office, then stood outside the door to count it, as Myles had done. Peggy, the short-sighted post-mistress, had on occasion left them both short, and so they made it their business to count it themselves, but so as not to cause offence, the check was done outside.

'She'd never mistake a twenty for a ten though,' Myles had once commented.

On totalling the correct amount, he pocketed the money and walked the hundred yards to Conroy's. Myles was seated at the bar and had already got the order in.

'There you are, Mr Quilter,' he said, as he slapped the stool beside him. 'Sit down there and tell me your worst.'

Myles Hickey was the lovable drunk of the village. He was known to the local teenagers as 'Doc Holliday', because of his love of drink, gambling and his violent smoker's cough. Aside from this, his boyish good looks made him a favourite with the female American tourists who flocked to the village during the summer months. Many an evening he was to be seen sitting out in Conroy's beer-garden, running his hand thoughtfully through his jet-black hair, as he related stories of great deeds of bravery from his days in the FCA, stories which were met with screeches in loud American accents from the tanned beauties who gaped in admiration at him.

While all this was going on, Jim, who was fifteen years older, would sit in the coolness of the bar and look out at the goings-on. Big Madge would shake her head as she shuffled about inside the bar. 'Isn't he some bullshitter?' she would say.

It was Myles's love of drink and his weakness for tanned American thighs that had caused the break-up of his two-year marriage to Áine. This resulted in a severe beating from her two brothers, a beating that had left a four-inch scar across his forehead. Always the opportunist, Myles had used this wound to impress his open-mouthed fans, explaining in great detail how he had dived on a live hand grenade to save the life of his company commander while on secret manoeuvres in the Glen of Imaal. It was a story that was always good for a couple of pints.

'I saw John Burns down at the river,' said Jim, raising the glass to his lips, drawing almost half of it off in one gulp and wiping the white moustache with the back of his hand. 'He's a right ignorant bollocks, that fella.'

Myles threw his eyes upwards and sighed heavily. 'Oh Jesus, please don't tell me that story again.'

Jim gave a roguish smile. 'What story?' he asked.

'You know well what story. The one you tell when you drink gin. The big, long, sad and boring one about how John Burns codded your father out of twenty acres of ground that he got off him for the price of a few nights' drink and how he developed it after and made a fortune on it. That story. I'm telling you now if you start you can shag off and drink on your own.'

Jim laughed out loud and slapped Myles on the back. 'You're a fierce man, Hickey. I'll save the story for another day. I'll say one thing though. He might be an ignorant thief, but he's a dab hand at the fly-fishing.'

Myles shook his head in confusion. 'I could never understand that,' he said. 'Why would a fella stand for the whole day, up to his balls in water, just to catch one or two salmon when, as you know, all you need is a stone of lime, lash it in, and in a few minutes you'd have twenty of them.'

Jim threw back the rest of his pint. 'You're missing the point, my man,' he replied. 'Fly-fishing is an art. It takes a lot of skill and a good aim.'

Myles laughed and moved away towards the dartboard. 'So does pissing when you're drunk,' he smiled. 'C'mon Jim, don't go mad on me now.'

He placed the pint down carefully on the narrow ledge of the alcove and switched on the spotlight, took the three darts which were huddled together in the bullseye, and began to throw them expertly, the little finger of the casting hand pointed upwards.

'I'll play you for the rest of that farm of yours,' he joked, as he retrieved the darts from the board.

Jim rose slowly from the stool and moved towards him. 'Same again please, Madge,' he called out over his shoulder. 'And a little less froth this time.'

Big Madge Conroy sighed as she put down her glossy crossword puzzle magazine and moved to the beer taps. Thursday was, as she called it, her penance day. By four o'clock, Jim and Myles would be drunk and roaring for sandwiches so as to stave off the hunger until the chip-van would arrive. She prepared herself for an evening of drunken wit and crude jokes, most of which would be directed at her.

'Isn't she a fine lump of a woman all the same? 'Twould take a fair jockey to tame Madge.'

Roars of laughter would resound throughout the bar, all joining in except for Madge herself. She had heard it all before. She had barred Jim and Myles from the premises more times than she could remember. Yet, even though she silently cursed their arrival every Thursday, she had a hidden fondness for the two of them, a fondness tinged with sympathy.

Jim took the darts and prepared to throw. 'Five-oh-one so,' he said and landed the first one into the treble twenty.

Myles rubbed the chalk-dusted sponge across the blackboard. 'Fluke,' he smiled.

Jim rolled his shoulders as he prepared to throw the second dart. 'No fluke, lad. I think it's only fair to warn you that I feel very lucky today.'

What Jim didn't know was that misfortune was to catapult him into the public eye, and very soon.

CHAPTER TWO

John Burns sat on the verge of the riverbank, dangling his feet in the water. A recently landed salmon of considerable size flapped on the grass beside him, taking its final gasps of the warm air.

He had perfected the art of fly-fishing over many years, learning the hard way: many the nearly landed salmon had given its final whip on Burns's line before splashing away to freedom. But not any more. Now, whenever Burns hooked one, he would reel and release, reel and release, slowly breaking down the will of the fish, until finally he would haul it in triumph to the awaiting net. He would laugh at the 'amateurs', as he called them, men who would fish beside him at the weekends, with their rods bent almost in half, spitting through gritted teeth, 'Got ya now. Come in ya bastard.' Struggles like this would inevitably result in the line snapping, and the 'amateur' falling backwards into the water, then there would be more cursing as the drenched fisherman would make his way back to the bank, wringing the water from the sleeves of his recently purchased fishing jacket. Burns would simply nod and smile, never revealing any of his fishing secrets to his fellow-fisherman.

He liked to make his own flies, and preferred to do so in silence. In any case, most of the amateur fisherman appeared at weekends only, whereas Burns's wealth meant that he could indulge in his favourite sport any time he liked.

He held the vice between his knees and began to tie the shining black wire around the feathered hook. He looked sideways at the gleaming fish. It was lifeless now.

Then Burns's thoughts turned to his wife, Claire. His temper rose. How dare she threaten him after all he'd done for her! And that ageing tart, Jenny Maguire. She's the problem. She's the one giving all the advice. Telling Claire to go to the guards, tell them what's going on, show them the bruises. That bitch! It would be more in her line to mind her own business. Burns hammered the ground with his fist. To hell with the two of them. Let them go to the guards. John Burns would deal with the guards too.

He picked up the fly rod and prepared to cast. He gritted his teeth and waited for his anger to abate. What the hell was the big deal? It was only a few slaps.

Jack Hegarty sat in the tiny day-room of Dunsheerin Garda Station. The room was silent, except for Hegarty's hollow sucking on his empty pipe and the sound of turning newspaper pages as he leafed through the sports results.

A policeman for thirty-five years, he had served in stations on the border, in Dublin and in Galway, and had spent the past eight years in the peace of his native county. His wife and two teenage daughters had been reluctant at first to forfeit the fast pace of city life for the enforced tranquillity of Dunsheerin, but had settled in well, much to Jack's pleasure.

He liked being amongst his own people. Country people had, he believed, a respect for the gardaí that is lacking in cities. Dublin people, he found, would always speak their minds, whereas country people would weigh a situation up carefully before speaking, and would always choose the right approach – country cuteness. When Hegarty had first arrived in the village, a couple of cute locals had 'mistakenly' addressed him as 'sergeant' and, on being informed that he was merely a humble guard, retorted, 'Well a fine man like you *should* be a sergeant'. Hegarty always saw through it. 'Less of the handy chat and get that thing taxed,' he'd reply.

Much as he liked his relatively crime-free work in Dunsheerin, he would often miss the *craic* and camaraderie of the big city station. As a young man in Dublin, he had relished the challenge thrown down by the criminal, the running battles and the good-humoured banter afterwards in the bar on the quay. Although he had gained a reputation for being something of a 'hard man', he disliked violence of any sort, believing in the old police adage that only when the time for talking has passed does the time for timber arrive. He also believed that everyone was entitled to at least one chance, no matter what their circumstances, but never voiced his opinion, for fear of ruining his reputation with the gouger fraternity.

Taking the pipe from his mouth, he inspected the empty bowl. He had given up smoking it two years previously as a result of the constant complaining of his wife about the dangers of cancer and the browning of her curtains. How he longed to fill it up again and watch the tobacco sizzle to life as he took a long, satisfying pull! But no. The tar that he tasted from the bowl would have to do.

He looked up at the faded face of the electric clock that hung above the door. He had spent the best part of the last hour at the counter helping an old-age pensioner to fill out her passport application form. She was seventy-seven years of age, as deaf as a stone and had just won an all expenses paid trip to the Holy Land, compliments of the local GAA.

'What's your date of birth?' he had roared at her, so loudly that a passer-by had stopped and looked curiously through the window of the station.

'What, boy?' she had shouted back, inching her head closer to his.

'What's your . . .' he repeated even louder. 'Ah Jaysus.'

'I'm going to the Holy Land,' she screeched at him.

'I know, girl, but they won't let you on the plane without your passport.'

She stood back and looked curiously at him. 'What's the matter with you, boy?'

After a further ten minutes of roaring at each other, she reached into her woven shopping basket and took a faded piece of parchment paper from between the packet of tea and pound of butter.

'Will I need this?' she shouted, holding the tattered birth certificate aloft.

The blood ran from his head in relief. 'Yes,' he replied softly.

However, by the time he had explained about the two photographs and the fee required, he was fit for nothing.

A local farmer who had come to the station to get a tax form signed had turned away at the door when he heard all the commotion inside. 'Jack has a right one in the cell,' he told the others at the co-op.

'Fair dues to Jack,' said another. 'He'll take no shit.' All present nodded in agreement.

In the peaceful aftermath, Hegarty folded the newspaper, stood up and arched his back. It was nearly time for his meal-break. He wondered what his wife had on the menu that evening. He hoped that it wasn't a salad. She had put him on a strict diet of lettuce and thinly sliced corned-beef in an effort to reduce his weight. He was seventeen stone. What he wouldn't give for a greasy fry-up and a long after-tea smoke! The creaking of the small iron gate and the sound of stiletto heels interrupted his mouth-watering thoughts. Claire Burns and Jenny Maguire appeared in the doorway.

'We're so sorry to trouble you, Jack,' said Claire. 'B–but could you spare us a few minutes?' Tears were rolling down her face.

Hegarty held his hands outstretched. 'My God, girl, what's the matter?' he asked, leading her inside the counter to a chair.

Jenny, who had remained silent until then, pointed with a painted fingernail to the station window.

'It's that bastard of a husband of hers, Jack. And please don't insult us by pretending that you didn't know what was going on.'

Hegarty glared at her as he directed her towards another chair. 'What the hell are you talking about, woman? Listen just calm down and tell me what the problem is.'

Jenny remained standing. Her voice rose slightly as she spoke. 'The problem, *Guard* Hegarty, is that for the past ten years John Burns has been beating his wife to a pulp on a daily basis.' She tugged at Claire's sleeve. 'Go on,' she urged. 'Show him the marks that you got from him last night.'

Hegarty watched as Claire undid the sleeve button of her white blouse and rolled it up to reveal the large black bruise on her arm.

He shook his head slowly. 'Jesus, I . . .' he started, then stopped and sat down beside Claire. 'And this has been going on for ten years? Why did you not report this to me before now?' He spoke as softly as he could.

Claire just shook her head and sobbed.

Jenny folded her arms and pursed her lips. 'Well, it's reported to you now,' she said abruptly. 'So what are you going to do about it, *Guard*? Or is he going to get away with it because he's the local big-shot?'

Hegarty was tiring of Jenny's attitude. 'Listen here now,' he started. 'I don't need any advice from you, Jenny, on how to do my job. Once I have a written statement of complaint I can assure you that I'll deal with John Burns, big shot or not.'

Claire rose quickly from the chair and grasped his arm. 'Oh good God, Jack, no.' Her voice was filled with panic. 'This can't be made public. It would ruin John and would probably make things worse.'

She turned and pleaded with Jenny. 'For God's sake, tell him. There can't be any court. No one must know that we came here about him.' She spoke through the tears. 'Oh why did I listen to you?'

'Calm down now, Claire. Just calm down,' said Hegarty. 'If you want this to stop, then it will have to go through the system. It can be done discreetly. I'm a good friend of the District Court clerk. Cases like this are never dealt with in the open court. I can . . .'

He stopped as Claire all but screamed at him. 'No! And that's my final word on it.'

She wiped the tears from her face and brushed past him towards the door.

Jenny started to follow but Hegarty blocked her path, saying, 'I know that woman since we were children and I'm back in the village for the last eight years. Why in the name of Jesus did she not come to me? How bad is it?'

Jenny lowered her head for a moment to compose herself and touched his arm. 'I'm sorry for what I said to you, Jack,' she said in a low voice. 'I'm just so angry. Claire and I think the world of you. It's just that we thought that you might be able to sort him out without going to court. It's worse than you can ever imagine, Jack. She lives in terror of him. Anything can set him off. A wrong word, a meal that's not up to his standard, a bad day's fishing. It's got to the stage now that he doesn't even need an excuse. Last night she told him that she was having an early night and he just punched her for no reason. He's a vicious bastard. I don't think he's right in the head, Jack, to be honest.'

She looked up at Hegarty. His expression had changed from disbelief to anger.

'What can you do about him, Jack?' she asked. 'I mean, she won't make a statement, so what can be done?'

'Where is he now?' asked Hegarty, ignoring her question.

'The same place that he can be found at this time every week,' she replied. 'Fishing at the small bridge, of course.'

Hegarty nodded. 'Go and look after Claire,' he said. 'John Burns isn't the first bully I've had to deal with. Tell her not to worry. No one will know that I've been to see him.'

Jenny nodded her understanding. 'He'll go off the head when he realises that she reported him. I mean, what about after, when he goes home? What if he attacks her?'

Hegarty led her towards the door. 'I can assure you that won't happen,' he said.

Outside Claire stood waiting on the footpath clicking the heel of her shoe nervously, glancing up and down the street in a vain attempt to look as if she was merely waiting for someone. Jenny took her by the arm and looked back at Hegarty, who stood in the doorway.

'So you'll sort that out for me, Guard,' she smiled.

'Consider it done,' he replied and went back inside.

He sat down at the dayroom desk and gathered his thoughts. His ignorance of what had been going on angered him. Eight years in the village and not even a hint of it. Eight years of no one saying anything. Who else knew? Why had he not been told? Was he the only one who didn't know that John Burns was terrorising his wife for the past ten years?

He grabbed angrily at the walkie-talkie on the table and settled himself before he spoke.

'Two two three to six five come in.'

'Go ahead, Jack,' came the instant reply.

Hegarty paused for a moment before he spoke. 'Listen, Kieran. I'm going to do a job shortly. Nothing major. I just have to see someone about a cross dog. Will you be able to look after things until I get back? I'll take the first meal-break and deal with it then. Over.'

'No problem, Jack. I should be back there in the next fifteen minutes. Close the door and work away.'

'Good man,' said Hegarty.

Kieran Costigan drove the patrol car at a leisurely speed, one hand on the steering wheel, the other resting on the open window ledge to catch the warm evening breeze. He waved at the locals as he passed. They waved back enthusiastically, delighted to see the patrol car in their area, but at the same time wondering why it was there.

Costigan had not endeared himself to them when he had first arrived in Dunsheerin, arousing their early dislike of him by clearing Conroy's and Clancy's bars on the dot of half past eleven while on his first night of foot-patrol. In the following months, a sudden flurry of car tax renewal forms arrived at the motor tax office and the wearing of seat-belts came into fashion locally overnight.

However, as time wore on, his original enthusiasm mellowed and the people's suspicion waned. Playing football with the local team and scoring a vital point in the winning of the junior championship furthered his popularity. They started to trust him, but they did not fully trust him yet.

The night of post-match celebrations at Conroy's was one of congratulations and caution. 'Fair dues to you, Kieran,' one local had said. 'You've done us proud. And I'm glad I'm not driving tonight. I must have at least four pints drank.' Then he moved away to shouts of 'Go way, ya arse-kisser. You must have at least two gallons on board.'

Hegarty had advised Costigan, 'Don't get pissed too often with the locals, lad. There's nothing they'd like better than the company of a drunken guard for protection while they drink after hours porter.'

Hegarty had been in charge of the station since the sergeant had gone on sick leave for a couple of months. It had happened that the sergeant had been trying to advise the local curate on the benefits of a good golf swing, but the clergyman was a novice to golf and he swung a three wood back quickly, catching the sergeant under the chin and sending him hurtling into the nearby bushes.

He had turned up for duty the next day, but was found lying across the day-room table by a local who had come to the station to get his dole form signed. He was taken home in the squad car and advised by the local doctor to take things easy for a few days.

Two months later, having grown fond of his life of leisure and having only a few months left in the job anyway, he had decided to prolong his holiday. Although he was a very amiable man, the sergeant's absence gave young Costigan a sense of freedom.

At the next lane off the road he turned the patrol car back in the direction of the village. He thought about Hegarty's message. 'Going to see someone about a cross dog' meant that he had private business to attend to, business that was outside his work as a guard. It was their radio code just in case the superintendent in the district headquarters had his radio on and was listening in. Kieran had used it many times himself in the past when he wanted to go off early to play in local football games or to make an early start home to his native county at the weekend. But this was the first time that Hegarty had used it.

CHAPTER THREE

Jim Quilter was feeling unwell. Having drunk twelve pints and savaged two baskets of Madge's sandwiches, his stomach had begun to rebel. He belched so loudly that the youngsters at the pool table fell into fits of laughter.

'Are you sure that was ham, girl?' he asked sheepishly as he moved off in the direction of the toilet.

Myles was concerned. 'It's not like Jim to feel queasy with only twelve pints in him,' he said, leaning across the counter to the big woman. 'I thought that ham smelt a bit iffy,' he went on, raising his head like a prosecutor waiting for an answer from a defendant.

Big Madge leaned across the counter, towering

over him. 'Listen, you little bastard,' she sneered. 'If he can't take . . .' She stopped in mid-sentence as Jim returned from the toilet.

'Are you all right, craythur?' she said, then turned to the glass optics behind her and lifted a small tumbler to the brandy bottle. 'Here,' she said softly, putting it on the counter in front of him, 'this'll settle your stomach.'

Even the sight of the free drink could not restore the colour to Quilter's face.

Myles eyed the glass. 'To tell you the truth,' he said, rubbing his stomach. 'All this excitement has given me a tummy upset myself.'

Madge raised her hand in rescue. 'Hold on, lad,' she smiled, then disappeared into the kitchen with another glass, only to return a few moments later and it foaming with liver salts.

'There you are, boy,' she said, placing the glass in front of Myles. 'That's the best cure of all for an iffy ham complaint.' She threw her head back and roared with laughter at her own joke.

'Big smart bitch,' said Myles under his breath.

Jim hovered over the glass of brandy, a brandy that was given more to ensure his presence there the following Thursday than to cure his aching belly.

'I can't drink it,' he muttered. 'I'm going home to my bed.'

Seizing his opportunity, Myles grabbed the glass of brandy and threw it back with a gulp. He raised the empty glass to Madge before slamming it down on the counter.

'Your health, girl,' he laughed, pushing the other sizzling glass towards her. 'And you can give

24

this scour water to some constipated tourist.'

She made a move to come outside the counter. 'Get out . . . the two of ye,' she shouted.

Myles feigned a wounded look. 'We're going anyway,' he said, putting an arm around Quilter's shoulder and leading him to the door, like an injured footballer being taken to the line.

Outside, they both sat down on the windowsill to rest in the evening sunshine.

'C'mon, smarten yourself, Jim,' said Myles. 'Will we go to Clancy's for a couple?'

Quilter stood up and rubbed at his face. 'No. You carry on. I'll probably see you there later.'

'Are you sure?'

'Yeah, go ahead,' he nodded.

'Fair enough, boy,' said Myles, patting him gently on the back, and he turned away in the direction of Clancy's.

'What you need now, Jim,' he called back, 'is a few greasy fried eggs and a good strong glass of buttermilk.' He disappeared around the corner.

Jim took a few deep breaths and started out on his journey home. He looked forward to reaching the footbridge, where he knew the sound of the running water would have a healing effect on him. And John Burns would still be there. He was drunk now and he would say what he liked to Burns. He had bowed down to the likes of him for long enough.

On the other side of the street he saw Garda Jack Hegarty going into his house at the end of the village. His pace quickened, as he remembered the outstanding warrant against him for a drunk and incapable fine. He hoped that he hadn't been seen.

'Going home early this evening, Mr Quilter?' called Hegarty, without even turning around as he put the key in the door.

'Christ, he never misses a trick,' muttered Jim, slowing his pace to a stroll. He ambled along on the side margin of the road, staggering occasionally on the loose gravel. As he turned into the boreen that led to the footbridge, a long walking pole that had been left in the ditch caught his eye. It would ease the rest of his journey.

By the time he reached the footbridge, his stomach pain was almost gone. Nothing like a bit of fresh air to cure food poisoning, he thought as he placed his hands on the coolness of the iron crossbar and rested the pole beside him. John Burns stood below him in the water, the fishing rod swaying to and fro above him like a well-oiled pendulum.

'Any luck, John?' Quilter shouted at the top of his voice.

Burns almost dropped the rod with the fright and staggered backwards in the water. He looked up at the bridge, his face filled with rage.

'You again. Go home, you drunken eejit. Don't you know better than to be shouting when someone is trying to fish? Or what kind of an *amadán* are you at all. Go home to bed for yourself for Jesus' sake.'

Jim smiled down at him and raised a hand to his ear. 'Sorry, John, I can't hear you with all the noise. What are you saying?'

Burns yanked at the rod as the fly lodged in the heavy weed on the other side of the river. He roared in anger. 'You drunk prick. Look at what you made me do now.'

Although he struggled with the rod, he continued with the tirade of abuse. 'You're a good-for-nothing the same as your oul' lad was. Now fuck off back to what's left of that place you call a farm.'

Jim's grip tightened on the railing. He swayed to and fro, shouting in anger at the same time. 'What did you say to me, you bollocks you? I'll tell you one thing, you're a lucky man that you're in the middle of that river or I'd come down there and beat the shite out of you.'

Burns did not reply but gave a wave of protest and turned his attention back to the trapped fly.

Jim searched the ground beneath him and picked up a fist-sized stone. He threw it with all his might into the calm pool of the river below him. Before Burns could admonish him, Jim had grabbed the pole and was moving away.

The strained fishing line twanged like a guitar string in the evening breeze as Burns called on all his knowledge of fishing to free it from the dense weed. He reeled and released, reeled and released until with one final jerk, the entire line jumped up and settled in a tangle in the water in front of him. It had snapped just above the newly tied fly.

'Damn you to hell, Quilter,' he roared up at the empty bridge.

Claire Burns sat at the marble counter-top in her spacious oak kitchen, her hands cupped around a crystal brandy glass, her head lowered in thought as she listened to Jenny. She had not spoken on the way home from the garda station but had just sat trance-like in the passenger seat, Jenny talking excitedly and promising that her ordeal was over. She looked up at the sound of the brandy cork popping for the second time in a matter of minutes. Jenny poured herself another large glass.

'It was the only thing to do, Claire. Jack Hegarty is a good man. If anyone can deal with him it's Jack. And like he told me, you don't have to worry about it becoming public. Although if I were you I'd have told the world a long time ago.'

Claire spoke sternly: 'How many times have I told you that it would only make matters worse? It's very easy to give advice, Jenny. "Go and get a barring order. Get him out of the house. Report him to the guards. Get his name in the papers. Ruin him." And then what? What do I do then?' She waved her hand around the kitchen. 'Yes, I would have a mansion of a house to myself. I could come and go as I pleased and be the happiest woman in the world?' She shook her head. 'No, Jenny, love. What you seem to be forgetting is that my husband's one of the most powerful men in the county. I would spend the rest of my days in more fear than I am in now.'

Jenny slammed her hand down on the worktop. 'That's rubbish talk, Claire, and you know it. The law has changed in this country. The day when a man could abuse a woman and get away with it is long gone.'

Claire gave a wry smile and finished her drink. 'The law,' she mocked. 'Do you really think that John gives a damn about the law or what it might threaten to do to him?' She shook her head and gave a sympathetic smile. 'Poor Jack Hegarty,' she murmured. 'He really doesn't know what he's letting himself in for.'

Jenny pulled up one of the high chairs and sat beside her friend at the counter. She took the glass from between Claire's hands, half filled it, then placed it on the counter and looked out the window as she spoke. 'It breaks my heart to see you like this.' Her voice cracked.

Claire placed her hand on Jenny's shoulder and turned her around gently. Tears welled in her eyes. 'I'd never get through the day without you,' she said. 'Only for you, I would be dead long ago.'

Jenny stood up from the chair and began to pace up and down. 'He's the one who should be dead,' she spat. Her eyes narrowed in anger.

Claire nodded in agreement. 'How often I have wished it!' she almost whispered. 'How many times has he slept beside me while I lay awake at night plotting his death! I imagined how good it would feel to plunge a large knife into his heaving chest and watch the look of surprise on his face before he took his last breath.'

Jenny's mouth fell open in shock. 'You don't really mean that, do you?' she asked.

Claire looked up and smiled as if awakening from a pleasant dream. She laughed at the expression on Jenny's face.

'Do you really think that I could murder my husband? Really, Jenny. Do you think that I would be capable of that? No . . . no.' Her voice trailed off. 'But still . . .'

Jenny shook her head. 'No Claire, that's not what I mean.'

The two women sipped their glasses in silence. Then their eyes met momentarily before they both burst into laughter. The three large glasses of brandy they had drunk were beginning to take effect. Their laughter grew louder.

'It's just that neither of us has the guts to do it,' squealed Jenny.

When the laughter had abated, Claire wiped at her eyes with the corner of a tissue. 'At least I haven't lost my sense of humour,' she said.

'What time is he due home?' enquired Jenny.

The mention of her husband was like a punch in the chest to Claire. Her face tightened and the laughter stopped. She glanced up at the kitchen clock above her. 'In about three hours' time. He usually gets back at around five o'clock.'

She looked across the kitchen at Jenny. 'Will you stay with me?' she said. 'It's just that I want you to see how he reacts to the visit from Jack Hegarty. I just know that we've made a big mistake by going to him.' Her voice shook.

Jenny approached her and placed her hand around her shoulder. 'Don't worry,' she comforted her friend. 'I'll be here with you.' She picked up the telephone receiver. 'I'll just ring home to say I'll be late.'

She moved across the kitchen to where the telephone hung on the wall and picked up the receiver. As soon as she had dialled the number she slammed the receiver back quickly on the phone. 'To hell with him,' she said casually, returning to her chair.

She picked up the brandy glass and finished the entire contents in one mouthful.

'Did you two have an argument?' Claire asked.

Jenny shrugged with indifference and laughed. 'An argument!' she said in mock surprise. 'How could anyone ever argue with Gerald? An argument would be too stressful for him.'

Her tone changed to disgust. 'Christ, he's as about as exciting as a wet day in November.'

'He's a very pleasant man,' Claire said.

Jenny threw her eyes up and huffed. '*Pleasant*,' she repeated. 'Having sex is pleasant, Claire. Having an orgasm is pleasant. And those are two things that my pleasant husband has no interest in.' She leaned forward on the counter. 'I knew on our wedding night that I had made a mistake.'

'Don't say things like that,' said Claire.

Jenny waved her hand to dismiss the protest. 'He produced a pair of *ironed* pyjamas from his suitcase. Jesus, I thought it was a joke. Then he put them on and brushed his teeth.'

Claire blurted out a laugh.

Jenny smiled and joined in with her. 'It was like getting into bed with a giant ball of wool.'

'And did you have . . .' asked Claire, then stopped and shrieked with laughter at the serious expression of her friend.

Jenny smiled and nodded. 'They were buttoned up to the top and I just ripped them off him. My first job as a married woman was to sew them on the following day.'

Tears of laughter ran down Claire's face. Jenny was pleased that her story had cheered her friend to such a state. 'He was the worst virgin I ever met,' she laughed.

Claire raised her hand to her face to hide her smile. 'Why did you never tell me this before?' she asked. Jenny threw her arms out as if in surrender. 'Well, it's not something that you just fire out at dinner parties,' she explained. 'Gerald, why don't you entertain our guests with the story of our wedding night?' She waved her hand delicately to the imaginary host. 'Better yet, why don't you show them your pyjamas while I go and shag one of your friends?'

After a few moments the laughter abated and Claire shook her head in admonishment. 'Jenny Maguire, you're terrible. Poor Gerald. What a lovely man!'

'Yeah,' said Jenny casually. 'Lovely.'

Jack Hegarty made his way quickly through the village. He was wearing a civilian jacket over his uniform shirt and was on his way to the footbridge. He picked at a piece of corned beef that had become lodged between his front teeth and as he moved, he worked through in his head what he would do and say on his arrival. The journey took only five minutes at his smart walking pace.

John Burns sat below him on the riverbank, his fishing box open and the fly-tying vice held between his knees. Hegarty watched him working for a few moments before announcing his arrival. And now, he was ready.

Burns looked up as he heard the sound of

Hegarty climbing over the railing, then turned back to the vice.

'Good afternoon, Guard,' he said casually. 'Is it fishing-licence duty you're on?'

Hegarty eased himself down the steep bank beside the footbridge without answering and slapped at the thighs of his trousers as he approached.

'No then,' he said, just as casually as Burns had spoken. 'It's wife-beating duty I'm on.'

He placed his hands in his pockets and looked into the river waiting for a reaction. None came. Burns continued to work on the vice and spoke as he took a length of thin wire from the fishing box.

'Shouldn't you be up in the Terrace so? I hear that they beat their wives night and day up there after drink.'

Hegarty sat down on the dry grass beside Burns and watched him tie the fly.

'By all accounts, John, a man wouldn't have to go as far as the Terrace to find a wife-beater these days. Apparently they can be found in the finest houses around.'

Burns slammed the lid of the fishing box shut. He had bantered long enough. He turned and glared at Hegarty.

'What's your business here, Guard? Can't you see that I'm trying to have a peaceful evening's fishing? So say what you have to say and let me be, like a good man.'

'Claire and Jenny Maguire came into the station today . . .' started Hegarty.

'Hah!' interrupted Burns in protest.

Hegarty held up his hand. 'Now John, you can

listen to what I have to say and then I'll listen to you. It appears that you have been beating your wife regularly over a period of ten years. I've seen the bruises that you gave her last night and I've seen enough beaten women in my time to know that the injuries she has were inflicted by someone else. You.'

Burns stood up quickly and pointed his finger down at Hegarty. He struggled at first to get the words out.

'Why you . . . listen here now, Guard . . . I'll tell you one thing, you have some cheek, boy . . . I've a good mind to get my solicitor . . . You have some cheek accusing me of that . . . making allegations against me that I beat my wife. I'm going to report you to the chief superintendent, boy.' He swayed from one foot to the other with anger. 'By Jesus you have some cheek.' He walked a few paces away then returned quickly and again pointed a trembling finger down again at Hegarty, who was slowly shaking his head from side to side.

'Did she make a complaint against me or didn't she?' demanded Burns.

Hegarty stood up from the grass and moved close to him. 'She didn't make an *official* complaint if that's what you're asking. Because if she did, I'd be dragging your bullying arse over the top bar of that bridge right now . . . *boy*.'

Burns took a step back from him. Although the fact that his wife had not made an official complaint increased his confidence, there was unusual anger in this village guard's voice. He started to reach down for the tackle box.

'Then you have no business here, Guard,' he said in a low voice, 'have you?'

Hegarty spoke calmly as he looked around. 'I'm just here to tell you to stop. That's all I can do at the moment. Apart from being a guard at all, I have known Claire for many years and she's a good and kind woman.'

He stood up and looked directly at Burns. 'A word of warning for you,' his eyes narrowed as he whispered. 'If I ever hear that you've touched her again or even threatened her...' He paused for emphasis before the punchline. 'Then I'll deal with you like I dealt with all the incurable wife-beaters I've met over the years.'

Burns looked puzzled for a moment then suddenly laughed out loud. 'I don't believe it,' he shouted, raising his arms and swinging around. 'I'm being threatened by the local flatfoot, PC Hegarty.'

When he turned back, his tone had become scornful. 'Who the hell do you think you are? Do you think that you're a sheriff in the Wild West or what?'

He pulled vigorously at the pocket of his fishing jacket and retrieved the pencil and notebook that he kept for recording the weight of his catches.

'You're going to answer for this, boy,' he nodded with assurance and began scribbling furiously on the paper. 'Threatened by the local guard,' he said slowly. 'And you needn't worry about the wife complaining any more. I'll sort out that problem when I get home.'

Hegarty clenched his fists at his side then raised one in front of him.

'What!' mocked Burns. 'What are you going to do? Hit me?'

Hegarty lowered his fist slowly and turned away.

Burns called from behind him, 'That's right, Guard. Quit while you're still ahead. It would be more in your line to put a few of the drunks in this village behind bars. That good-for-nothing Quilter threatened me as well today and threw stones at me. Go and do something about him.'

Hegarty climbed over the top pole of the foot-bridge and pointed down.

'Remember what we've discussed now,' he said and walked away.

'Yeah . . . yeah, Guard,' sneered Burns before sitting back down on the riverbank.

CHAPTER FOUR

Jim Quilter spoke aloud to himself as he moved around the stone floor of his cottage. The cylinder of gas which he used to boil his kettle had just expired with a blue-flamed splutter as he held the lighting match over the ring. He searched around the small kitchen for pieces of wood and loose gorse bush twigs, with which he could light the open fire.

He had slumped in a state of unconsciousness in his armchair for nearly an hour, before a blinding headache behind his eyes had awoken him. He would have to move quickly before it got worse. A quick cup of strong tea and a smoke was needed before returning to the village to rejoin Myles

Hickey. He rattled at the money in his pockets as he searched for the kindling. There was still a good night's drinking left.

He went outside for a moment and returned with a lump of bog oak the size of an average man. He took the small hatchet that rested beside the dresser and proceeded to chop furiously at the wood, knocking slices of its rotten side away, chips of the wood catapulting across the room. When he was satisfied that he had enough, he gathered it in his hands and hunched with it towards the open fire. Moments later the sparks were flying in all directions.

He watched the fury of the fire increase as he filled the kettle and stamped on the sparks that had landed on the floor. 'Better than petrol,' he thought to himself, nestling the kettle into the centre of the fire. He took a flattened cigarette box from his pocket and sat down to wait.

His hangover was developing rapidly. First the headache had got worse, and now he was beginning to feel cold. He decided to busy himself by washing the dirty mug and dishes that lay in the sink. However, once he had washed the mug, he lost interest in the project. He threw a tea bag into the mug and convinced himself that the kettle was boiled.

His encounter with John Burns flitted in and out of his thoughts as he drank his lukewarm tea. He didn't mind the language and abuse that was hurled at him, but the comment about his father stung.

His father had been a hard-working man in his time. A gentle and well-liked man who could only ever see the good in people. For the first time in a long while, Jim felt the pangs of loneliness and sadness that can only come from the loss of a father. He looked up at the faded black and white photographs of his parents on the high mantelpiece above him. It had been so long since he had even thought of them. What would they think if they saw him now? He stood up and brushed the depressing thoughts aside. He still had a night of fun ahead of him. It would be no state of mind to go drinking in. A man should never drink when he's depressed.

The one-hour walk to the village would be ample time to change his humour. He whistled loudly as he washed the mug under the gushing tap. Still, what Burns had said would not be forgotten.

John Burns sat on the riverbank with his wader boots dangling in the water below him. He munched pensively on a cheese and tomato sandwich, staring blankly ahead. Jack Hegarty would pay dearly for his threats, as would Claire for her indiscretion. As for Jenny Maguire, he would ban all visiting privileges, something he should have done a long time ago. Although he felt confident that his friendship with the local superintendent would be enough to suppress the matter if it ever came to light, he still had a few nagging doubts in the back of his mind. Some drastic measures would have to be taken. Killing his wife was out of the question, a thought he had entertained many times while fishing. He would surely be suspect number one in light of recent events.

Killing the three of them, however, was something to consider. He laughed at the absurdity of the very idea.

His thoughts reverted to his original plan and he set it out in chronological order. On his arrival home, he would threaten his wife discreetly, as only he could. He had seen the look of fear on her face many times. He knew how to put it there. He was an expert at it now. As for Jenny Maguire, well, she would be a challenge. Unlike Claire, she had become a tough and well-educated woman, unafraid of the power of men, a dangerous, bra-burning bitch.

But she had her skeletons. What about the affairs she was having? He smiled with contentment. Even in her youth she had been a slut. Well, if a whore wants to keep her legs open, then she should learn to keep her mouth shut. It would have to be made clear to her that before one begins to discipline others one must first discipline oneself.

He laughed out loud as the thought of what the expression on Gerald's face might be with the revelations. Poor, stupid Gerald.

As for Hegarty, it would be a simple matter of a visit to his friend the superintendent. How could such an upstanding officer allow one of his men to continue serving in the small village after he had threatened its leading employer with physical violence? An apology and a transfer to the local town would be inevitable, and satisfactory. Try as he did to convince himself that this would be the outcome, the fear of failure sent a shiver down his back.

What if Claire stood her ground and made an official complaint? Jack Hegarty might not be the sheepish village policeman he was hoping for and the superintendent might do a Pontius Pilate. Then the whole thing would be out in the open. 'Burns the wife-beater,' 'Bully-boy Burns'.

How could he face his employees? Worse still, how could he face his wealthy counterparts at the Lions Club? His money could not save him from their discreet silences and excuses that they had to be 'somewhere else'. Partners for the four-ball competition in the golf club would be hard to come by.

He threw the remainder of the sandwich back in his lunch-box and reached for the fly-tying vice. Although he had a large selection of flies in the tackle box beside him, the simple pleasure of creating a new one would help calm his panic. In any case, the salmon had stopped biting since that thug Quilter had upset the life of the river with his act of stupidity. He would try something new to tempt them.

Behind him and to his left he heard the sound of approaching footsteps in the grass. He did not look back. Instead he drooped his shoulders and sighed heavily. How the hell could he concentrate with this racket going on around him? He would have to buy the fishing rights to the damn river and ban all this human traffic from it. It would be the only solution.

The footsteps drew nearer and stopped directly behind him. He turned around and looked up, the glare of the evening sun silhouetting the form above him. The blunt weapon struck before he could speak, the first blow catching him just above the left ear and spinning his head violently to the right, the vice falling from between his knees into the water below.

The second and third blows glanced off his shoulder and arm as he raised them in a vain bid to protect himself. He grabbed at the riverbank in an attempt to rise, but there was nothing but water beneath his feet.

The fourth and fifth blows landed with fury on the back of his head. He slumped on the ground, breathing in short spasms. His assailant stood in silence above him.

There was no pain now. Just a numbness and a fading of the evening light. His grip relaxed as he felt himself falling over the edge and slipping peacefully into the cool calmness of the river. His hands opened and closed in the water.

He was not going to go out like this. He was a survivor. How many times had he taken on the best and won? Why should this be any different?

The last thing that John Burns heard, before he lapsed into the unknown, was the sound of footsteps running away through the long grass of the riverbank.

CHAPTER FIVE

Kieran Costigan slammed the station ink-stamp down hard on the dole form and added it to the pile on the mantelpiece. The man who had brought it held his hand out.

'Will I bring that to the post office myself, Guard?' he asked.

'No, I'll bring them all down later,' said Costigan. 'You work away.'

He grinned at what he had said. 'And that was an off-the-record comment,' he added.

The man laughed as he walked out the door.

Costigan glanced at his watch. He was tempted to call for Hegarty on the radio but there was always the danger that there would be no reply, and the local superintendent might have his walkie-talkie tuned in. Still, he knew that it was unusual for Hegarty to take such a long unofficial break.

He would give him another fifteen minutes and then go and search for him in the patrol car. He sat down at the desk and swung his legs up on it. He flipped the keyring over and back on his index finger like a gunfighter. 'Cross dog, my arse,' he muttered, then rose suddenly to his feet.

His urgency was dispelled when he heard the familiar sound of Hegarty's steel-tipped shoes approach on the footpath outside. He sat back down and grabbed one of HQ's circulars from the tray on the desk and stared studiously at it as Hegarty entered the day room.

'What kept ya?' he asked casually without lifting his eyes from the page.

When Costigan eventually looked up, he saw Hegarty standing pale-faced outside the counter. Costigan's mouth fell open when he saw the expression on his colleague's face.

'What is it, Jack?' he asked, his eyes narrowing with concern.

Hegarty walked slowly around the counter, his hands in his pockets, his eyes fixed on the floor.

'I'm in the shit, lad,' he said softly.

Costigan stood up. Hegarty walked around him and stared out the window. Costigan held his hands out but said nothing.

'That job I was doing earlier . . .' said Hegarty. 'Oh Jesus,' he sighed, lifting his eyes to the ceiling.

Costigan pinched the shoulder of his jacket and

turned him around. 'Will you tell me, for Christ's sake,' he urged.

Hegarty sat on the corner of the dayroom table, his arms folded, and began to relate his encounter with John Burns, pausing only in mid-story to enquire if Costigan had heard any rumours of Burns's brutality. He appeared relieved when Costigan said that he hadn't had a clue about it. When he had finished his account of the events, he slapped his thighs and stood up.

Costigan shrugged. 'Is that it? I mean is that what all the fuss is about?' he asked casually. 'John Burns saying that he's going to complain that you threatened him for beating his wife? Where does he go with a story like that? Big deal, Jack.'

Hegarty smiled weakly. 'That's what I like about you, lad,' he said. 'You remind me of me when I was younger. Thirty years ago I'd have picked that little bollocks up with one hand and wouldn't have given it a second thought. Look at me now. Worried about losing my pension. Maybe you're right.'

Costigan gave him the thumbs-up and grinned.

Hegarty took off his civilian jacket and hung it on the grey metal stand in the corner.

'So, do you think ye'll win next Sunday,' he asked. 'Or is it going to be another free football lesson from the town?'

'Aw yeah, very smart,' started Costigan, then stopped and cocked his ear up. 'Jesus Christ, what's that?' he shouted, jumping up and racing towards the door.

Hegarty pressed his face against the window to

look up the street. As the sound of screeching grew louder, Hegarty recognised the voice.

'Aw for Jaysus' sake,' he groaned as he slung his tunic on and walked out to join Costigan at the station gate. 'Would you look at the garch of that,' he said angrily, buttoning up his tunic and watching as Jim Quilter struggled towards them in an intoxicated sprint.

'Have you anything for the September court?' asked Hegarty softly.

Quilter was a hundred yards away and roaring like a bull in a pen as he approached.

Costigan shook his head slowly. 'Not even a tax case,' he replied.

Hegarty pointed towards Quilter: 'God works in mysterious ways, his wonders to perform.'

'Help . . . help,' roared Quilter running towards them. He grasped at Costigan's shirt and pulled violently at it, the buttons from the top and second holes popping out, the clip-on tie falling on the ground.

'What's the matter with this drunken gobshite?' growled Hegarty, reaching over Costigan's shoulder to take Quilter by the collar of his tweed coat.

'River,' panted Quilter. 'Salmon . . . body . . . Burns . . . John Burns . . . Jesus mercy.'

Hegarty pulled him away from Costigan.

'Come here you,' he said. 'Take it easy now. Calm down or I'll put you in the cell.' He shook Quilter until he stopped ranting. 'What's the matter with you, man? Spit it out.'

Costigan pulled the buttonless collar of his shirt together and clipped on his tie. 'Look at the state of me, Quilter,' he protested. 'You're some bollocks.'

Ignoring this comment, Quilter grabbed at the two guards, one with each hand, and gulped in several mouthfuls of air before beginning: 'John Burns is dead,' he whispered. 'His body is in the river and there's a lot of blood on his head.'

Hegarty and Costigan stared at each other for a brief moment before Hegarty averted his eyes and looked back to Quilter.

'Are you sure?' he asked. It was a question that came naturally when dealing with the likes of Quilter.

'Well he wasn't fuckin' swimmin', Guard,' squealed Quilter, the tears starting to fall from his eyes.

He breathed in fast spasms as he watched the two policemen and waited for them to react. Hegarty nodded to Costigan in the direction of the parked patrol car and took Quilter gently by the arm.

'Take it easy, man,' he said, opening the rear door of the car. 'C'mon and show us. Sit in there, Jim.'

Hegarty sat into the passenger seat and removed his notebook from his tunic pocket. Costigan rubbed his hand nervously across his face and started the car. He drove slowly up the street. He feigned a smile and threw his eyes to heaven at the people who stood watching from the footpath and had seen Quilter charge through the village. Hegarty scribbled furiously as he listened to a mumbling Quilter recall how he had seen the body floating in the river as he crossed the footbridge.

'Should we not contact headquarters to let them know?' Costigan interrupted.

Hegarty merely shook his hand at him and looked into the back seat. 'Continue,' he ordered.

Quilter took a cigarette butt from the top pocket of his jacket and rubbed at himself, looking for a light. 'I've no shaggin' match,' he sighed.

Hegarty rooted in the dashboard and side door panels for a moment before shaking a box and throwing it over his shoulder.

'Here. Get on with it.'

'I can't tell you any more,' said Quilter. 'I was making my way back to town and I looked over the footbridge and saw Burns, stomach down in the water. Then I ran to the village.'

'Did you see anyone else?' asked Hegarty.

Costigan held his breath as he turned the patrol car up the narrow laneway that led to the footbridge.

'Not a sinner,' replied Quilter, panting through the smoke.

Costigan drove the patrol car as near to the footbridge as he could and the three of them got out. He stood for a moment looking over the roof of the car at Hegarty, who was gazing straight ahead to the footbridge. Costigan felt a sudden wave of discomfort. Quilter moved forward, beckoning them on with his hand.

'C'mon. What's the matter with ye?' he shouted back at them.

Costigan swallowed hard and glanced sideways at Hegarty. 'Christ, Jack,' was all he could say. Hegarty gave no response.

Costigan slammed the door and quickly brushed

his thoughts aside. Quilter was already climbing over the top bar of the bridge.

'Hold on there,' shouted Costigan, as he slid down the earthen bank. 'Don't touch anything.'

Hegarty stood above them on the footbridge and narrowed his eyes. He did not follow as Costigan had done. Instead, he walked back and forward across the short bridge looking down at the river. He did this twice more, then climbed down the bank to join the others.

Quilter looked at the two of them and pointed with a shaking hand.

'Over there,' he muttered, and remained where he was, watching the two guards walk along the riverbank. He fumbled in the pockets of his coat for his cigarettes and lit one, his hand trembling.

He moved closer to the others.

Hegarty sat down on the riverbank and removed his shoes and socks, then rolled up the ends of his trousers. He inhaled as he stepped into the cold water, then, reaching out, he pulled on the back of John Burns's coat. The body floated towards him.

Together, Costigan and Hegarty, with the help of a reluctant Quilter, lifted it on to the riverbank. Costigan grimaced as he looked at the body.

'Jesus . . . the whole back of his head is open,' he gasped.

Quilter took a long drag on his cigarette. 'Do you think he was murdered?' he asked.

Hegarty climbed up on the bank and squeezed out the sodden leg of his trousers

'No, Quilter,' he said, looking angrily at him. 'He had a fight with the salmon. Ya eejit ya. Here,

Costigan, get on the blower. Contact the super and tell him we have a murder. Then get something to seal off this area.'

Quilter was getting into the spirit of things. 'What can I do?' he asked expectantly.

Hegarty rolled down his trouser legs and looked up at him, then held out his hand.

'Give me that dirty rag of a coat to cover this body,' he said, taking off his own tunic and removing his notebook and pen from the top pocket.

Quilter watched as he placed the tweed coat on the top half of the body and the tunic over the legs. He patted his pockets and leaned forward anxiously.

'My fags,' he whispered. 'They're in the coat.' He was afraid to get too close.

Hegarty searched the pockets and handed over the cigarettes.

'Just in case you've forgotten, Quilter, I'll remind you again. There's going to be a lot of talk about this in the next few days. What I don't want to hear is yourself and Doc Holliday bullshitting about it below in Conroy's. It'll be in your own best interest. Not forgetting, of course, that you are, after all, the number one suspect.'

Quilter broke into a spasm of smoker's cough.

'Whaat?' he gasped.

Hegarty smiled.

'What about the salmon there?' asked Quilter, pointing to it.

Hegarty glared at him. 'Forget it,' he growled. 'I'm not having you eating the only decent witness that we have so far.'

They both listened to the car radio crackle in the

distance as Costigan relayed the message.

'Don't quench that cigarette here,' shouted Hegarty, as Quilter was about to put his foot on it.

'Why not?' he asked, with genuine curiosity.

'Because this is a murder scene, you amadán. You're not even supposed to be smoking here let alone trampling the ground with your size twelve drinking boots.'

Quilter spat in the palm of his hand and quenched the cigarette in it, then shoved it into his pocket.

'Happy now, Guard?'

'Thrilled,' replied Hegarty. 'Now sit tight until the cavalry comes.'

Chief Superintendent Pat Brosnan sat looking at the stack of multicoloured files on the table in front of him, some of them over four inches thick. He smiled with satisfaction as he stacked them and replaced them in the filing cabinet. In the boredom of his office in headquarters, he could not resist taking them out from time to time to relive each murder case in turn. Seventeen solved in the past three years was going to take some beating by his successor when he would retire in three years' time.

He took each murder case as a personal challenge, driving his men hard to find the vital clue which would lead to the capture of the culprit, sending them back time and time again to check on some small omission in the statement of a witness. He was affectionately known to the men in the Murder Squad as 'The Hammer'. His broad frame, a height of six feet two and his dark piercing eyes could break down the toughest suspect when he got him in his grasp.

After each successful interview, during which he had melted a false alibi or moved closer to the solving of the case, he would leave for the privacy of another room and bang the nearest flat surface with his huge fist in delight.

'Getting closer,' he would whisper through gritted teeth.

While the others in the squad would be backslapping during the celebrations in a nearby pub, Brosnan would sit quietly in the bedroom of his bed-and-breakfast in the town where the murder had been committed, methodically checking through the file to ensure that some 'overpaid ambulance chaser', as he called members of the legal profession, would not find some technicality which would lead to the dismissal of the case. No stone would be left unturned. He had seen too many killers and other criminals walk free from the courts because of legal arguments brought by men 'with dried horse-shit on their heads and verbal horse-shit they had learnt from case books in the Law Library'. Now, whenever Brosnan brought a killer before the court, it was for a conviction.

He would sit at the rear of the courtroom, paying little attention to the legal jargon, his gaze fixed firmly on the men and women of the jury, searching for the smallest sign. A shake of one of their heads in disgust at the killing, a look of anger at the accused.

When the 'guilty' verdict would be announced, he would rise slowly from his seat and cross the road to the nearby bar where he would smoke a King Edward cigar and drink a large brandy. It was the only time he ever indulged in alcohol.

The telephone rang on the desk behind him. He closed the cabinet door and answered it.

'Yes . . . Dunsheerin. I have a fair idea where . . . I understand . . . Has the pathologist been notified? Right. Give me a few minutes. No. I'll travel in my own car.' He was about to replace the receiver. 'By the way,' he enquired, 'who's the superintendent who covers that village?'

The skin on his face stretched as he clenched his jaws shut with the answer.

'Yeah,' he said. 'I was thinking that it was him.'

He put down the phone and took his coat from where it hung at the back of the chair. As he left the office, he stopped to look around, the filing cabinet swelling with paper, the desk-top computer which he had never learnt to use, but which looked good whenever a visiting police force came on a tour of the building. And finally, the large wooden desk with its green leather worktop over which he had sweated for so many hours. In three years he would be leaving it all for compulsory retirement and a life of boring leisure. He had given nearly forty years of his life to the job and was soon to be replaced.

'Once more into the breach,' he said to himself and pulled the door closed behind him.

CHAPTER SIX

Hegarty struggled with a large ball of orange builder's twine that Costigan had commandeered from a nearby house that was under construction.

'Jesus, lad . . . is this the best you could do?' he grunted as he pulled at it.

Costigan dropped the three timber stakes and sledgehammer on the ground and smiled as he watched him struggle. His suspicion of Hegarty had waned. He was confident that the big man could not be capable of such an act. He had seen him lose his temper many times in the past. The clenched fists, the veins standing out on his neck. But not this. Jack Hegarty could not have done this.

'Well, you said you needed something to seal off the scene,' he smiled.

'Yes lad, I know,' said Hegarty, 'but I meant a good length of rope. If some fella walks into this, he's liable to hang himself.'

Defeated, he threw the ball of twine down to where Quilter was sitting.

'Here . . . get your nimble fingers around that like a good man.'

Quilter picked it up and began to unravel it quickly without even looking at it, like a child solving a familiar puzzle.

'Do you think we'll have to stay here much longer?' he asked as he worked. 'It's just that I promised Myles that I'd meet him and if I don't show, he'll be worried about me.'

Hegarty picked up one of the timber stakes and forced it into the soft ground with one thrust. He spoke in a rhythm of grunts as he hammered it down.

'Listen, the only thing that Hickey fella is worried about is sex and porter and the scarcity thereof.'

'That's a very poor outlook to have on life, Guard,' said Quilter as he continued to work on the twine. 'Friendship is something you obviously know very little about. Then again, I suppose you don't have many friends, being a guard.'

'Not like Hickey anyway,' puffed Hegarty as he stopped and rested his hands on the handle of the sledgehammer.

Quilter stood up and gave the end of the twine to Costigan, who took it and began to back away slowly.

'Myles Hickey is the best friend a man could have,' continued Quilter, as he directed Costigan back with his hand.

'Yeah,' replied Hegarty, checking the stake for firmness, shaking it with his hand. 'Next to a good sheep-dog you couldn't find better . . . Kieran, tie that around the first stake like a good man.'

Costigan fixed the twine around the timber stake and then walked back towards them, running his hand along the slack to smooth it. Hegarty wound it around the top of the second stake and then secured it on the third with a triple knot.

The three men stood back to survey their work.

'Well, lads,' said Hegarty. 'What do ye think?'

Quilter folded his arms and walked slowly up and down outside the thin orange line.

'You know, Guard,' he said, 'There are fellas in the Vietnamese army that would give their right arms for a trip-wire like that.'

Costigan sniggered.

'Well, it'll have to do until the lads from town bring something better,' said Hegarty, trying without success to stifle a smile.

'What time did you contact them anyway, Kieran?' he continued, looking at his watch. 'They should be here by now.'

Before Costigan could answer, Quilter, who had seated himself down outside the 'trip-wire', interrupted, shaking his head.

'They'd be quick enough if it was a drunk and disorderly summons they were delivering . . . Jesus, a man can't have a social drink these days without being dragged to the nearest Garda barracks.'

Hegarty eased himself down beside Quilter, watching him as he lit another cigarette, a forlorn look on his face.

'Tell me,' enquired Hegarty, leaning towards him, like a priest hearing confession, 'would this *social* drink you're talking about be the time that yourself and Hickey drank eleven pints and a bottle of poteen and stood outside the convent gates shouting, "C'mon, ye're safe with us, we're virgins too." Would it, Quilter?'

"Twas only a bit of *craic*,' huffed Quilter, shaking the match box before squeezing it into his trouser pocket. 'Anyhow, I was surprised at the guard's lack of self-control. I didn't deserve to get the baton across the shins.'

Hegarty nodded solemnly.

'Agreed, Quilter. But calling him a big ugly bollocks wouldn't have helped your case. Some fellas don't like that.'

Costigan edged towards the conversation and looked down at Hegarty.

'Who did he say that to?' he asked.

Hegarty looked up and winked. 'Big Feargal Bolger, the fella from the town. He was out on patrol here one night and met Lord Jim here and his assistant outside the convent wall.'

Costigan gave a short laugh.

'At least he got the "ugly" part right. Considering the man in question, I'd say he got off fierce light.'

Quilter sucked hard on his cigarette as he remembered the incident. There were still questions left unanswered.

'I thought that guards were trained to take abuse and keep the cool . . . that a man could say anything he liked to them and they'd just smile back.'

Hegarty stood up and brushed the dried grass from where it had stuck to his damp trousers. He grinned as he looked down at Quilter.

'Someone has been telling you lies, Mr Quilter. You see, they get all the abuse they can handle during training and when they come out, they're just waiting for an eejit like yourself to say something stupid to them. Then they snap.'

Quilter shook his head in disbelief.

Hegarty grinned and winked at Costigan who gave a nervous laugh, his eyes going to where the body lay.

Hegarty sensed the young guard's anxiety. 'Relax, lad. Help is on the way.'

He turned his attention back to Quilter and took his notebook out. 'Just one last question,' he said as he flipped it open. 'When was the last time that you saw John Burns alive?'

Quilter looked at him and then at Costigan, who had moved himself closer to listen. He put a shaking hand to his lips and closed his eyes as if immersing himself in deep thought.

'Em . . . this morning when I came into town,' he replied. 'Why do you ask?'

Hegarty pursed his lips and shrugged as he wrote Quilter's answer into the notebook.

'No big deal,' he said casually. 'It's a standard question.'

The speedometer wavered between seventy and eighty as Mike Daly of the Traffic Corps braked hard. He threw the gearshift down, and the car rounded a sweeping bend and accelerated away again. Superintendent Eamon Murray clung to the small handle above the rear door. Daly looked in the driver's mirror and smiled on seeing the pained expression on the face of his officer.

'Nothing like a nice drive in the country, Super,' he quipped in a cheery voice, pressing his foot down on the accelerator as he saw a straight stretch of road ahead.

'What amazes me, Daly, is that you have never actually killed anyone. What lunatic put you on a driving course anyway?'

'By God, then, but 'twas yourself, Super,' grinned Daly.

The superintendent gritted his teeth as they approached a hair-pin bend, pressing forward hard against the driver's seat and flopping back helplessly as the patrol-car pulled out of the turn.

Mike Daly was a man who loved to enforce the road traffic laws, a love which made him extremely unpopular both in the town and in outlying villages. His speciality was lorries, and he got a great deal of satisfaction from getting as many offences as possible from the one vehicle. His personal best was thirty-six. His older colleagues in the Traffic Corps believed that he had either been hit by a truck as a youngster or that his mother had been raped by a lorry driver, such was his hatred of heavy goods vehicles.

Apart from this one idiosyncrasy, Daly was a

likeable character with a sharp sense of humour, and would banter with the traffic offenders at the side of the road, belittling their offences. 'Ah sure 'tis a thing and nothing,' he would say. Most of them would drive away, chuckling to themselves about the 'hilarious guard', only to receive a bale of summonses in the post a few weeks later.

The distraught defendants would shout down the phone to the man in the communications room in the station, ''Twas the young fella in the white squad. Jesus . . . I thought he was joking, he was laughing and everything.'

The man in the communications room would struggle to remain serious. 'He's a gas man, isn't he?'

'Gas man, my arse,' would be the usual infuriated reply before the phone would be slammed down.

'Listen, Daly,' said Superintendent Murray, 'one dead body is enough. It's not as if it's going anywhere.'

He sat back quickly as Daly turned around.

'Do you not trust me, sir?' he asked.

'It's not you,' he replied, signalling Daly to turn his head around, 'it's the fella that's going to pull out in front of you that I'm concerned about. And the sad thing is, it's usually the innocent gobshite in the back seat that pays for it. So for Christ's sake, slow down or I'll prosecute you myself for dangerous driving.'

The superintendent exhaled slowly with relief as the noise of the engine abated. He eased back into the seat and took out his cigarettes, thinking of the evening ahead. For his entire service as an officer he'd had it 'handy', as the lads in the station would say. His biggest challenge in that time was to bring down his golf handicap to single figures, and to look efficient whenever the Minister for Justice visited.

And now this.

Twenty minutes earlier, he had been sitting in the station canteen, drinking tea and advising a couple of sergeants on the intricacies of proper crime prevention when the telephone had rung. Young Guard Costigan had informed him of a suspicious death that had taken place in Dunsheerin. John Burns the millionaire. The Murder Squad was racing to the scene, led by Chief Superintendent Pat Brosnan.

Jesus. Of all people, Pat Brosnan. What had he done to deserve this kick in the arse from the past? He had avoided him successfully for twenty years. Even at a retirement party for a mutual friend some years before, he had spent most of the night moving between the hotel lobby and the toilet, anxiously awaiting the big Kerryman's departure. A half an hour he had spent washing his hands and pretending that he was feeling unwell to the people there who knew him.

He exhaled the smoke slowly as the memories came rushing back.

The small station. Sergeant Pat Brosnan sitting behind his desk, looking up angrily at him.

'You're a waster, Guard Murray,' he had roared. 'The man responsible for recruiting you has deprived some crossroads of an eejit. Go on . . . get out of my sight!'

Eamon Murray was suddenly brought back to the present as the car jolted over a large pothole. He leaned forward and nervously stubbed the remainder of his cigarette in the ashtray.

Daly eyed him in the rear mirror, regretting that he hadn't taken a later meal break. If he had, then he wouldn't have been collared to drive the superintendent to Dunsheerin.

'Go to the footbridge,' came the order. 'Do you know where it is?'

Daly nodded. 'Tell me, Super, is there a chance that this could be our first murder in the district? One of the lads in the station was saying that the body had head injuries.'

Murray drummed his fingers on the ledge of the door and stared blankly out the side window.

'That's right, lad,' he said quietly. 'Apparently it's John Burns.'

Daly turned his head back quickly. 'John Burns,' he repeated. 'Jesus, Super. Isn't he your golf buddy?' he said, turning his attention back to the road.

The superintendent grimaced behind him.

'*Was*, Daly,' he gritted through his teeth. '*Was*.'

Claire wiped the tears from her eyes and reached over to shake her friend's arm.

'We could pretend that it was a robbery,' squealed Jenny through the laughter. 'Or even a sex crime.'

The laughter had reached its peak. Claire held her sides and stood up.

'What about all those fellas who hang themselves in wardrobes and they're found wearing women's knickers,' continued Jenny. She deepened her voice. 'The man was found in what could be described as suspicious circumstances.'

Claire rolled herself along the counter as she laughed, then stopped suddenly.

'Did that actually happen?' she asked innocently.

'Of course it did,' said Jenny. 'I read about it in one of those Sunday tabloids. I must bring it over to show you.'

Claire raised her hand. 'You'll do no such thing, Jenny Maguire. John can't abide filth like that, as he says. I got one of them for a laugh one morning and before I could read it he had thrown it in the fire.' Her voice lowered as she remembered.

The smile fell from Jenny's face as she watched her.

'Yes. I remember that day all right,' she said. 'That was the time that you should have gone to Jack Hegarty.' She stood up and walked towards Claire. 'That was at the beginning of all of this. That was the time to stop him. He's the one who should be in the tabloids.' Her voice faded into a whisper.

Claire turned to her. 'Thank you for staying with me.'

Jenny smiled and lifted an eyebrow to the bottle on the countertop.

'Why would I not stay and drink the most expensive brandy in the county?' she smiled. 'After all it would be rude to leave now.'

She waited for a smile to show on Claire's face.

Both their faces were red now from the combination of laughter and brandy.

'Maybe it would be better if you came to my house for a couple of days,' said Jenny. 'Give him time to cool down after meeting Jack Hegarty. Leave him on his own for a couple of weeks to see what it's like. My sex-machine is going on business to Dublin for a couple of days so it will be a real girls' party. We can go to that classy new restaurant that you were telling me about.'

Although Claire did not interrupt, she shook her head the entire time that Jenny spoke.

'What's the matter with you?' asked Jenny in exasperation.

'I can't do that,' replied Claire. Her voice was stronger now. 'The one thing that I won't do is run. I want to be here when he comes back. I want to see the look on his face when he walks through the door. He won't touch me while you are here.'

'Then promise me this,' said Jenny. 'If he raises his voice or threatens you that you will come to my house.'

Claire sipped at her glass and shook her head again.

'I can tell you exactly what he will do,' she said. 'He will come through the door and stare at me for a few seconds like I had betrayed him. Then he will grunt at you.'

She pointed to the corner of the kitchen. 'He will kick his waders off and throw them over there making as much of a racket as he can. If you speak to him he won't answer. If he has caught something he will throw it into the sink and then retire to the sitting room. And then when you leave, depending on how Jack Hegarty handled him, he will either beat me up or not speak to me for weeks.'

Jenny inspected her fingernails one by one carefully.

'Bastard,' she muttered. 'Of course you are half to blame for this yourself,' she continued, without looking up. 'By letting him get away with it you have made this twice as bad.'

Claire gasped and slammed the glass down on the counter-top, a chip from the crystal base breaking off and landing on the terracotta tiled floor.

'What did you just say to me, Jenny?' Her voice quivered and rose as she continued. 'What are you saying? That all this is my fault. How the hell can you say such a thing to me?'

Jenny stood up and searched for the piece of glass on the floor and, on finding it, placed it on the counter beside Claire's glass. She pursed her lips as she sat back down.

'Don't get angry with *me*,' she said. 'Why don't you save some of it for the tough guy when he comes home?'

'And do what, exactly?' asked Claire, still angry.

'Hit him with something,' shrugged Jenny and glanced around the kitchen. 'What about that cast-iron pan?' she said, pointing to where it hung above the counter-top. 'If you give him a good whack of that across the head it might put some manners on him.'

Claire glared at Jenny then reached up and took the heavy pan down. She weighed it in her hand for a couple of seconds then handed it over.

'But wouldn't that kill him?' she asked curiously.

Jenny tapped the base of the pan in the palm of her hand.

'What do you think?' she asked.

Claire looked bemused. 'What do I think about what?' she asked.

Jenny stood up and swung the pan with both hands.

'Bang,' she shouted. 'Right on the back of his big bully head.'

'You're drunk,' laughed Claire.

Jenny took her by the arm and squeezed. Claire was unnerved by the urgency in Jenny's voice.

'Do you want him dead, Claire? Do you want him gone for good?'

Claire shook her arm free and took a step back. She stared at her friend in front of her, armed with the iron pan, willing the right answer from her. Both of them breathed rapidly.

'Yes,' whispered Claire.

Hegarty pulled at the legs of his damp trousers as he watched Daly and the superintendent climbing down the embankment. Daly cursed loudly, losing his footing and sliding on his backside to the bottom.

As they approached, Hegarty looked at Costigan.

'So this is the assistance that you got. Christ, I wouldn't look for assistance like that to break up a hen-party,' he whispered from the corner of his mouth.

The superintendent, moving towards the

covered body, looked suspiciously at Quilter, who was sitting on the grass, taking long pulls on a cigarette.

'What's the position here, Guard Hegarty?' he asked with authority.

'Well, sir, Mr Quilter here found the body about a half an hour ago, reported it to me and I removed it from the river and sealed off the scene.'

The superintendent made to speak.

'It would appear from the wound on the body,' continued Hegarty, enjoying his moment in the limelight, 'That some person or persons tried to remove his head with a blunt instrument.'

The superintendent glared at him. He had never liked Hegarty. Too much of a country guard and not enough spit and polish about him.

'I don't appreciate your flippant attitude to this, Guard. Show me the body.'

They moved around the orange line and Hegarty lifted the tweed coat.

'Jesus Christ!' gasped the shocked officer, raising his hand to his mouth and turning away.

'That's what I said,' muttered Quilter.

Daly eyed the body from where he stood at the other side of the line.

'Nasty one all right,' he said, sucking air hard between his teeth.

'Now then,' said the superintendent, struggling to keep the bile from rising, his eyes watering with the effort, 'the GP from the town, the pathologist and the Murder Squad have been notified and should be arriving shortly.'

He pointed to Quilter.

'Have you questioned this man and taken a statement from him?'

Hegarty shook his head.

'Then we will bring him to the station with us, Guard Hegarty. Daly, you and Guard Costigan remain here to preserve the scene. No unauthorised person gets in. Understood?'

He eyed Costigan up and down. Something was out of place.

'Button that shirt properly, Guard,' he ordered, and pointed in turn to the vacant buttonholes on the guard's shirt. Quilter muttered an apology as he rose to his feet.

The superintendent continued: 'We have a murder to investigate. Is it too much to ask that we look professional?'

He turned, without waiting for an answer.

'Hegarty, who covered the body?' he enquired.

'I did, Super . . . out of respect for the deceased.'

The superintendent tossed his head back and began to walk towards the embankment, speaking angrily as he went.

'You'll be deceased when Chief Superintendent Brosnan sees it. Have you ever heard of fibre evidence, man? I can see it in court now, "The only strange fibre found on the dead man, my lord, belonged to the tunic of a big guard who knew nothing about preserving murder scenes." We're off to a great start!' He started to climb back up the bank.

'Nice one, Jack,' whispered Daly and grinned.

Hegarty shouldered him as he passed, Quilter following sheepishly behind. The superintendent was already seated in the patrol car when they reached the top of the bridge. Hegarty opened the back door for Quilter.

'Am I arrested or something?' he asked nervously, settling himself in the seat.

'Well, let me put it this way,' replied the superintendent, turning back to look at him. 'You're, shall we say . . . helping the gardaí with their inquiries.'

'In simple language, does that mean I'm going to get the shite beat out of me?' Quilter laughed nervously.

As there was no reply forthcoming, he eased back into the seat and took the flattened cigarette box from his pocket to examine its contents.

'Can we stop for fags on the way?' he asked. 'I'm out.'

'Yes, Jim . . . we can,' replied Hegarty.

CHAPTER SEVEN

Daly walked up and down outside the orange line. A frosty silence had developed between himself and Costigan as a result of his smart comment to Jack Hegarty. Daly regretted having made it.

'So,' he said finally, 'how are things in Dunsheerin?'

Costigan looked at him.

'Well, apart from the occasional head being smashed in, things are just great,' he replied coldly, turning away again.

Moments passed and Costigan turned angrily towards Daly again.

'Tell me, Daly . . . does being a complete bollocks come naturally to you, or do you have to work at it?'

'It was only a bit of slagging, Costigan. Hegarty is long enough in the job to take it. Lookit,' he continued apologetically, 'I didn't think he was that sensitive.'

The moments ticked away in silence.

'Jesus!' said Daly eventually in exasperation. 'Now, look, I don't want to spend the rest of the evening in the company of a dead man and a thick man, so can we just drop it?'

He sighed and sat down on the grass.

Costigan knew that this was as close as he was going to get to an apology. In any case he had something else on his mind. He sat down beside Daly.

'There's something I want to ask you,' he said. 'A favour if you like.'

Daly smiled at him. 'A square you mean,' he said, happier now that his position of villain had been changed. 'Who is it?'

'You stopped Seamus Casey a few weeks ago driving without tax.'

'Yeah, so what?'

'Well, he's a decent man with five kids and he's promised me that he'll get it in order as soon as he can scrape the money together. His circumstances aren't the best. Will you give him a break?'

Daly paused as he pulled at a blade of long grass and began to chew pensively on it.

'As you well know, Guard Costigan,' he said, 'I don't square cases.'

'This is a Mickey Mouse tax case,' Costigan said.

Daly shook his head.

'My principles wouldn't allow it, Kieran. The

law is the law and it's the same law for the rich and for the poor.'

Costigan lay back on the ground, defeated, and sighed heavily at the sky.

'You're a heartless prick, Daly,' he said quietly.

Daly chuckled to himself. 'You know a day doesn't pass but someone calls me that. Even on my days off, the mother-in-law comes around to remind me.'

They both laughed. When they stopped, Daly shook his head and took out his notebook. 'When was it?'

Costigan edged himself closer to inspect the flicking pages. 'The tenth of last month,' his voice lowered in shock as the names flitted before his eyes. 'Jesus, Daly, is there *anyone* in the town that you haven't prosecuted?' Daly stopped and rubbed his hand pensively under his chin. 'Well, let me see now. I haven't done yourself or Hegarty yet.' Costigan smiled and shook his head.

'Is it true that you stopped the parish priest for speeding last year?' he asked.

Daly smiled, remembering the incident.

'Yeah. Fifty-two in a thirty zone, and a big, silver cross hanging around his neck. His excuse was that he was on his way to visit a widow. And I told him that if he kept going the way he was that he'd be visiting a few more.'

Costigan laughed. 'And did you bring him all the way to the court after?'

Daly nodded. 'Everyone from the Pope down tried to square it. You know the usual. The quiet, holy voice on the phone.'

He imitated a delicate whisper. 'Hello Garda, this is Father Brian. We played a hurling match against each other a few years ago. You caught poor Father Liam unawares last week.'

Daly tossed his head back and laughed. 'Kiss the back of my bollocks.'

'C'mon, Daly,' said Costigan, shaking him from the laughter. 'What's the story with Seamus Casey?'

Daly turned his attention back to the notebook and stopped at one of the pages. He took a pen from his top pocket and drew a line through it.

'Fair enough so, Kieran,' he grinned. 'I'll let him off this time, but if I catch him again he's for the holly.'

He stood up and watched the smile widen on Costigan's face, then turned and looked at the body, lifting the corner of the coat that covered it with the tip of his shiny black shoe.

'Who would do such a thing to a harmless old geezer like him?' he asked quietly. The humour was gone from his voice as he spoke.

Costigan shook his head.

'Don't know. All I know about him is that he had plenty of money and an adoring wife.'

'Mmmm, a rare enough thing,' mused Daly as he let the coat back down on the body, then turned to Costigan.

'Speaking of wives,' he smiled. 'I hear that you've fallen on your feet with that young O'Driscoll one. I believe that it's only a matter of time now.'

Costigan looked up at him with a face of mock seriousness, but could not hide his proud smile.

'What rumour did you hear now?' he asked, then immediately regretted it when he saw the grin widen on Daly's face, followed by a short chuckle.

'Forget I asked,' Costigan said quickly.

'No, no, Kieran,' said Daly. 'I feel it's my duty to tell you the rumour that's going around. It's just that the lads were saying that she's a fine big girl and that she should be put forward for this year's Rose of Tralee contest.'

'Big girl! What do you . . .' started Costigan, then held his breath for the inevitable punchline.

Daly held his arms out in triumph. 'But the only problem is that the local foundry has refused point blank to make the dress,' he laughed and threw himself on the ground beside Costigan, legs in the air as he balanced on the small of his back, sniggering at his own joke.

Costigan stared angrily at him. He could think of no insulting counter-punch through his anger. He did not know Daly's wife.

'Have you no respect for the dead?' he asked solemnly and nodded to the body in front of them.

Daly gave him a surprised look. 'Don't tell me you've never seen a dead body before.'

'Of course I've seen dead bodies before,' said Costigan angrily. 'But not with the head all smashed in and blood all over them. Nothing as ugly as that.'

Daly smiled and lay back down on the grass. 'I must show you my wedding photographs sometime,' he laughed.

The superintendent slammed the door of the car outside the Garda station. He was angry for two reasons. Firstly at Hegarty for his ignorance on the importance of fibre evidence, and secondly at himself for snapping at him. Hegarty, he knew, would be an important part of the investigation that was to follow; his local knowledge and knowledge of the deceased man's friends and, more important, his enemies, would be of great assistance to the investigating team.

Remembering the golf match with three other members of the Lions Club team planned for the following day, which would now have to be cancelled, only added to his irritation.

He tried hard to quell his annoyance.

'Right, Jack,' he smiled weakly, 'let's see what Mr Quilter here knows about the incident.'

He gave Hegarty a friendly pat on the back as they went inside.

Across the road, beside the chip-van, Myles Hickey balanced precariously on the heels of his shoes and, although his powers of vision had drastically deteriorated with his intake of drink, he had still seen his friend being escorted into the Garda station by Hegarty and another well-dressed man. In one hand he held a bag of chips, soggy with vinegar, his other hand taking one slowly and holding it up for examination before placing it in slow motion into his mouth.

Now and then, a passer-by would be invited to indulge in the feast with him.

'Wanna ship?' he'd slur, holding the greasy brown bag at arm's length in front of an unsuspecting female. She'd smile and quicken her pace to pass him.

He took a step towards the kerb, then staggered backwards, the bag falling on the ground and bursting into a sodden mess.

'Boll . . . ocks!' he muttered, bending down at an angle to pick it up, then changed his mind as his head began to spin. He straightened up and looked across the road, his mouth hanging open.

'No friend of mine is going to be locked up,' he shouted as he started for the kerb, and walked out on the road, waving his hands furiously and cursing at the car that screeched to a halt and blew its horn loudly.

Inside, Hegarty, who had heard the noise, turned and looked out the day-room window, watching Hickey approaching the gate.

'Ah . . . Jaysus, no,' he sighed, rising to his feet and brushing past Quilter and the superintendent, making his way quickly to the front door to intercept the arrival of Hickey.

His height dwarfed the swaying drunk at the door.

'What do you want, Hickey?' he whispered as he moved closer.

Hickey straightened himself up and looked at the frowning face above him.

'Goo . . . good evening, Offisher Hegarty,' he said, his head bobbing from side to side on his shoulders. 'I want to . . . to see my friend Jim . . . I'm . . . shh . . . I'm all right, Guard . . . D-Don't you know me?'

He extended his hand to Hegarty. 'Leave it there, Guard . . . You're . . . all . . . right.'

Hegarty looked up and down the street, over the smaller man's shoulder.

'Hickey,' he whispered as he looked around. 'I'm going to give you five seconds to disappear. If you're still here on the count of five, then you'll never forget the number six. One . . . two . . .'

Hickey lifted his hands in surrender.

'Fair 'nuff, Guard,' he said as he held his hand out to balance against the wall and turned to walk away.

Hegarty watched him go.

When he was about thirty yards away, Hickey turned back and raised his clenched fist in the air, the top half of his body appearing to revolve on the bottom.

'Justice!' he shouted. 'Justice for all.' Then he fell over a refuse bin that had been left out on the path for collection.

'Gobshite,' said Hegarty quietly as he walked back inside.

The superintendent was seated behind the day-room desk. He rested his hands on his lap, rolling his thumbs in the silence and narrowing his eyes to give a look of knowing suspicion. Quilter sat opposite him, looking around at the posters that hung on the station wall. Posters that warned about the dangers of not wearing a seat belt, another about not having a roller-bar on a tractor and finally one about the beetle that would destroy the country's entire potato crop if it got the chance.

Quilter read them all. He had been in the same room many times in the past, but never as sober as he was now.

'Now then, Mr Quilter,' said the superintendent, when he saw Hegarty returning to the room.

'I want you to tell us in your own words exactly what happened.'

Quilter watched him as he took a blank sheet of unlined paper from the desk drawer. His pen hovered above it.

'Well, . . .' began Quilter, 'I remember seeing him earlier today as I came in to collect my dole.'

'What time was that?' asked Hegarty as he scraped a chair across the stone floor.

'Around a quarter past twelve,' replied Quilter. 'He was . . .'

The superintendent interrupted: 'Carry on. There's a good man. Give us the full picture.'

Hegarty gave him a glance of disdain.

'He was fishing,' continued Quilter. 'I said hello and he got a bit upset because I suppose I disturbed him.'

'Ah ha,' said the super.

'Was he on his own when you saw him in the morning?' asked Hegarty.

'Yeah.'

'And everything appeared normal to you?'

'Yeah, like I said, he was fishing.'

'And you didn't have any conversation with him?'

'I told you already, I just said hello. He gave me a dirty look and said nothing . . . He could be a right ignorant bollocks when he wanted.' Quilter blessed himself. 'The Lord have mercy on his soul,' he added.

The superintendent made a stroke of his pen across the paper and it was then that Hegarty noticed that he was not making any notes, but had merely doodled a car on the blank sheet of paper.

He shook his head as he took out his notebook and began to write what Quilter was saying. 'Carry on, Jim,' he said.

'Well I was feeling a bit sheepish below in Madge's and so I decided to go home. Burns was still fishing when I passed him. I went home and had a cup of tea and a rest. And when I was coming back I saw Burns in the river. Floating dead in the river.'

The superintendent leaned forward on the desk and pointed his pen at Quilter. 'Then can you please explain for us why you made no attempt to save him? How did you know that he was dead? He could have been drowning. Can you explain that one for us?' His voice had risen to a high pitch.

Hegarty turned his head slowly. 'The river is three feet deep, Super,' he muttered.

The superintendent nodded for a couple of seconds. 'I see,' he said softly. 'Carry on, Guard.'

'Tell me, Jim,' said Hegarty, as he wrote. 'How did you see the body in the river from the footbridge? I looked down from it at all angles and couldn't see it. It would have been hidden by a clump of reeds.'

Quilter averted his eyes and looked at the floor, to hide a guilty look that swept across his face.

The superintendent leaned forward in the silence of the room, placed his elbows on the table and looked from Hegarty back to Quilter.

Quilter remained silent, looking at the floor.

'C'mon, lad,' said the superintendent, 'If you have something to confess, just spit it out.'

His heart raced as he watched Quilter's head rise.

The arrival of Chief Superintendent Brosnan would not be such a rough experience if the case were solved when he arrived. The superintendent smiled. He could already feel the congratulatory pats on the back at the golf club.

Quilter stuttered.

'I . . . I . . .'

'Yes? . . . Yes?'

'I saw the salmon,' Quilter said finally as he bowed his head in shame.

'What!' shouted the superintendent as he rose from his chair and walked quickly around the table. 'What shaggin' salmon is he talking about, Guard?'

'I believe, sir,' said Hegarty, 'That he's referring to the last fish caught by the late John Burns. The one beside the body.'

'Oh . . . *that* salmon,' said the superintendent, calming himself.

Quilter looked up. 'I saw the salmon on the bank as I was coming back to town. There was no one around and so I thought I'd claim it. There's a legal word for a claim like that.'

He clicked his fingers.

'Stealing,' said Hegarty.

Quilter continued: 'When I went to pick up the salmon, that's when I saw the body. I knew that he was dead when I saw the big cut on the back of his head. Then I ran to the village and told Guard Hegarty. Will I be charged?'

The superintendent gave a short cough and walked back around to his seat.

'No, Mr Quilter. As you can see, we have a little more to do at the moment than enforcing the fishery laws.' He pointed to the door. 'We'll be talking to you again in due course . . . and, as our American colleagues would say, don't leave town.'

Quilter looked curiously at him as he rose from the chair.

'I'll see you out,' said Hegarty standing up.

Quilter smiled weakly. 'Don't I get a blanket to put over my head like they do on the television?' he asked.

Hegarty took him by the arm and led him to the front door.

'The blanket should have been put over your head when you were in the pram,' he said. He pulled him to a sudden stop at the door. 'I get the feeling that you're not telling the truth. I wonder why I have that feeling,' he whispered.

'What... what do you mean, Guard?' Quilter asked, holding his hands out. 'Do you think that I had something to do with killing him?'

There was a short silence between them as Hegarty stared at him. He put his hands in his pockets and spoke over Quilter's shoulder, as if surveying the street.

'What I'm saying is that you have not told the whole truth. You have coloured your story and by doing that you have aroused my suspicion.' He fixed his eyes on Quilter. 'A dangerous thing to do, as you well know, Jim.'

Quilter breathed rapidly, his hands clenched to stop them shaking.

'I . . . I don't know what you're saying to me, Guard. I don't know what . . .'

'Go home and have a think about it,' said Hegarty. 'We'll be coming to see you in due course anyway.'

'I told you the truth,' insisted Quilter, his voice rising.

Hegarty shook his head.

'Maybe so,' he whispered, 'but not the whole truth.' He turned around. 'Go home, Jim,' he said, then went inside and closed the door.

Quilter stood alone on the path for a moment, contemplating his situation. What had he missed? Or rather what did Hegarty know? He turned and walked slowly away.

Hegarty stood at the door of the day-room. The superintendent sat behind the desk, looking discontented and disappointed.

'We'd better notify Burns's wife, Super,' said Hegarty.

'Yes, Jack,' replied Murray absentmindedly. 'Yes, we better.'

Hegarty took the sheet of paper with the drawing from the desk.

'Is there something wrong?' he asked, examining it.

Murray rubbed at his face.

'He should be arriving at any moment now.'

'Who?'

'Chief Superintendent Pat Brosnan. Head of the Murder Squad.'

'Pat . . . ah yeah,' said Hegarty. 'Sound man, Pat.'

'You know him?' asked the superintendent in surprise.

' Yes. We served together in the city when we were young fellas . . . in the same unit. Decent man, Pat . . . only if he likes you, of course. Otherwise he can be a right thick donkey.'

Hegarty placed the paper back down on the desk.

'Do you know, Super . . . you'd have made a great artist,' he said with a smile.

The superintendent chewed absentmindedly on his thumbnail and after a few seconds looked up at Hegarty.

'What were you and that Quilter fellow talking about outside?' he asked. 'Nothing off the record I hope.'

Hegarty gave a casual shrug. 'No. I was just reminding him about a warrant I have here for him,' he lied. 'He's an all-right enough fella without drink.'

The superintendent drummed his fingers on the desk.

'Mmmm,' he mused. 'I wonder.'

CHAPTER EIGHT

For a man with what most people would consider to be a horrifying job, Frank Long had an excellent sense of humour. He had been the state pathologist for nearly six years and in that time had struck up a great relationship with the Murder Squad.

The most popular story amongst the squad related to a post-mortem that he had performed in Dublin in the presence of a curious, fresh-faced recruit.

'There's no need for you to stay, Guard,' he had told the young man. 'Your identification of the body is sufficient.'

The recruit, however, stated that he would like to stay and see what 'all the fuss was about'.

Half-way through the post-mortem, as the chest was sawn open and the rib cage pulled apart, Long noticed to his delight that the recruit's face was beginning to lose its original rosy colour. With a snip, he removed the pink lungs and held them up for examination.

'Ah, a non-smoker,' he smiled, before throwing them into the red basin held by his assistant nearby.

'Pity he wasn't a non-drinker as well. Then he wouldn't have cut that telegraph pole in half with his car,' said the recruit.

'How very true, Guard. Well now, what have we here?' Long moved his hand around inside the lower half of the cadaver, then, taking the scalpel, removed a dark red body part and held it in front of the recruit, shaking it in his hand like a piece of jelly. 'And this of course is the *liver*!' he exclaimed, like a man who had just opened his Christmas present. 'And a fine piece of liver it is too. I must bring a pound of it home to the good woman.'

The smell, the basin of innards and the pathologist's sense of humour were all too much for the recruit. Long heard a slight belch from the young policeman. It was, as he used to call it, 'the belch before the storm'.

'I think I've seen enough,' muttered the recruit, one hand replacing the notebook in his tunic pocket, the other pressed hard against his mouth, his cheeks swelling with air.

'Ah, don't go yet, Guard. I must show you the brain. Tom, get the bone saw.'

Tom, the assistant, picked up what looked like a

small angle-grinder blade attached to an electric tooth-brush and turned it on.

Zzzzzzzzz.

'And now,' declared Long, 'the *pièce de resistance*.'

But it was too late. The door of the morgue slammed behind him as the recruit rushed out into the corridor, searching frantically for the door with 'Men' written on it, or anywhere, for that matter, where he could release the digestive volcano that was about to erupt.

In the end, unable to ask directions, he charged into the toilet reserved for wheelchair-users, hurdled over a man seated at the mirror combing his hair and, without a second to spare, reached the low toilet bowl into which he emptied everything but the lining of his stomach.

Back in the hospital morgue, Long dabbed the tears from his eyes. 'Another successful post-mortem, Tom,' he smiled.

Later, in the corridor near the exit, he saw the recruit sitting on a window ledge, his head in his hands, taking deep breaths, his shoulders shivering. His face was ashen pale, though the circumferences of his eyes were a fiery red.

Long recognised it as the effect of the violent rush of blood to the head induced by the force of vomiting, when it feels like your eyes are going to pop out of your head.

The young guard made a pitiful sight. Long sat down on the ledge next to him.

'I was like that too, lad. I remember the first time I had to cut someone open. I did it very professionally of course, then I spent the next eleven days throwing my guts up. I lost a stone and a half. I was going to market it and call it the post-mortem diet plan.'

The recruit lifted his head and tried to smile.

'By the way,' continued Long, 'your drunk driver died of a broken neck. Not another scratch on him.'

'Tell me, Mr Long,' asked the recruit, looking at him straight in the eyes. 'How come you can take death so easily that you can joke about it?'

'Well, Guard, my job is not unlike yours in that at times both are unenviable. I'm much better paid than you, of course,' he laughed. 'But if we take our jobs too seriously, we become a pain to ourselves and everyone else. A job like ours without a joke cracked now and then is a life sentence.'

He rose to his feet and began to walk away. The recruit got up and accompanied him to the end of the hall. They parted company at the door, both taking deep breaths in the evening air.

'My last word to you, son,' said Long, 'is this: Remember . . . a body is just a body.'

And so it was with the body of John Burns.

Frank Long snapped at his rubber gloves as he hunkered beside it, turning the head back and forth to examine the wounds. He could feel Costigan and Daly behind him, where they stood with arms folded, leaning sideways over his shoulder to get a view of what was happening.

'Well gentlemen, I can confirm your worst suspicions,' he said, standing up and arching his back.

'He's dead, and it wasn't suicide.'

He smiled at the two guards, although he had taken an instant dislike to Daly who had all but cross-examined him before he would let him near the scene.

'I'm the pathologist, Guard. Don't you recognise me from the television?' he had joked.

'I have instructions to let no one near the scene,' Daly had said sternly. 'However, if you can prove to me that you are indeed the pathologist, then you may pass.'

'Perhaps you would like me to take out your brain, Guard. Somehow I don't think that task would be too difficult,' snapped Long, losing his patience.

But for the intervention of Costigan, the pathologist would not have been allowed to examine the body.

Daly noted the name and time of his arrival at the scene in his notebook.

'It would be vital evidence in the trial if ever the perpetrator is caught,' he had told Costigan.

Long carried out all the necessary examinations on the body of John Burns under the ever watchful eye of Daly.

'Any sign of Pat Brosnan?' Long enquired as he peeled off his rubber gloves. 'He should be here by now.'

'He probably went to the station first. The super and Garda Hegarty are there,' said Costigan.

'Very good. Is this your first murder scene, Guard?' Long asked Costigan, ignoring Daly.

'Yes, sir.'

'Well all the same, you know the score . . . no unauthorised person to be let near the body and that does *not* include the state pathologist,' he said sternly, looking at Daly whose eyes were averted to the ground.

'Pat Brosnan and his squad should be here shortly. No removal of the body until I give the all clear . . . got it?'

He picked up his case and made for the footbridge.

'Who does he think he is, giving orders?' said a clearly irritated Daly when Long was out of earshot. 'I wonder if that Mercedes he's driving is taxed?'

'That would be one for the local papers all right, Daly,' laughed Costigan. 'State pathologist removes guard's brain after prosecution for no tax.'

'You know what, Costigan?' asked Daly changing the conversation. 'I didn't have any meal break this evening. And even though we're in the presence of a corpse . . . I could eat a farmer's arse through a hedge.'

CHAPTER NINE

There was a single loud rap at the door of the station.

'It's okay, Super,' said Hegarty. 'I have a fair idea who it is.'

He made his way quickly to the door, preparing himself to grab Hickey by the scruff of the neck, drag him out of the hearing range of the super and give him the kick in the arse which he usually reserved for a Saturday night.

He pulled the door wide open and leaned backwards on his heels in preparation for the lunge forward. There in the doorway stood a man who was familiar to him. A tall man in his late fifties, dressed impeccably in a white shirt, navy blue tie and a long black overcoat. Although the time of the year did not warrant them, he held a pair of dark gloves in one hand and slapped them rhythmically into the other.

They looked at each other for a few seconds. Then the man spoke: 'Jack, my ould stock, Hegarty.' He put the gloves in his left hand and extended his right. 'It's been a while.'

The voice, although it had been almost twenty years since he had last heard it, solved the puzzle for Hegarty.

'Pat Brosnan!' he exclaimed, his face lighting up with a broad smile. 'Well, Pat Brosnan!' he said again, taking the outstretched hand, shaking it with vigour, while with his other hand he slapped the right shoulder of the man before him.

'Jesus . . . You haven't changed a bit . . . come in, come in,' said Hegarty, all but pulling Brosnan over the door step.

'Great to see you, Jack. How's the wife? You must have a gang of kids at this stage.'

Brosnan was very pleased at this reception.

'Two daughters, it's like having three wives, all giving out about something different,' laughed Hegarty.

Superintendent Eamon Murray had heard the conversation in the hall. He rose from behind the desk and straightened his tie and jacket. The moment he had been dreading all evening had finally arrived.

Hegarty and Brosnan walked through the door of the day-room, a story of days gone by just about to break between them. Brosnan stopped in mid-sentence when he saw the superintendent.

'*Superintendent* Murray,' said Brosnan with mock emphasis.

There was silence in the room as the two men looked at each other. Hegarty eyed each in turn.

'Oh, so you two know each other as well,' he declared heartily. The tension in the room was palpable. He had to try to diffuse it. 'This is turning out to be more like a reunion than a murder investigation.'

Neither officer commented. They stared hard at each other for a moment before Murray's face relaxed.

'Chief Superintendent Brosnan . . . how are you?' he asked conventionally, but with a sharp edge in his tone.

'Fine, fine . . . and you?' replied Brosnan moving forward, his hand extended. 'You've jumped a few ranks since we last met,' he continued. 'I would never have believed that you were an officer at heart.'

'Ah yes,' interrupted Hegarty as he watched them give a brief shake hands. 'As Napoleon once said, "Inside every foot-soldier's rucksack is a Marshall's baton."'

It was a knife for them both.

Hegarty detested the bullshit that passed between officers, particularly at Garda dinner dances and parties for retiring members, the mock-camaraderie which disguised the reality that each one was waiting for the next to fall at some fence or other, thereby creating a vacancy in some 'handy number'.

When Costigan had decided to sit the sergeants' exam, Hegarty had spent the months before trying to dissuade him, not because he did not want him to succeed, but because he could foresee the hardship and the endless arse-kissing that would inevitably lie ahead. Costigan came from a large middle-class family, a family devoid of all political pull.

'Many men have been promoted in this job because of their ability,' Hegarty had once told Costigan. 'Then again, many men have got up on a politician's back and ridden him to the top. It is, as they say, the way of things.'

Costigan had thought it was a bad case of sour grapes that made Hegarty talk as he did.

Introductions dispensed with, Brosnan clapped his large hands together.

'Now I believe we've a murder to solve, so let's get down to business. My lads are already on their way to the scene. It's getting too dark to carry out any real search of the area, so what I want for now is to keep the scene sealed off. Superintendent Murray, you organise that, if you can. Jack, you're the man with the local knowledge, I want to visit the scene. Is there a next-of-kin?'

'Yes,' answered Hegarty, 'his wife – she doesn't know yet.'

'Right gentlemen, let's get cracking,' said Brosnan, holding his hand out and directing Hegarty to the door.

Murray, who was already on the phone, gave a wave as they departed.

'The superintendent here,' he said into the

phone. 'Send me out five men. I'm at Dunsheerin station. Yes . . . on overtime if necessary.' He paused for a moment then raised his voice. 'Listen boy, I don't give a toss about the Munster final. Get them out here as quick as you can.'

Hegarty and Brosnan settled themselves in the front seats of the car.

'Tell me, have you a suspect for this one, Jack?' asked the chief, snapping his seatbelt shut.

'I'm afraid not,' replied Hegarty, accelerating away.

Brosnan shuffled himself in the seat. 'Ah well, we can only do our best,' he said. He slapped Hegarty on the arm without warning. 'By God, but it's been a while, Jack. When was the last time we were in a squad car together?'

Hegarty laughed. 'I don't know, Pat, but I bet that we had a prisoner in the back.'

Brosnan grinned to himself. 'Jesus, those were the days.' He glanced sideways at Hegarty. 'Isn't it funny how fellas lose contact when they go to different stations?'

Hegarty nodded. 'Ah, they lose contact all right. But they never really forget.'

'I suppose not,' smiled Brosnan.

'What's the story with yourself and our beloved superintendent?' asked Hegarty without warning. He could wait no longer.

'Jesus, you haven't changed a bit have you, Jack,' said Brosnan with a shake of his head. 'You're as tactful as ever. That question has been burning a massive hole in your throat, hasn't it?'

Hegarty shrugged his shoulders. 'Not at all,' he

said casually. 'It's just that when the two of you met, I thought that I'd have to referee a boxing match. Anyone could see that ye hate one another's guts. How do you know him anyway?'

'What kind of a super is he?' asked Brosnan ignoring Hegarty's question. 'And please don't give me that "Yerra he's all right" line.'

Hegarty smiled and paused for a moment.

'Well, he's a low-handicap golfer. He ignores the lower ranks when he meets them socially with his high-class pals. He's a complete disaster in court and if the truth be known, he knows sweet shag all about the job.'

Brosnan closed his eyes slowly.

'Yep. That's him all right,' he said softly.

'Well,' said Hegarty expectantly. 'What's the story? And don't water it down,' he added with a smile.

Brosnan gave a heavy sigh.

'Do you remember when I got promoted to sergeant and transferred out of the city?' he asked.

Hegarty nodded.

'Well,' Brosnan continued. 'I was put in charge of a three-man station out the country, not unlike the set-up here. There were two ould lads and myself. 'Twas a big change, I can tell you. We had four crimes for the entire year and the one gobshite was responsible for the four of them. I was bored out of my arse.'

Hegarty laughed. 'It takes a bit of getting used to all right,' he said.

'Well, I couldn't,' continued Brosnan. 'I wanted to get back in the thick of things. I wanted to get up the ranks and I'm not ashamed to say it. I got on to a friend of mine in headquarters and he told me that if I held tough for another year or so and kept quiet that I'd get back to the city.'

'And did you?' said Hegarty, rushing him as the journey to the footbridge was drawing to an end.

Brosnan winced and ground his teeth as he remembered. 'One of the ould lads retired and I was sent a recruit.'

Hegarty beamed with delight. 'The super!' he laughed.

'Yeah,' said Brosnan with disgust. 'The super. 'Twas the longest eighteen months of my life.'

Hegarty slowed the patrol car to shuddering point and changed to a lower gear. He glanced across. 'Go on,' he urged.

'Do you remember "The Shank" that used to be on our unit in the city?' asked Brosnan.

Hegarty frowned in puzzlement.

Brosnan helped him along. 'Tall, thin fella, deep voice. Do you remember? The station sergeant used to say that every time he had a turnip for dinner he doubled his brain power.'

Hegarty slapped at his thigh. 'Ah yes, "The Shank". I remember now.' He deepened his voice to imitate his colleague of old. ''Tis an awful thing when young fellas break windows.'

Brosnan laughed. 'That's the man.' He raised his thumb for emphasis and pointed over his shoulder in the direction from which they had come. 'Well "The Shank" was a rocket scientist compared to the fella back there. I tell you, Jack, your super is everything that I hate about the way this job is turning out. Jesus, but he was a bone-idle bollocks if ever there was one.'

Hegarty could sense the hatred in Brosnan's voice.

'Yeah, but that was a long time ago, Pat,' he said. 'Things couldn't have been that bad.'

Brosnan waved his hand dismissively. 'It has nothing to do with that, Jack,' he corrected. 'When I think of all the fine men who were passed over for promotion so as to make a place for a waster like him. It just makes me sick. At least I got my crack at him.'

'What do you mean?' asked Hegarty.

Brosnan rubbed his hands together.

'I was on one of the interview boards when he tried out for promotion to sergeant. I nearly got sick reading his application form. "The job is smothering in the dark ages," he told us. And that coming from a fella who never felt a gouger's collar in his life.'

'But he got promoted though,' said Hegarty.

'Not that year!' Brosnan growled in response.

'He'll surely make chief now,' said Hegarty and inwardly cursed the stupidity of his comment.

'Of course he will,' agreed Brosnan quietly. 'It wouldn't surprise me if he bluffed his way to the very top. He must be an expert at it by now.'

Hegarty pulled the car to a halt at the foot-bridge and jerked the handbrake up hard.

'Sure didn't *you* get where you wanted after,' he smiled. He waited for Brosnan to nod in agreement then gave him a gentle elbow. 'Tell me now, Pat. Are you a low-handicap golfer yourself?'

Brosnan grinned as he reached for the door handle. 'Get out of the car, Guard,' he roared.

Jim Quilter sat alone in the corner of the packed lounge bar. His view of the act which was taking place in the centre of the floor was blocked by the mass of people who stood in front of him.

'Hup ya boya, Myles,' shouted the clapping female who then jumped up and down squealing with laughter.

Quilter sighed and sipped at his glass. He had tried unsuccessfully to get Hickey's attention. But Hickey had other things on his mind. He was, as they both referred to it, 'with chance of a ride'. The music from the accordion and bodhrán grew faster and faster as did the clapping and cheering.

Quilter stood up and looked over the young girl's shoulder.

There in the centre of the floor was Hickey stripped to the waist, a woman on either arm as he swung around in time to the music. His eyes rolled in his head as their speed increased. He loosed his grip on the women and raised his arms in the air. The sweat poured from his deathly white face and bare chest.

'Jesus Christ, he's going to vomit,' said Quilter out loud.

The young woman in front of him glanced backwards and held her hands to her face as she screeched with laughter. Hickey spun round once more then lost his balance and headed straight for the musicians. The music stopped suddenly, the musicians holding their instruments above their heads as Myles sped towards them.

All this time, the publican, John Clancy, was making a futile struggle through the crowd, his arm reaching over the shoulders to grab Hickey.

'You're barred for life, ya mad bastard,' he shouted to roars of laughter.

He moved forward and pulled Hickey from where he had pinned the bodhrán player to the toilet door. A silence filled the bar. An uneasy silence like that which falls over a noisy classroom when the principal walks in.

Quilter looked at the people as they muttered their way back to their seats. All these people who were oblivious to the fact that a man lay murdered less than two miles away.

'I'm going. I'm going,' protested Hickey as John Clancy pulled him towards the door. 'Where's me shirt, ya tunderin' shite?'

Before he could continue, Hickey was pushed out through the front door. Quilter searched the floor and the nearby stools.

Hickey shivered on the path outside. He rolled his fists in front of him and staggered backwards.

'Come out here and say it,' he shouted.

His eyes widened with fear as the door opened. Then he lowered his drunken head and snorted. 'Jesus, Jim, ya frightened the livin' bejesus outta me.'

Quilter threw the bundle of clothes at Hickey's bare chest.

'What in the name of Christ are ya at?' he asked angrily. 'I've been trying to talk to you for ages.

Did ya not see me calling you? I had something very important to talk to you about.'

Hickey held out his jacket. 'Hold that.'

He struggled with the sweat-soaked sleeves of his shirt then looked up with a drunken gaze of urgency. 'Jim. Jesus, Jim.'

'Yes.'

'Jim, my friend . . . I forgot . . . how could I forget?'

Hickey shook his head in self-disappointment.

Quilter awaited the apology. Hickey pointed to the door.

''Twas a new pack. Will you go back in and get them for me? Please, Jim.'

'What in the fuck are you talking about?' asked a confused Quilter.

'My fags,' revealed Hickey. 'I left them on the counter. Maybe I didn't. Search that jacket.'

Quilter rolled the jacket in a ball and threw it forcefully at Hickey.

'Stick your fags up your arse, Hickey,' he shouted and began to walk away.

Hickey picked the jacket up from the path and followed in a drunken stagger.

'Don't be getting all thick with me, Quilter,' he shouted.

He lunged forward and grabbed at Quilter.

'Jim . . . Jim . . . hold on,' he suddenly laughed as he ran beside him. 'Did ya see the big French one I was dancing with? Jesus, the size of her. She said that her father owns a grape farm in France and that I could go out and drink all the red wine I want.'

He moved himself in front of the walking Quilter and held his hands up.

'Will we go for the *craic*, the two of us?' he grinned.

Quilter stopped and held his arm out on Hickey's shoulder.

'John Burns was murdered this evening and Jack Hegarty thinks that it was me that did it.'

He waited for Hickey's reaction.

'Did you hear what I said?' he asked when none came.

Hickey swayed in front of him, his eyebrows furrowed in confusion. He put his jacket on slowly and looked up at Quilter.

'*Who* did ya kill,' he asked.

'Aw for . . .' started Quilter and began walking away.

'So that's why you were in the station,' said Hickey from behind him. 'Now I remember. Jack Hegarty, yourself and that other fella. Well I never thought 'twould come to this . . . My friend a murderer.' He shook his head in disbelief.

Quilter took him by the jacket and shook him.

'I didn't kill anyone! I was the one that found the body,' he said angrily. 'But I had a few words with Burns before he was killed.'

Hickey removed Quilter's hand from his jacket.

'Jim, I don't care if you killed him or not. He was a bollocks anyway.' He glanced up and down the street of the village then raised an eyebrow at Quilter. 'Listen we shouldn't be talking here. Come on to my place. I have a bottle.'

He set off in long purposeful strides ahead of

Quilter, the occasional stagger betraying his state of mind. He looked up as Quilter joined him at his side.

'Is he really dead, though?' he asked.

Pat Brosnan climbed carefully down the side of the footbridge. As a younger man he would have vaulted over the top railing and jumped the six feet or so to the riverbank. He had kept himself fit by taking long walks and swimming once a week. However, his dedication to the Murder Squad had led him to neglect this regime in recent years. He consoled himself with the fact that the energy that he had expended in that physical activity could now be used to work the mind twice as hard. He stood on the edge of the riverbank, looking at the dusk-lit water that winked up at him. He paused for a moment, lost in thought, then snapped back and moved towards the body. He did not bend to examine it, but merely stood beside it, his hands in his overcoat pockets as he looked around. He nodded towards Daly and Costigan.

'You're going to need your coats, lads. It's getting a bit chilly.'

He beckoned Daly towards him with his finger. 'What's your name, Guard?' he asked.

Daly stuck his chest out. 'Garda Mike Daly, sir,' he said, almost standing to attention. 'Attached to the Traffic Corps,' he added.

Brosnan eyed him up and down. 'Not any more, Daly. At least not until this matter is solved. Remain here at the scene until two a.m. and be in the Garda station tomorrow morning at ten sharp. You'll be doing questionnaires.'

He leaned forward. 'Do you know what *they* are?' he asked.

Daly nodded. 'Self-explanatory I'd say, Chief,' he smiled.

'Don't be a smart arse, Daly,' growled Brosnan, pointing to the bridge. 'Go and get the coats.'

His attention was drawn from Daly by a young man dressed in plain clothes who, with the aid of a strong torch, was examining a section of ground beside the body.

'Sullivan . . . anything?'

'Nothing yet, Chief. It's best left 'till morning.'

Finbarr Sullivan was one of the few men in the Murder Squad who Brosnan knew would leave no stone unturned. A man whose actions were unquestioned by his superior. 'If it's there, then Sullivan will find it,' Brosnan would say.

He had been in the Technical Bureau for five years, and in that time, he had been instrumental in solving all but one of the seven cases with which he had been involved. Sullivan, like all great murder investigators before him, believed that forensic evidence was the best evidence.

However, this case was not going to be an easy one.

The ground leading to and around the body would have to be thoroughly checked. That meant the hands-and-knees method. Long river grasses would be difficult to examine, but Sullivan was always hopeful that the murderer would not be thorough enough in covering his tracks. There was always the chance.

He looked up from his work as he felt the presence of someone behind him. Jack Hegarty gave a backward nod of his head, indicating that he wanted a word.

'Yes, Guard?' said Sullivan softly, as if not wishing to disturb the eternal slumber of the body nearby.

'Well . . . It's about the body . . . I . . .'

'Yes, what about it? What about the body?' asked Sullivan, shining the torch on John Burns.

'I put a coat over the body when I removed it from the water . . . I probably ruined any fibre evidence.'

Hegarty fell silent. Sullivan gritted his teeth. Even in the failing dusk light, the guard could see the bones protruding in anger at the top of his jaw. He prepared himself for the worst.

Sullivan wanted to give him a screaming lecture on the proper methods of crime investigation and the preservation of the murder scene, yet somehow he felt sorry for the elderly guard. He knew by the look of him that Hegarty was close to retirement age. What good would it do either of them?

'A slip, Guard. Forget about it. Just don't lose that overcoat until we've eliminated it along with any other fibres.' He smiled.

'Thanks, lad,' came the relieved reply.

Hegarty walked back to the footbridge where Brosnan was speaking to four men in plain clothes. They were not from the division, so

Hegarty figured that they were Brosnan's men chosen especially for the investigation. He walked past them as they listened attentively to their superior. Hegarty wanted nothing to do with the Murder Squad detectives. The one whom he had just met made him feel like a child who had broken his mother's favourite vase.

'Six a.m. sharp,' called Brosnan as he climbed up to join him on the bridge. 'That's *six* . . .' he emphasised loudly, pointing to the four men below. Brosnan knew that Sullivan, dedicated as ever, would be carrying out his investigations at first light, but it was harder to keep these men in line, the men who had the tedious job of taking statements and filling out questionnaires with the locals.

'Right, Jack, let's go and break the news to the next of kin,' said Brosnan, sitting into the patrol car.

At the end of the narrow road that led to the footbridge, a number of people had gathered. A single guard at the mouth of the road held his arms outstretched, as if holding back a huge crowd. He turned on seeing the lights of the squad car and directed it onto the main road with a half-hearted wave of his right hand.

'What's goin' on, Guard?' asked the onlookers.

'Has there been an accident?'

'Is there anyone hurt?'

'Ah go on, Guard, tell us . . .'

All hoped privately that some serious incident had occurred. Something to throw a smattering of excitement into the ordinary life of the run-of-the-mill village.

'There's nothing to concern yerselves about,' shouted the guard. He swung his arms as if ushering cattle through a gap. 'Come on, now,' he urged. 'Away with ye.'

CHAPTER TEN

During the three-mile journey to the Burns residence, Pat Brosnan reached into the inside pocket of
his overcoat and withdrew a fresh new copybook
which had been folded in half. Attached to the front
cover by its clip was a gold Cross pen, which he
removed and clicked a few times. Having flattened
the cover on his lap, he wrote the name 'John
Burns' on it and creased open the first page. He jotted down the mental notes he had made at the
scene. He stopped now and again to think, tapping
the pen against his lips. Hegarty watched him out of
the corner of his eye, straining to see what was
being written.

'Take it easy, Jack,' said Brosnan as the car

struck a small pot-hole, the jolt causing the pen to slip from his hand. 'Never rush when you've got bad news.'

Hegarty eased his foot off the accelerator and changed to a lower gear. After a few minutes, Brosnan finished writing, clipped the pen on the front cover, folded the copy in half and replaced it back in his inside pocket. He sat back in the seat and folded his arms.

'Tell me what you know about the victim, Jack. This John Burns, what sort of a client was he?'

'Well,' replied Hegarty pushing himself back at arm's length from the steering wheel, 'he was a self-made man, worked hard all his life to get what he wanted. No doubt stepping on a few people on the way up.'

'No shortage of enemies?' interrupted Brosnan.

'We all have enemies, Pat, and I'm sure Burns had his. But off-hand I can't think of one who would split open the back of his head, if that's what you're asking me.'

The car shuddered across the wide cattle grid at the entrance and moved smoothly up the tarmacadam driveway. Brosnan looked out at the tall trees that lined both sides and at the illuminated lawns with the three-tiered fountain in the centre.

'Bit of a pity really to leave all this behind,' he said quietly as the car pulled up at the steps of the house. 'I suppose you'll do the needy, Jack. The blow will be softer coming from someone she knows.'

'Sometimes I really hate this job,' sighed Hegarty as they both started up the steps.

'No you don't, Jack. You wouldn't have survived this long if you hated it,' said Brosnan as he pushed the doorbell, its echo resounding inside the hallway.

They could hear the sound of voices inside, then the tapping of high heels on the solid floor.

'Jack Hegarty,' smiled Jenny, standing back to open the door wide, beckoning the two men to enter. 'Come in, we're just making the tea. Come in, Claire will be delighted to see you.'

Hegarty made an attempt to speak, but was cut off by Jenny's excited chattering. A smell of drink and perfume wafted in the air as she spoke.

'Well, Jack,' she gushed, pointing at Brosnan. 'Aren't you going to introduce us?'

'This is Chief Superintendent Pat Brosnan from Dublin. I really don't know how to tell . . .'

'Stop your mumbling at the door, Jack,' she laughed. 'Come in gentlemen, come in. Leave your coats there.' She pointed to the mahogany stand and walked quickly towards the kitchen door, her stiletto heels tapping loudly on the gleaming marble floor.

'This way, gentlemen.' She stopped at the door and looked back with concern. 'Jack. Did you sort out John Burns?' she asked. 'What did he say? Claire is dying to know what happened.'

Brosnan gasped and dropped his coat on the ground in front of the hallstand. He looked sideways at Hegarty as he bent down to pick it up. Hegarty swallowed hard and shook his head quickly in response.

'What the hell is going on, Jack?' asked Brosnan in a whisper through his teeth.

Hegarty shook his head again. 'Not now, Pat,' he

pleaded. 'Let's get this over with and I'll tell you outside.'

'Aw, Jesus Christ,' whispered Brosnan.

Jenny stood smiling as she waited for them.

'Claire,' she called out as she opened the kitchen door, 'you'll never guess who it is.'

She stood back to allow the two men to pass in ahead of her.

'It's Jack Hegarty and . . . and?' She took Brosnan by the arm. 'Oh, *what* did you say the name was again? I'm sorry. I've a terrible memory.'

'Chief Superintendent Pat Brosnan,' clipped Hegarty, growing tired of the giddy hostess.

'A chief superintendent no less,' said Jenny, her voice changing to mock-seriousness, letting go of Brosnan's arm. 'Well, we won't hold that against you.'

She giggled up at him.

'Well, I must go to the little girls' room. You're in safe company here, Claire.'

Claire stood at the counter smiling, shaking her head from side to side.

'I'm so very sorry, Jack. What must this man think?' she said, putting her hand up to her mouth in an attempt to wipe away the smile. 'You know what Jenny can be like. You're very welcome, both of you.'

She nodded in acknowledgement to Brosnan, who was standing behind Hegarty.

'Anyway, you're just in time for a cup of tea,' she continued, taking the chinaware from the counter and placing it on the table. 'Sit down . . . sit down, make yourselves comfortable.'

'Claire, I'm sorry,' said Hegarty, 'but this isn't a social visit. I'm afraid I've got some bad news.'

Both men remained standing.

'What is it, Jack? Is it about the complaint I made today? What did he say? Did he lose his temper with you?'

Brosnan ground his teeth and closed his eyes.

Hegarty stepped forward and held his arm out. 'No, Claire, it's not that . . .'

He was visibly grappling for the words as he stepped towards her. There was a pause. A pause which was too long in the circumstances.

'I'm afraid it's your husband, Mrs. Burns,' blurted Brosnan, coming to the aid of Hegarty. 'He's been murdered.'

No sooner was it out of his mouth then he silently cursed himself for the sudden outburst. In all his dealings with death, he had never got that part right. He had rehearsed the breaking of such news many times, twisting the words to ease the blow, 'the watering down of death', as he called it. He had searched for the right formula and had discussed it with his colleagues over the years. Nothing made it easy. Brosnan too had laughed at the story of the insensitive guard delivering the death message:

'Are you the Widow McCormack?' he had enquired of the woman at the door.

'I'm no widow,' she had replied indignantly. 'My husband is at sea.'

'Well you are now,' grunted the guard, walking away. 'He's at the bottom of it.'

Brosnan clenched his fists behind his back, looking across the table. Hegarty stood a few feet away with his eyes to the floor. Both looked more like schoolboys who had been sent to the headmaster's office than investigators of a murder. Neither knew what to say next.

Claire Burns swayed slightly to one side and, before Hegarty could round the long kitchen table to catch her, fell back awkwardly against the kitchen counter, the cup and saucer slipping from her grasp and shattering into tiny pieces on the tiled floor. Hegarty put his arm around her and gently eased her to a chair.

'Water, Pat,' he hissed. Brosnan hastily took one of the cups from the table, filled it at the sink and placed it before Claire. Hegarty took the cup and, as if helping a blind person, placed Claire's hands around it.

'Here . . . take some.'

Claire sipped a little, then put the cup down slowly and rested her face in her hands.

'Oh my God!' she cried out. 'Dear Jesus . . . no . . . no . . . no.'

The two men looked at her helplessly.

'He's all I've got, Jack,' she sobbed, turning and placing her head on Hegarty's shoulder.

He rested his chin on her head, and patted her back.

Moments of silence followed, broken by intermittent sobs from Claire.

Brosnan stood at the end of the table. His mind was in turmoil. He looked from Claire to Hegarty and back again.

Suddenly the kitchen door swung open and Jenny pranced in, smiling and carrying a crystal brandy glass.

'No tea for me, Claire. I just . . .'

She stopped in mid-sentence.

'What's the matter?' she exclaimed, obviously shaken by the scene which greeted her. 'Claire . . . what is it? Tell me . . .' She moved around the table, stumbling slightly as her heel crunched on the broken china.

Hegarty got to his feet and, without speaking, offered the chair to Jenny.

'It's John!' wailed Claire, embracing her friend tightly. 'He's been murdered.'

'What!!' said Jenny, holding her back at arm's length and looking up incredulously at the two men who stood sheepishly at the table.

'It's true, I'm afraid,' nodded Hegarty. 'His body was found by the river.'

The two women looked directly at one another.

'Oh my God,' said Jenny and once again embraced her sobbing friend. 'Oh Jesus, Claire . . . I'm *so* sorry,' the tears welling in her eyes. The women hugged each other tightly, each one sniffling into the other's shoulder.

After a few moments Jenny broke free of the embrace and stood up. She looked up directly at Jack Hegarty. She wiped a tear from her eye and sniffed loudly before she spoke. Her voice was full of anger.

'Have you caught the person who did it?' she asked. She scowled at Hegarty.

'We're doing all we can at the moment. But as of yet . . . nothing,' he replied.

'I can assure you that no effort will be spared in getting the person responsible, Mrs Burns,' added Brosnan, looking down at Claire.

'There is also the matter of the identification of the body.' Hegarty spoke in a low voice. 'I know that it's a bad time . . . but it's something that has to be done . . . tomorrow I'm afraid. Do you think that you'll be up to it, Claire?'

'You needn't worry yourself about Claire, Guard,' interrupted Jenny. 'You go out and catch the person who did this.'

Claire sighed heavily and got up.

'There's no need for that, Jenny. Yes, Jack, I believe that I am up to it. Thank you for coming . . . and you too,' she added, nodding in Brosnan's direction. 'What exactly do I have to do?'

'Don't worry about that now, Claire,' said Hegarty gently. 'I'll collect you tomorrow and explain it to you then.'

'I'll go with you,' whispered Jenny, giving Claire a supportive squeeze on the arm.

'Thank you again, Jack . . . I just can't believe that this has happened to us,' said Claire, her voice breaking as the tears began to flow once again.

'Is there anyone you'd like us to contact?'

'No . . . no, Jack, thanks . . . I'll manage.'

Both men nodded and backed towards the kitchen door.

Jenny led them along the hall. Brosnan was first out the door and stood on the top step. He looked back and watched as Jenny took Hegarty's arm and said something in a low voice that he could not make out.

'Good night then,' said Brosnan as they made their way out into the coolness of the summer night.

Hegarty walked in silence around to the driver's side of the car. He unlocked the door and looked across at the tall man standing there, motionless, his wide frame silhouetted by the bright lantern lights that hung above the front door.

'What is it, Pat?'

Still no move from the big man, who stood there with his hands in the pockets of his overcoat.

'Pat! What the hell is wrong?' whispered Hegarty through clenched teeth.

Brosnan looked at him like a man awakening from a trance. He stared at him for a few seconds then made his way to the passenger door and without speaking sat in.

Hegarty shrugged and sat into the driver's seat. Brosnan removed the copybook from his pocket and began to write as Hegarty drove slowly away from the front steps. As the car rolled across the cattle-grid, Brosnan tore the page from the book and slammed his fist violently on the dashboard.

'*Jesus Christ*,' he roared at the top of his voice.

Hegarty flinched with shock beside him. Brosnan lifted the hand-brake of the car and opened the door. 'Get out,' he shouted. 'Get out of the car.'

Hegarty watched as Brosnan made his way around to the driver's side and banged his fist on the windscreen.

'Get out of the car, Jack,' he shouted.

Hegarty stepped slowly out. 'What the hell is the matter with you?' he asked. 'Look, I can explain about what happened up there.'

Brosnan raised his fist in front of Hegarty's face and released the index finger from it.

'Why the Christ did you not tell me that you had seen the victim this evening? Or have you got so country-guard stupid that you didn't think it was important?'

'Give me a chance to explain,' pleaded Hegarty, raising his hands.

Brosnan inched closer, his finger almost touching the face of the man in front of him. 'Answer the shagging question, Guard.'

Hegarty had had enough. He pushed at the large frame in front of him back and raised his fists. 'Is this what you want?' he asked through gritted teeth. 'You were never able for me, boy. Now back off and let me speak.'

Both of them stood panting in the darkness.

'Well?' said Brosnan. 'Are you going to stand there like an eejit or are you going to explain all this to me?' He held his hand up and counted on his fingers. 'One. Why did you not tell me that you had seen the victim today? Two. Why did you go to see the victim? And three. What in the name of Christ is going on?'

Hegarty put his hands in his pockets and rested against the wing of the patrol car.

'He was beating his wife,' he said. 'I only found out about it today when herself and Jenny Maguire came to the station. I went to the riverbank and warned Burns that it had to stop.'

Brosnan cupped his face in his hands. 'Oh sweet Jesus,' he muttered.

'Anyway,' continued Hegarty looking at him. 'Claire Burns wouldn't make a statement of complaint so my hands were tied.' He stood up and moved towards Brosnan. 'I went to see him off the record,' he said. 'I know it looks bad . . .'

'Looks bad,' Brosnan snorted. 'Looks bad! Did you see the way that Maguire one looked at you? From the expression on her face, Jack, I'd say she thinks that *you* did it.'

'Ah now, bullshit,' Hegarty shouted at him. 'You know very well that I had nothing to do with it.'

They were both illuminated by the headlamps of a passing car. Hegarty continued when it was gone. 'I did *not* kill John Burns, Pat,' he said softly. 'You know me a long time and if that means anything then you'll believe me.'

Brosnan shook his head slowly. 'Why did you not tell me about your meeting with Burns?' he asked.

'I was going to,' replied Hegarty. 'To be honest I didn't think that it was that important. Anyway, I wasn't the last one to see Burns alive.'

'Who was?'

'One of the local characters by the name of Jim Quilter.'

Brosnan nodded and made his way around to the passenger side. He looked across the roof of the car at Hegarty.

'Have you anything else that you'd like to let the head of the investigation team know before we continue?' he said.

Hegarty shook his head. 'Nothing that I can think of.'

'Very well then,' groaned Brosnan, as he eased himself into the seat.

Hegarty sat in and started the patrol car. Brosnan started to write.

'I may live to regret this, Jack,' he said as he wrote. 'I can't understand why you waited to tell me about Burns.'

Hegarty sensed the disappointment in his tone. 'I can see now that it was stupid, Pat,' he said.

Brosnan nodded. 'By the way,' he said casually, 'assaulting a chief is a serious enough offence.'

Hegarty turned to him and watched as a smile broke on his face.

He looked back at the road and smiled himself. 'It's not an offence if the chief is a thick man.'

'Jack,' said Brosnan without looking up. 'From this moment on I want to see less of the country-guard bullshit and a bit more of the man I worked with in the city. No more surprises. Got it?'

Hegarty nodded in understanding and smiled to himself. Their outburst at the entrance to the Burns residence reminded him of the many violent arguments that they had had while working together in the city. Hegarty felt invigorated. Despite his cosy existence in Dunsheerin, at times he missed the thrill of urban police work and the buzz that went with it.

Brosnan closed the copybook and looked up. 'Is there a good lodging house in this place?' he inquired.

'In tourist areas they're called bed-and-breakfasts,' Hegarty corrected him.

'Yeah. Right,' said Brosnan. 'Just get me into one, like a good man.'

Hegarty drove to the end of the village and stopped the car. He leaned across to look out the passenger window.

'This is a good place,' he said and got out of the car.

Brosnan watched from the passenger seat as he walked up the path and rang the front doorbell.

A small woman in a dressing gown appeared in the doorway. Following a short conversation with her, Hegarty signalled with a wave of his hand. Brosnan stepped out and walked towards him.

'You're in luck. She has one room left. What about your luggage?'

'It's in my car, I can collect it tomorrow morning.'

The two men nodded their goodnights on the doorstep and Hegarty turned to walk away.

'One more thing, Pat. Don't leave any documents lying around and don't tell her anything. She's like the friggin' *Daily News*, this one. You'll be finding out yourself.'

'Jack?'

'Yeah?'

'A fresh start tomorrow. OK?'

Hegarty nodded. 'A fresh start, Pat,' he agreed.

'Good man. See you at the station at six a.m. sharp.'

Hegarty saw Rose Scully extending a hand of welcome to Brosnan in the hall. He pictured the conversation in his mind.

'What county man are you? What's happening in the village? Are you here because of that? Would you be a friend of Jack's?'

'God help you, Pat,' Hegarty said to himself, pitying his friend who would be held captive by the old woman's chat for at least a half-hour.

He was driving back towards the Garda station, but changed his mind. He would go and check on young Costigan instead. At this stage, he reckoned that the young guard would be in dire need of a cup of tea, having spent the entire evening at the murder scene. He would let him go for an hour or so.

As for Daly. Well, he could starve.

CHAPTER ELEVEN

The two men sat on low, cushioned stools at the darkened end of the city-centre bar, the smaller of the two playing nervously with a beer mat.

'What can I get you?' chirped the waitress, her white blouse illuminated by the ultra-violet strobe light. The bigger man looked up.

'Two Mulligans, plenty of ice.'

The waitress nodded.

'Oh . . . and by the way,' he added, 'what are you doing after? I'm very good with my hands you know.'

His friend snorted a laugh.

'You'll have to get them out of the straight-jacket first, love,' she smiled, rolling a wisp of gum across her teeth and turning to go.

'Stuck up bitch.'

Recovering quickly from the rebuff, the big man leaned menacingly across the table.

'What the *fuck* is the matter with you?' he spat through clenched teeth. 'It's like looking at a dead man. It's a bit late for regrets now, ya know.'

He fell silent as the waitress approached and banged the drinks down on the table.

Tony Kearns put down the beer mat and looked across at the other man, the events of the past twelve hours racing through his thoughts.

The early morning drive down to the country, Seanie beside him in the passenger seat, playing nervously with the two-foot iron bar as he disclosed to him the purpose of the trip. The hour-long wait on the roadside near Dunsheerin village and the high-speed journey back to the city. The violent argument between them in the car.

'Did you do it?' he had demanded, as the car screeched away towards the main road, 'Did you fuckin' do it?'

'I think so,' came the breathless reply from Seanie, examining the blood-stained iron bar before throwing it on the floor of the car as if it were white hot.

'You *think* so? . . .You fuckin' *think* so?' he'd shouted incredulously.

'I... I hit him a couple of times . . . he fell into the river. I'd say he'll drown anyway.'

'Aw for fuck sake!'

Tony's knuckles were white on the steering wheel, pressing his foot down. The country ditches galloped past.

He was an excellent driver who had stolen his first car when only twelve years old. He and his friend Jimmy had taken an Opel Berlina from a city-centre car park and had driven around for a few hours before hearing the wail of the patrol car behind them. In a panic, he had increased speed, losing control and mounting a roundabout, striking a young man who was returning from soccer training.

He was to be Tony's first victim.

In the sixteen years that followed, his joy-riding would injure more than ten people. But it was never intentional. One night his luck had run out, driving a stolen fuel-injection BMW. His four passengers had dared him to drive at a motorcycle garda whom they had seen waiting for them in a side street. As they sped towards him, an unmarked car had roared out from the side street opposite. In the seconds before it smashed into the BMW Tony had seen the violent expressions on the men inside, men who had had enough. He would never forget the sound of the impact, his useless efforts to reverse the wrecked car away from the summary punishment that would follow. The shattering of glass. The shouts of the others as batons rained down on them. He had woken in the cell the following morning, a crumpled copy of the charge sheet beside him, his entire body sore and shaking.

'Your age has saved you before,' the judge had boomed. 'Not this time, Mr Kearns. I'm going to give the city a break. Three years.'

Tony, sandwiched between two guards, had looked wildly at his solicitor who moved quickly across the courtroom, shrugging his shoulders.

'Excuse me, Guard. May I have a word with my client in private?' the lawyer had asked.

'No you cannot,' the guard had replied. 'You can speak to him in prison.' He enjoyed being on the winning side.

'Listen, Guard, I'm entitled to . . .'

'You're entitled to nothing. You had your crack at it and you made a balls of it.'

The guard had lowered his voice and leaned confidentially towards the solicitor. 'I don't know how you can sleep the night, defending the likes of this scumbag.'

'Everyone is entitled to their rights, Guard.'

'Yeah. But thankfully they have to pay for their wrongs,' the garda had shot back, pulling the helpless Tony off the stand, the two of them moving down the corridor.

'We'll appeal!' his solicitor had called out. 'Don't worry.'

It was in prison that Tony had met Seanie. They had shared the same cell for the twelve months that Tony had served of his three-year sentence. Seanie was serving a two-year sentence for grievous bodily harm. Some drunk had called his girlfriend of three weeks a slut, and Seanie had given him a cut that required fifty stitches to the face. He had always carried a hunting knife for protection.

Prison was nothing like what Tony had seen on television. There were no organised gangs. No top dogs keeping the prison officers in check and running the jail.

'We're all just lags here,' Seanie had once commented, as he rolled a cigarette with his rationed tobacco. He had told Tony of his ambition to get involved with the biggest and most organised gang of criminals on getting parole. He promised to put in a good word for Tony once he got established.

'There's always room for a good car thief,' he had said.

True to his word, Seanie had called. It was almost two years later. The job was simple. Tony would have to steal a car and drive Seanie to a village down the country. For this simple task he would receive the sum of two thousand pounds.

'Ah come on, Seanie, tell us . . . is it house-breaking?' Tony had pleaded in the weeks leading up to the trip.

'You'll know on the day. Just keep your mouth shut about it,' he had been told.

Seanie had smiled to himself, wondering how the small man would react when he discovered that they were travelling down to a village to kill a local businessman. He had broken the news a few minutes into the journey. Tony had said nothing at first.

'You wanted in,' Seanie had said. 'Well, this is your chance. You do this right and you're made for life.'

Tony had listened, eyeing the iron bar that was resting on Seanie's lap.

'Made for life . . . made for life . . .' Tony repeated over and over in his head, swirling the contents of the small glass in front him. The waitress waited for payment.

'Would you like a tip?' Seanie asked her innocently.

'Yeah,' she replied rummaging around the change-glass on the tray.

'Well, here's a good tip for ya,' leered Seanie. 'Go way an' get a good balling for yourself!'

He guffawed loudly as he toasted the waitress with the glass of spirits.

She silently mouthed 'Fuck you' and walked away.

Seanie smiled and leaned across the table. 'Listen sunshine, you're the one who wanted to get into the big time. Well you've done it. You're in,' he said, taking a swig that drained the glass.

Tony looked around nervously. 'Oh, I'm thrilled to hear I passed *the test*. What's next? Shooting the fuckin' president?'

'You don't have to worry any more. No one saw us and we wiped the car. We're in the clear.'

Seanie waved his hand in the direction of the bar.

'Oi! Gorgeous. Two more Mulligans. Make 'em doubles.'

'What about the weapon? Where's that?' Tony hissed.

Seanie smiled and patted the right-hand side of his army jacket.

'What! You mean . . .?'

'Yeah,' smirked Seanie. 'It's my non-flexible friend. I never leave home without it.'

Kearns stared at him wide-eyed.

'Seanie, you are without doubt the biggest fuckin' eejit that I ever had the misfortune to meet. You mean to tell me that you've held on to the one thing that can link us to . . .'

Tony suddenly fell silent, aware that his voice was getting louder as his disbelief was growing. He looked around and began again in a whisper. '...the one thing that can trace us to *it?*'

'Look Tony, I've had it since I joined up with the outfit. I did my first job with it, a fella on the southside . . . small shop . . . owed some money and wouldn't pay.'

His tone made it sound almost logical.

But Tony wasn't listening. He just sat there, his forehead in the palm of his hand, shaking his head from side to side. Seanie sighed heavily.

'All right . . . all right . . . Jesus! If it means so much to you I'll dump it in the canal. What's keeping those drinks?' He raised his voice towards the waitress.

Later, on exiting from the pub, they decided to take a leisurely stroll along the canal. They stopped in the centre of one of the bridges. Tony looked nervously around him and suddenly nodded. Seanie leaned forward on the stone wall and casually removed the bar from the inside of his army jacket.

'Goodbye, my love,' he sniggered as the bar fell lengthwise into the black water below.

'Christ! It nearly made as big a splash as the ould fella,' he joked, as they walked away.

Claire Burns lay fully clothed on the four-poster bed, her arms by her sides, her eyes wide open, staring at the ceiling. Through the open bedroom door she could hear Jenny approach, talking to the doctor.

She could feel nothing. It was as if her body had failed her and its spirit had fled. The conversation was faint in the distance. She could barely make out Jenny's chattering.

'I found her on the bedroom floor. The whole thing has been a terrible shock. She was fine when she was in the kitchen. She just said that she wanted to change.'

'I see,' said the doctor. He was an elderly alcoholic who had grown weary of his profession and had a reputation for being rude and abrupt. He looked down at the patient. 'Sit up for me, Claire. There's a good woman.'

He took her wrist and looked around the room as he waited. 'Oh yes,' he said turning back to her. 'Sorry about John. Terrible thing. Just terrible.'

'What's the matter with her?' asked Jenny who stood behind him, her hands clasped together.

The doctor shook his head.

'Nothing much really. It's just a mild form of shock. Nothing that a good night's rest won't cure.'

Jenny threw her eyes to heaven. A good night's rest was the doctor's cure for every ailment. The same advice was given for everything from Alzheimer's to pre-menstrual tension.

'Does she not need something to help her sleep?' asked an irate Jenny.

The doctor held his hand on Claire's forehead and shook his head once more.

'A waste of good medicine,' he said. 'People are always looking to get needles stuck in them nowadays. They want a miracle cure for everything.

Tablets for this, tablets for that. Long ago people would just get up and do a good day's work.'

Jenny folded her arms angrily and waited for the ranting to stop.

'What's this now?' asked the doctor in surprise.

Jenny leaned over to look. The doctor was rubbing his hand gently over the bruise on the inside of Claire's arm.

'How did this happen?' he asked, looking up at Jenny.

'I fell,' said Claire still looking up at the ceiling. 'I fell in the garden.'

The doctor narrowed his eyes with suspicion as he continued to examine the bruising.

'An unusual place to fall,' he said. 'On the inside of the arm I mean, not the garden,' he added by way of explanation.

'Would you like a cup of tea?' Jenny interrupted his thoughts.

The doctor stood up. 'I rarely drink tea, Mrs Maguire,' he smiled.

'Something else then?'

'Yes indeed. Why not something else?' he said and looked down at Claire. 'You get a good night's rest now.'

'Good night, doctor,' she called after them as Jenny led him from the room.

Fifteen minutes later Jenny returned and threw her arms up in desperation.

'I thought he'd never leave,' she gasped. 'By the way, he drank the rest of the brandy.'

Claire gave a weak laugh. Jenny sat herself on the edge of the bed and took her hand.

'What have I done?' Claire asked her. 'I wished so hard that he was dead and now he is. It's as if I willed it.'

'Don't be ridiculous,' huffed Jenny. 'You did no such thing. You had nothing to do with it. You didn't kill him.'

Claire turned her head away on the pillow. 'But who did?'

Jenny stood up and clasped her hands in front of her as she walked up and down beside the bed.

'Well, I'm no detective,' she started. 'But if I had to take a guess I'd say that it was . . .'

She paused. Claire turned back to look at her.

'. . . Jack Hegarty.'

As if injected with life, Claire sat upright on the bed.

'You must be joking,' she protested. 'Jack Hegarty would never harm anyone. Why would you say something like that?'

She fluffed the pillows behind her and folded her arms awaiting an explanation.

'Well,' started Jenny, 'when we left the station today, I could see that he was in a temper. And everyone knows what he's like in a temper.'

Claire held up her hand.

'There's a very big difference between effing and blinding at the village team from the sideline, and going out and killing someone.'

'Nevertheless,' continued Jenny, 'he has a temper. And he went and met John at the river after we left. I think that they argued and Jack Hegarty killed him.' She shrugged her shoulders. 'It stands to reason.'

'I don't believe it for a minute,' said Claire. She gave a sudden look of dismay at Jenny. 'How was he killed?' she said. 'I never asked how he was killed.' Her voice rose in panic as she spoke. 'I mean was he shot or strangled or . . .?'

Jenny sat on the bed and took her hand. She rubbed it gently as she spoke.

'He was hit on the head with something,' she said. 'I asked Jack Hegarty when he was leaving.'

'Hit on the head,' repeated Claire softly, as if picturing the scene. 'Poor John.'

Jenny released her hand and stood up quickly. 'Poor John,' she mocked. 'Poor brutal John. You don't mean that, surely.'

Claire stared at her for a moment. She knew that her friend was right.

'I feel a kind of sorrow, I'm not sure what kind. It's a bit like the sudden sorrow you feel if you kill something on the road. I've been thinking about it here on the bed. But try as I can to feel the sorrow of a widow, I just can't do it.'

'Why should that surprise you?' asked Jenny. 'You should be glad he's dead.'

Claire nodded her head. 'I *am* glad,' she said. 'And that's why I feel so ashamed.'

Hickey pulled the grey serge blanket around his shoulders and settled himself in the torn armchair beside the stove.

'If I were you, Jim, I'd go straight to the papers,' he advised. 'Look at all those fellas in England. How much money did they get for their stories?'

Quilter sat opposite him on a high chair, the twine from the seat ravelled and falling on either side.

'Are you still drunk or what?' he erupted. 'Have you been listening to one shaggin' word that I've said?'

Hickey nodded. 'I don't think that you realise the money that you can make from this, Jim.' He held his hands out in front of him, the blanket falling from his shoulders. 'Picture the headlines. "A miscarriage of justice," the story of the man wrongly accused of a crime that he did not commit.' He snapped his fingers. 'Like yer man Harrison Ford in that film, ah Jaysus. The what . . . the . . .'

'Hickey,' interrupted Quilter. 'Hickey, will you shut up like a good man?'

He shook his head in disappointment. 'Not one shaggin' word,' he muttered to himself. He looked around in the darkness of the small kitchen. 'Tell me, Hickey, have you any light in this place? 'Tis like Dracula's castle.'

'Didn't pay the bill for a while. Sure isn't it a bright night outside? Anyway what was I saying? Oh yeah, you'll have to go on the run like yer man. And then when it's all over you can sell your story to the papers.' He stood up suddenly. 'Wait there. I'll get us a drink and we can plan it.'

Quilter watched as Hickey made his way through the semi-darkness to the kitchen press and searched through it, ejecting saucepans and various dirty pieces of kitchenware. His teeth gleamed as he wrapped his hand around the bottle.

'Where did you get that?' asked Quilter, watching him rinse two mugs under the tap.

'I won it in the raffle in Madge's at Christmas. Do you not remember?'

'And you still have it,' said Quilter in shock as he took the mug from him.

Myles nodded and grinned, cracking the seal.

'May the bad luck of the year go with you,' he said to the bottle top and threw it over his shoulder. 'You may stay for the night now.' He poured a large one into Quilter's mug. 'Tell me this now,' he said as he sat back down and placed the bottle on the floor between them, 'did they accuse you of the murder?'

'No, Myles, they didn't.'

'Did they beat the shite out of you while you were in the station?'

'No . . . no they didn't.'

Myles sighed heavily and flopped back in the chair. His hopes were dashed. He could think of nothing further.

'So what *did* they do? I mean I saw Hegarty taking you into the station and I questioned him about it, y'know. Did he tell you?'

'Em . . . no . . . he didn't.'

'Well, I had him shaking in his boots outside the station . . . froze him to the ground with questions about your arrest. I bet that's why they chickened out. If you know your rights, Jim, no one messes with you.'

'I suppose you're right, Myles . . . I suppose you're right.'

Although Quilter was aware that Myles was talking a lot of shite, he felt safe in his company, safe in the house of a friend who would never see him in a hold, drunk or sober.

Silence followed. The two men stared into the darkness as they drank.

'Well, what do you think about going to the papers?' asked Myles. 'You'd be a rich man out of it. They're always on the lookout for a good story. 'Twas only the other day I was reading about this fella who turned into a woman . . . the old snip snip. Tough lines I'd say, Jim . . .'

'Listen, Hickey,' said Quilter, angered by his friend's lack of seriousness. 'Hegarty will give you the exact same operation for free if you open your mouth about this. Not a word to anyone . . . Understand?'

'Fair enough, my friend,' replied Myles, and drained his mug with one mouthful. 'You're missing a big opportunity to make a few quid, though.'

Quilter sighed as he cradled the mug.

'You know, I think that Hegarty thinks that I had something to do with it,' he said suddenly.

'What makes you think that?'

'He told me outside the station that I didn't tell him the truth.'

'And did you tell him what you told me?'

'Yeah . . . but I left out the bit about giving Burns a piece of my mind.'

Myles tut-tutted softly as he reached down for the bottle. 'That was a bit of a mistake I'd say, Jim,' he said. 'You should never lie to the police.'

Quilter laughed out loud. 'Would you ever shag off,' he said slowly. 'You never told Hegarty the truth in your life.'

Myles continued in a serious tone. 'If I were you, Jim, I'd go on the run.' He snapped his fingers again. 'To France . . . we can go to France to yer one's place.'

'With what?' said Quilter. 'Half a bottle of whiskey and twenty quid? Will you give over about going on the run. I haven't done anything wrong.'

Myles tapped the top of the bottle against his chin. He was lost in thought. 'I wonder where a fella can get a false passport.'

Quilter leaned forward and snapped the bottle from him.

'For the love of Jaysus, will you shut up and drink.'

CHAPTER TWELVE

Brosnan lay back on the bed, his fingers inter-locked behind his neck. Having just endured an hour-long quick fire round of questions with Rose Scully, he was mentally drained.

'You should be in our job, Missus,' he had joked as he left her to climb the two flights of stairs to the top room.

He glanced at his watch now. Two a.m. In four hours' time, he would be down at the local station, directing fifteen men in the murder investigation, assigning each to his own particular task. He rubbed his palm across the growing stubble on his face, listening to it bristle in the silence of the dimly lit room. He regretted now not collecting the tightly packed case from his car outside the village Garda station. He always made a point of appearing fresh and clean-shaven whenever he addressed the squad on the first day of a case.

'Enthusiasm is contagious,' he would tell any officer who had given up hope of solving a case.

He got up suddenly and moved across to the edge of the bed and sat there, fumbling in the pocket of his overcoat for his copybook. He glanced through the scribbled jottings. He wished that it was six a.m., that he could set the group of yawning, yet highly competent detectives to work. The men who would groan at one another in the hallway as they left with a handful of questionnaires. Men at whom he would grind his teeth and roar during the investigation, knowing that they were capable of much better.

He closed his eyes and tried to sleep. He smiled suddenly as he thought about the argument with Hegarty. The big guard standing in front of him with his fists raised and ready to defend his honour. Convincing himself that he was not a suspect was easy. Too easy perhaps. Although the friend in him had dismissed the idea, the detective kept repeating in his mind, 'Overlook nothing'.

And of course there was the super. How did that fella go from an eejit of a guard who couldn't even make out a summons, to the rank of superintendent? What big stroke had he pulled over the years, or more importantly, who was his golf-club sponsor? From Hegarty's description, it was obvious that he hadn't changed one bit.

Jack Hegarty stood at the back door of the house, fumbling and cursing at the set of keys in his hands. He had never arrived home as late without giving his wife some advance warning.

On finding the correct key, he sighed heavily and unlocked the door. Reaching blindly across the wall, he switched on the kitchen light and stood motionless for a moment, looking around as if he were a stranger who had entered. The solid-fuel cooker, which his wife had lit late in the evening to keep the summer chill from the house, had at this stage quenched. He decided to make a quick cup of tea and ponder the events of the day before retiring to bed to tell his wife, but then cancelled the idea, the lure of the warm bed being too much for him.

It had been a long two hours at the riverbank while Costigan and Daly had gone for their meal-breaks. He had changed his mind about letting Daly starve at the murder scene for the night, but as usual he had torn the arse out of it. Costigan had taken a mere half an hour to grab a cup of coffee and a sandwich at his digs, while Daly had driven back to the town and gorged himself on a feed of chips, onion-rings and a snack-box.

'They can kill everyone in the shaggin' place now,' he had joked at an angry Hegarty when he returned. 'Sorry about that, Jack.'

Hegarty had glared at him, but it was water off a duck's back.

'Those Italians mightn't have been any good to the Germans, but by God, they know how to fill a snack-box.'

Hegarty tiptoed up the stairs in the darkness, unbuttoning his tunic as he went. He hoped that his wife hadn't slipped into too deep a slumber, but the coolness of the kitchen indicated that she had been in bed for a considerable time. He undressed quietly in the room and slipped under the covers, moving his cold feet slowly across until they touched hers. It reminded him of when he used to do night duty in the city, returning home in the early hours, freezing with the cold. Slipping quietly into the bed he would grasp his young wife, squeezing the heat out of her. She would awaken immediately and scream loudly in their flat. 'Jack ... You're ice cold!' After the initial shock, she would turn and hug him, and with that, the worries and strain of the night's work would disappear.

He felt the same way tonight. He rolled over and put his arms around the sleeping woman. Her warmth was comforting, but she did not wake. Hegarty released his grip on her and turned with disappointment, punching the pillow.

He sighed heavily.

It had always worked before.

He decided to try again, this time sitting up in bed, resting his hands on his lap.

'Oh God!' he sighed. 'Oh God!'

There was a quick movement beside him as his wife turned over half way and looked at him through squinting eyes.

'What the hell is the matter with you, Jack Hegarty?' she snapped. ''Tis late enough you brought yourself home. Go to sleep.'

Hegarty knew by her tone that it would take a statement of shocking proportions to get her attention. He thought for a moment.

'There's a killer on the loose,' he announced gravely.

His wife sat bolt upright in the bed and looked at her husband as he sat there rolling his thumbs, a habit which irritated her greatly.

'What did you say?'

'I said . . . there's a killer on the loose. Did you not hear me the first time, woman?

He was confident now that he had her full attention.

She reached over and switched on the bedside lamp, then turned, blinking at him.

'Who's been killed?'

'John Burns. His body was found down by the old footbridge late this evening.'

'Oh dear God!' she said, blessing herself quickly. 'What happened him?'

'Well, we're not sure yet. It looks like a blow to the back of the head.'

'Oh, dear God,' she repeated and held her hands up to her face. 'Look, I'll go and put on the kettle.'

She heaved herself to the edge of the bed. 'And then you can tell me all about it. Poor John Burns.'

'No . . . no . . . no,' said Hegarty, reaching out to put his arm around her. 'I'm up in a few hours and I don't intend to spend them giving you ammunition for the gang of chatterers in the local supermarket. Let me get some sleep and I'll tell you all about it tomorrow morning. That is, of course, if there's a man-sized fry on the table at half five.'

'You don't expect me to be able to sleep after getting that piece of news, Jack,' she said crossly, shaking her arm loose from his grip.

He watched her as she took her dressing gown from the back of the chair and put it on.

'Don't go to sleep now. I want to hear all the details when I get back.'

She shut the door gently and Hegarty threw himself back on the pillows, sorry now that he had opened his mouth.

He rested his tired head in the warmth of his wife's pillow and fell asleep almost immediately.

It was six a.m. and the entire investigation team had gathered in the small side room of Dunsheerin Garda Station. The room which had been used to store property found through the years had been hurriedly cleaned out, its contents, fragile or otherwise, jammed into a brush cupboard under the stairs, the two big guards who had been assigned the task shouldering the door closed until the latch caught.

The men crowded inside the room, the uniformed gardaí from the nearby town nodding greetings at the unknown Murder Squad detectives, the whisperings at the back about overtime, sub allowances and the murder. Brosnan stood behind a large, ornate oak desk, incongruous in its small surroundings.

He began to speak. The huddle fell silent.

'I want five uniformed men to the scene, one to relieve the lad on scene preservation. He must be nearly dead with the hunger at this stage.'

There was a muffled laugh. Hegarty threw his eyes upwards.

'Each of you has been given a handful of questionnaires. I expect them to be filled out properly. Anyone over the age of ten years is to be asked what they know. The three of you going to the scene will assist Finbarr Sullivan. You will do exactly as he says and only when he says it. You all have a particular task to do. This book, or jobs book, as we call it,' he said, slamming his hand down on the grey diary in front of him, 'will show you what the task is. If you have any questions, ask the squad detectives. That's all. We will meet back here again at two p.m. sharp.'

The crowd shuffled towards the door, questions already being asked and answered.

'One last thing,' called Brosnan.

The heaving mass stopped, the heads turned back.

'Once again we are under the spotlight. Don't let us down. I want the person responsible for this crime. Overlook nothing. That's it.'

As the room cleared, one of Brosnan's men squeezed his way back through the crowd, edging himself between two heavy uniformed men who, in their haste to get out to the coolness of the summer morning, ignored his efforts. He puffed loudly when he reached the table and picked up the grey book.

'Thanks, Chief,' he panted at Brosnan before turning and again attempting to force his way out to the front door.

'Mulcahy,' said Brosnan to Hegarty, nodding in the direction of the detective, 'he's my second in command.'

Superintendent Eamon Murray rolled back the sleeve of his tunic and glanced at his watch. He silently cursed his luck. In less than two hours, his three companions from the Lions Club would be teeing off, less one member of the four-man team. He hoped that they would understand.

'Superintendent,' called Brosnan, awakening him from his misery.

'Yes, Chief,' he replied, his arms falling to his side.

'I want constant and efficient supervision of your men during this investigation. Men at the preservation of the scene are to be relieved regularly until examination is complete. I can only assume that you have cared for the spiritual needs of the deceased.'

'Yes, Chief,' the superintendent lied. 'That has been taken care of.'

'Good. Get in contact with Frank Long to arrange removal when he's finished his preliminary . . . and deal with the press as well.'

'What will I tell them?'

Suddenly things were beginning to look brighter for Murray, who was relishing the thought of a high-profile appearance on national television.

'Just be brief . . . body found . . . following a definite line of inquiry. The usual . . . Just don't say anything that might, God forbid, get you demoted.'

'Are we?'

'Are we what, man?'

'Following a definite line of inquiry.'

No sooner had Murray asked the question than he was sorry. Brosnan looked at him. It was a look that Murray knew well.

'Of course we're not. But would you go on the nine o' clock news and tell the population, "We've discovered the body of a murdered man near a local river, but unfortunately we haven't the faintest shaggin' idea how it got there" . . .? Use your loaf, man.'

'Yes, Chief.'

The superintendent turned and walked out of the room like a scolded child, his eyes never leaving the floor This was the Brosnan that he knew and disliked.

He clenched his teeth in humiliation as he closed the door of the day-room behind him. This could not go on. He held the rank of superintendent and would not have his authority belittled by that ignorant bully. He decided to wait for an opportunity to get the big man on his own and give him a piece of his mind. He would show him what an efficient policeman and officer he had become.

A quick search uncovered the telephone book. He fumbled through the pages and, on finding the number, he picked up the receiver and dialled.

'Hello, is that the presbytery? This is the superintendent at the local station. Will you be there for a while? Good. I'll be up for you in a minute. Right.'

He replaced the receiver gently, opened the day-room door and walked quickly out of the building.

Hegarty rested his thigh on the corner of the oak table as he watched Brosnan scribble in the copybook. When he had finished writing, the big man straightened up and removed his overcoat.

'No need for this today, Jack,' he declared.

'Looks like it's going to be a scorcher.'

He folded the copybook in half and put it into the inside pocket of his grey jacket.

'C'mon, Jack,' he said, hanging his coat on a hook at the back of the door, 'let's go and see if Sullivan has uncovered anything for us. He's had a two-hour head start.'

Costigan was just climbing the footbridge when they arrived at the scene. He looked like a part of the German retreat from Moscow, coat collar up, blank expression, eyes heavy and reddened. Daly had left some four hours earlier, protesting as he went about having to be in the station for ten o'clock.

'Good work, lad,' said Brosnan cheerfully as he passed him. 'See you at two o'clock.'

Costigan turned back and watched the grey-haired head of the chief superintendent vanish down the embankment.

Brosnan stood at the foot of the climb with Hegarty and looked around. The scene was much smaller in the daylight than it had appeared in the fading light of the previous evening.

A short distance away, Finbarr Sullivan was well into his work, bent at the hips, moving slowly forward, his arms outstretched. On either side of him, two men in grey Garda overalls walked in similar fashion, their arms by their sides. The three of them looked like the front row of a rugby scrum.

Nearby, the bureau photographer walked carefully around the body, snapping from all angles, sometimes moving backwards for a wider shot.

The pathologist, Frank Long, clicked his case shut and walked towards Brosnan and Hegarty.

'It's a nasty one,' he said, nodding back in the direction of the body. 'So far it looks like he died as a result of a number of blows to the back of the head. Mid-afternoon. I'll tell you more this evening after the autopsy. You can move him at any time now . . . the sooner the better.'

'Okay, Frank. Thanks,' said Brosnan, absent-mindedly staring at Sullivan.

He knew that medical evidence would play only a small part in this particular investigation. His hopes rested on Sullivan and what he would find. His curiosity overcame him. He knew how much Sullivan hated being interrupted while he was working but he needed to be told that the trail was still hot.

'Finbarr,' he called, and the three-man scrum broke, the man in the middle standing up and turning, his frown softening when he realised who had called him.

He spoke quickly to the two men beside him: 'Don't move. Take a break,' he ordered as he saw Brosnan and the big guard with the poor knowledge of fibre evidence approaching.

'Well?' enquired Brosnan expectantly.

'Doesn't look like there was a struggle,' said Sullivan as he led them back to the body. 'This I found just inside the water.' He held up a plastic evidence bag containing Burn's fly-tying vice. 'See this?' he continued, holding the palm of his hand over an impression on the grass at the edge of the riverbank. 'The vice was found in the water directly under this. It's where he was sitting when the killer struck.'

'Could that impression have been made by one of the men preserving the scene?' asked Hegarty.

'Not unless he wanted to get his feet wet, Guard,' replied Sullivan, reaching for the other evidence bags. He disliked having his theories questioned.

Brosnan knew better.

'Carry on, Finbarr,' prompted Brosnan. He nudged Hegarty when Sullivan wasn't looking and put his index finger to his lips.

'The impression left is that of the dead man's arse and the top of his thighs. His legs would have been hanging in the water. The impression is facing the river, Guard,' he said, staring at Hegarty. He cleared his throat and continued, his pointed finger drawing Brosnan's eyes on a guided tour of the murder scene. 'This is a fragment of bone and hair of the deceased which was found two feet away, to the right of the victim. A tackle box, found beside the impression on the grass, the fishing rod at arm's length from the impression.'

'So what you're saying is . . .?' said Brosnan expectantly.

Sullivan held his arms outstretched.

'This I believe is what happened. The victim was sitting here, his feet hanging in the water. He was either taking a rest, or else using that vice thing. The killer crept up behind him and struck.'

Sullivan hunched down beside the impression in the grass and continued.

'If the killer had approached from the foot-bridge as you two just have, then the victim would have seen him from this angle. Therefore, the attacker came from . . .' He stood upright and pointed forcefully in the direction of the two men who had been helping him, ' . . .there!'

Brosnan followed the direction of Sullivan's pointing finger.

'Finbarr, would the victim not have heard the killer approach from that side through that long grass?'

'I'm glad you asked me that. The grass is another indication as to the direction of the approach.'

Sullivan walked towards the long grass, beckoning to the two men behind him as he spoke.

'The grass has been recently trampled in both directions, showing that although the killer may have approached in stealth, he retreated in haste.' He pointed again.

'Two tracks, one coming, the other leaving. We're doing the one going from the scene at the moment. Looks like it finishes about twenty yards on into that cut hay field there.'

Hegarty moved forward, craning to see where the river grass ended.

'There's a side road at the end of that field. Flann O'Neill's house is at the top of the road. Maybe he saw something.'

'We can talk to him later,' said Brosnan. 'I want to see this.' He removed the copybook from his pocket and opened it. 'Ah yes. This fella Jim Quilter.' He moved towards the footbridge. 'Good work, Finbarr. Keep at it.'

Sullivan rejoined the two men in overalls and resumed his work.

'He's a first-rate policeman that Sullivan,' said Brosnan getting into the patrol car. 'We could all learn a few things from him.'

As they were pulling off, the superintendent passed by in his car. Brosnan looked at Hegarty.

'Jack, who's that fella with Murray?'

'What fella?' asked Hegarty innocently.

'The fella in the front seat of his car. C'mon, Jack, don't tell me that you're going blind in your old age. He's not one of ours, is he?'

'No. But if I were to make a guess, I'd say that the super is just ensuring that John Burns goes straight to heaven, if you know what I mean.'

Brosnan thought for a moment. Suddenly realising what Hegarty meant, he shook his head from side to side.

'Jesus,' he groaned, 'some things never change.'

Hegarty laughed and turned the patrol car on to the main road.

'Jim Quilter's house then,' he said.

CHAPTER THIRTEEN

Michael Carroll tucked into a large breakfast of bacon, sausage and tomatoes in the dining room of his eight-bedroom residence on the west side of the city. He turned his head occasionally to peruse the half-folded newspaper on the table beside him. His thirty-two-year-old wife of seven years stood in the doorway, leaning against the jamb, the strap of her silk negligée falling from her shoulder. She looked in disgust at her husband who was voraciously shovelling a large slice of bacon into his mouth.

'How can you eat that shit this early in the morning? Have you ever heard of heart-disease and cholesterol?'

Carroll glanced back in her direction.

'Why don't you make yourself useful and turn the radio on? And while you're at it, get dressed. You look like a prostitute.'

He turned back to his breakfast with a roll of his shoulders.

'Fu-uck you,' came the reply.

Carroll slammed down the knife and fork and made for the door like a bull charging at a red rag. He pushed past her into the kitchen, knocking her back with the force of his shoulder. With a snap, he switched on the stereo to Radio 1 and paced angrily back to the table.

His wife remained where she was in the doorway, rubbing her arm.

'Bringing one of your sluts out to dinner today, are you?' she sneered. 'Nothing like a bit of secretary's ass to work off a big feed of bacon and tomatoes.'

He turned in her direction, his eyes alight with disgust and anger. She laughed, and sauntered into the kitchen.

Carroll wiped his greasy mouth with the linen serviette and sat back to listen to the radio. He didn't have long to wait for the story. It was the main headline.

The body of an elderly businessman has been found near the small tourist village of Dunsheerin. The discovery was made by a local farmer at around teatime yesterday evening. This report from Sean Keohane:
—The tiny village of Dunsheerin is in a state of

shock, following the discovery of the body of local businessman, John Burns. The discovery was made at about six-thirty yesterday evening. The state pathologist, Frank Long, was at the scene early this morning, along with members of the Garda investigation team led by Chief Superintendent Pat Brosnan. Earlier, I spoke to local Superintendent Eamon Murray and asked him about the gruesome find.

—Well, Sean, we are treating the death as suspicious. At the moment, I can make no further comment. But I would appeal to anyone with information that might help in the solving of this heinous crime to come forward immediately.

—Do the investigation team have any positive leads at the moment, Superintendent?

—Emm . . . ye-es. We are following a definite line of inquiry, Sean.

—Can you elaborate on that, Superintendent?

—No . . . no, Sean. I'm not prepared to comment at the moment. Thank you.

—Thank you, Superintendent. This is Sean Keohane for Radio One at Dunsheerin.

Carroll leaned back in his chair and began to laugh. His full stomach shook.

'Ha! Bog warriors! Couldn't detect their bollocks if they were stuck to the end of their noses. Not . . . a . . . *fucking* . . . clue!'

His guffaws filled the dining room.

He stopped suddenly, cutting the laugh off with a cough when he felt her presence behind him.

'What's so funny?'

He didn't answer, but stood up. He looked at her for a moment and lifted her chin with the tip of the rolled newspaper, examining her. She stood there helpless, like a rag doll, hands by her side, her mascara streaked from the crying of the night before. Her breathing quickened, her chest rising and falling under the thin negligée. He sneered, and flicked the paper away. Her shoulders fell in relief.

'I'm going to work.'

She watched him go, peering through the lace of the diningroom curtain. Her eyes welled up with tears of anger and self-pity. The black sports car disappeared from view. She ambled back into the kitchen. The news headlines were being read again.

The body of an elderly businessman has been found near the tiny tourist village of Dunsheerin. Gardaí are treating the death as suspicious.

She sat down at the table and stared hard at the radio. Dunsheerin. She repeated the name over and over in her mind. It was the second time that morning that she had heard that name and it was strikingly familiar. She massaged her throbbing temples. Her excessive intake of gin and tonic at the previous evening's party to launch a new car at her husband's dealership had dulled her thought processes.

Where had she heard that name before? Or maybe she had read it somewhere. She slapped her hand down on the table, rattling the heavy silver cutlery. She raced to the window and checked the driveway, then ran up the long marble stairway, almost tripping mid-way on her long negligée. In the bedroom she tugged at each of the heavy oak drawers of the large wardrobe, rummaging her hands through each one in turn. She smiled with satisfaction as she withdrew her hand and held up the leather-bound filofax and sat back on the bed as she opened it.

'D . . . d . . .' she repeated out loud as she searched.

The page was empty. She cursed silently as she flicked on through the pages. Maybe she was wrong. Her doubts disappeared as she looked down and flattened the page. There in one single line written in black ink under M was 'McCann – Dunsheerin'. Beneath it a rough diagram of a road plan showing the main road and a turn off for a river.

'Liam McCann,' she thought. That shifty Northern character that her husband had brought home one evening. They had both stayed in the sitting-room for over an hour, talking in muffled whispers. When she had interrupted them to inquire if they wanted a drink, McCann had turned his face away from her as he answered, 'Whiskey, love.' She had disliked him instantly.

She snapped the filofax shut and knelt down in front of the drawer. She knew that she would have to replace it as she had found it. She had made the mistake before of searching through her husband's private belongings in an effort to prove his infidelity. When she revealed to Carroll in mid-scream that she had found his 'little black book', he had flung the heavy oak table on its side, raging with anger, purple veins throbbing in his neck.

'Is it not enough that I have the fucking cops checking my books all the time?' he had roared. 'Do I have to look over my shoulder for you as well?'

Her repugnance at his affairs overcame her fear of him that evening. Instead of cowering, she had remained seated holding her knife and fork, the table swept from in front of her, along with her poached salmon dinner.

'Cops? Checking up on you?' she had sneered. 'Don't flatter yourself. You're nothing but a small-time hood putting plates on stolen cars. The cops have better things to do with their time than to follow a ringer around.'

He had moved quickly across the room pinning her against the wall, holding her at arm's length by the throat, whitening her flesh as he squeezed.

His voice was low and menacing.

'You really have no idea, do you? Look around you.' He released his grip. 'You live in a house worth two million, the best of clothes and jewellery, two holidays in the islands . . .' He was calmer now. She rubbed her throat and listened. '. . . and you think we have all this from ringing a few cars? Well I've got news for you . . .' he said, bending to pick up the table and straightening it beside the chairs, ' . . .I am one of the top men in this city.' She had stared wide-eyed at him as he stood resting his hands on the back of a chair, like a chairman of a board addressing a meeting. She had wanted to laugh out loud, but the silence in the room and the look on his face conveyed the fact that it was not a joke.

'W-what you mean is . . .?'

Carroll stared across at her, the look of shock, yet eagerness to know more, etched on her face. He bit the inside of his lip. He regretted what he had said. He had made a point of never disclosing details of his business affairs to her. But he knew that she would not be put off lightly. His statement would have to be backed up by fact.

'You really don't have the faintest idea do you?' he smiled. 'Do you really think that I make all this money from flogging a few expensive cars?' He shook his head and tut-tutted softly at her. 'Protection rackets, girl. Drugs. Prostitution . . . whatever it takes to make a few extra quid. Somebody comes to me with a problem and I solve it for them.'

'You mean . . . like the Mafia?' she gulped.

She reminded him of a child engrossed in a fairy story. Her innocence touched him. Carroll smiled.

'Yeah . . . something like that. We wouldn't have as many members though. But what we have are loyal to a man.'

His sudden violent outburst and the physical abuse of earlier in the evening had frightened her. But what she was hearing now frightened her even more. She had reached up blindly across the mantelpiece, nervously grasping for her cigarettes and lighter.

'I think I've said enough,' said Carroll, walking towards the door, 'Oh . . . one other thing . . .' He pointed a finger in her direction. 'I don't ever want to hear any of this back. Otherwise I might have to get one of my loyal followers to tear your fuckin' lungs out and show them to you.' He grinned for a second, then frowned. 'OK?'

She had nodded quickly in understanding.

'Good!' he had called from the kitchen. 'Now bring me a drink in the front room. There's a good gangster movie on the telly.'

She had stood and listened to his laughter until it was muffled by the closing of the sitting-room door.

She pushed the oak drawer closed now and made her way slowly downstairs to the kitchen, her mind in a daze. The radio blared beside her. Her hand shook as she reached into the press for a coffee mug. She clenched her fist to steady it.

The news was about to finish.

Anyone with information can contact their local Garda station, or Dunsheerin Garda Station, on 066-668836. That's all for now. Next news is at nine o'clock.'

She snapped back to reality.

'It's him,' she said out loud.

Brosnan hammered his fist against the shaky wooden door and then stepped back to search the windows for a sign of life.

'Jim Quilter,' he shouted and hammered the door again.

Hegarty appeared from the side of the house, stepping gingerly through the mud that surrounded the leaking water-barrel at the corner.

'No sign of him, Pat?' he asked. Brosnan shook his head and looked around the yard, blinking in the strong sun.

'This is some place to be living,' he said with disgust. 'Christ, I wouldn't keep cattle here.'

Hegarty made his way to the front door and gave it a single bang of his fist.

'Get up, Quilter.' He leaned heavily on the door and placed his ear against it to listen. There was a loud crack as he fell inwards, the latch of the door giving way to his large bulk.

'Oh, sweet Jesus,' said Brosnan, running to his aid.

On seeing that he was all right, he examined the broken jamb where the latch had given way. Hegarty stood inside in the darkness of the cottage and looked out at Brosnan.

'For God's sake don't come in,' he said. 'The smell in here is only atrocious. I'll check the bedroom.'

Brosnan waited outside with his hands in his pockets, a wide grin on his face. The rusting horse-drawn plough under a large pine tree caught his eye, the sweat and toil of generations – and for what? He shook his head in dismay.

'Pat!' came the shout from inside. 'In here.'

'What is it?' he asked as he made his way through the door. He looked through the dark room to where Hegarty was standing in the bedroom with his back to door.

'What is it, Jack?' he asked again with more urgency. Hegarty turned around with a wide smile of delight and held out the faded newspaper. 'Nineteen thirty-six,' he beamed as he handed it to

Brosnan. 'A newspaper from nineteen thirty-six. The year that I was born.' Brosnan looked quizzically at him as he took the paper and glanced down at it.

'Look at the price of a bike there,' smiled Hegarty. 'God, there's history in that.'

Brosnan handed the paper back to him.

'Jack, where's your man?' he asked pointing to the bed.

Hegarty placed the paper down gently on the pile beside the dusty bedside dresser.

'He probably stayed with that other eejit, Myles Hickey, last night. He does that when he has too much to drink.' He walked out of the room. 'Come on. The house is just down the road.'

Brosnan followed him and stopped at the front door.

'What about this breaking and entering job that you've done on the door?' he called.

Hegarty brushed back past him and pulled the door closed as tight as he could. He rubbed at it with his hand.

'There now,' he smiled. 'Good as new.'

'I thought you'd given up breaking down doors,' said Brosnan as they sat into the car.

Hegarty laughed. 'A man is never too old for that,' he said.

The heat in the car was intense, and, as if on the same wavelength, they rolled down their windows together.

'This sun will kill us,' puffed Brosnan as Hegarty drove away.

After a few minutes he turned the car off the

main road on to a stony boreen. The car shook violently as it moved towards the small house at the
end. It was similar in size and condition to Quilter's
apart from two whitened stone nymphs that Myles
had crudely cemented on the low entrance pillars.

'Another fine residence,' said Brosnan sarcasti-
cally as he walked to the front door.

He knocked gently on it and waited. Hegarty
cupped his hands to his face as he looked in the
window. 'Good Jaysus,' he said softly and then
moved himself in front of Brosnan.

'Hickey . . . Quilter . . . get up ya pair of
wasters,' he shouted as he knocked loudly on the
door.

There was a groan of discontent from inside.
The door opened slightly and Myles, with half-
closed eyes and tossed hair, peered out.

'Yes? What is it?' he croaked.

Hegarty waved the vile smell of stale drink from
in front of him.

'We want to see Quilter,' he said.

Hickey blinked and stepped back, opening the
door fully.

'Have ye a warrant?' he asked as they stepped
inside.

Hegarty turned and glared down at him. 'I'll
give you warrant, Hickey,' he growled.

Quilter was stretching himself on the chair like
a cat and yawning loudly.

'Rough night, Jim?' smiled Hegarty, looking
down at the empty whisky bottle on its side.

Quilter shivered and looked up at them.

'We won't delay you long,' said Hegarty. 'I know

that you men have a hard day's work ahead. All we want is a few quick lines of a statement from you.'

'What time is it?' asked Hickey as he shuffled towards the sink. 'Will ye have tea?' he asked before anyone could answer.

Hegarty eyed the array of filthy mugs in the sink and looked at Brosnan.

'No thanks, Myles.'

He slapped his hands together suddenly.

'Now then, Jim. This is Chief Superintendent Pat Brosnan from Dublin. He's in charge of the investigation into the murder of John Burns. And seeing as you're the man who found the body, we have to get a statement from you. Do you understand?'

Quilter looked up at Brosnan and nodded.

'Good man, Jim,' smiled Hegarty and pulled up a chair. 'Now tell us in your own words again exactly what happened.'

Brosnan removed a few sheets of paper from his back pocket and sat down at the table. He spoke as he flattened them. 'Now then, Mr Quilter. In your own time if you please.'

Hickey shuffled across the floor and stood behind Quilter's chair with his arms folded. Hegarty looked up at him.

'Are you his solicitor, Hickey?'

'No.'

'Then sit down, like a good man.'

Hickey shrugged and moved to the long wooden bench against the wall.

Brosnan wrote as Quilter related the exact same story he had told Hegarty the previous evening.

When he was finished, he looked from one to the other.

'Well, that's it,' he finished.

Hegarty rubbed his hand across his lips.

'Are you sure, Jim?' he asked. 'What I mean is, have you told us everything?'

Brosnan looked at Hegarty and then back to Quilter. 'Tell us about the second time you met Burns yesterday again.'

Hickey leaned forward with interest. The other two men fixed their eyes on Quilter and waited.

'All right . . . all right,' conceded Quilter finally. 'I had an argument with him. He insulted my father.'

'And you threatened him, didn't you?' said Hegarty.

Hickey rose from behind him. 'Hold it . . . hold it,' he declared and stepped to the centre of the floor. 'Is he a suspect or isn't he? Answer me that.'

Hegarty closed his eyes and ground his teeth together.

'Hickey,' he muttered.

'No. No,' continued Hickey. 'If he's a suspect then you must read him the mirandas. I saw it on the television.'

Brosnan gave a puzzled frown at Hegarty.

'What is he saying, Jack?' he asked as he shook his head and stifled a smile.

'The mirandas,' declared Hickey. 'You have the right to remain silent. You have the right to . . . to . . . You have the right to . . .' His voice faded out as he failed to remember the rest. 'All that mullarkey,' he finished and nodded at Quilter.

Hegarty looked up at him.

'Jim is not a suspect,' he said. 'But he is making himself a suspect by not telling us everything.'

He turned back to Quilter. 'Now, Jim. Did you or did you not threaten him?'

Quilter paused for a moment before speaking. 'Yes,' he said finally. 'I suppose I did. After he insulted my father I told him that I'd beat the shite out of him.'

He shook his head.

'But I would never do it, Guard Hegarty,' he added quickly. 'I could never do anything like that. You know that, don't you.'

Hegarty looked at him for a moment and then at Brosnan who gave a knowing shake of his head, indicating that Hegarty should neither answer the question nor ask another. He rose to his feet and smiled at Quilter. Hegarty stood up to join him.

'We'll want to talk to you later, Mr Quilter,' said Brosnan, as he turned to the door.

Hickey looked at both of them. 'Is that it so?' he asked.

Brosnan nodded at him. 'That's it for the moment,' he said and followed Hegarty outside.

Hickey closed the door calmly after them and then turned with a look of panic. Quilter's eyes widened at the expression on his friend's face.

'We'd better start learning French, boy,' said Hickey. 'That big fella with Hegarty thinks that you did it. Did you see the look on his face when you said that you threatened Burns?'

Quilter looked down at the floor for a moment as if in deep thought, then looked up at Hickey in awe.

'How did he know?' he asked.

Hickey shook his head. 'I don't understand. How did he know what?'

'How did Jack Hegarty know that I threatened Burns?'

'Aw, yeah,' said Hickey pretending to understand. 'God this'll make a great story in the papers.'

Quilter frowned at him. 'Shut up and make the tea, Myles,' he said.

Outside, Brosnan had stopped at the gate and was looking back at the house.

'Well, Jack,' he said softly. 'What do you think?'

Hegarty leaned on the pillar and examined the statue as he thought. 'I don't really know, Pat,' he said. 'The one thing that arouses my suspicion is that he tried to keep the fact that he had words with Burns a secret.'

Brosnan snorted a laugh and turned towards the car.

'So did *you*, Jack,' he smiled. 'So did *you*.'

Hegarty thought about it for a moment and then laughed.

Brosnan leaned against the hot car.

'What we need is a witness. Let's go and see that fella who lives beside the scene.'

Hegarty nodded.

'Flann O'Neill,' he said. 'He's our man.'

CHAPTER FOURTEEN

The stiffened body of John Burns was unceremoni-
ously rolled over on to the heavy-duty plastic body
bag, the flaps placed around him, the large zipper
pulled closed, sealing him into the black cocoon.
The undertaker, along with three guards, gripped
the nylon handles and, on a count of three, lifted it
to the foot of the incline. Above them on the
bridge, two men reached down to assist in the haul-
ing of the corpse over the top railing. The hearse
was parked on the side of the road, awaiting its
grim cargo. The local hospital had refused permis-
sion for the body to be transported to the morgue
by ambulance, so the superintendent had called on
the services of Ned Hennessy.

Hennessy was known locally as 'Dead Ned'. Not, as one might expect, a reference to his profession, but rather to his appearance. Ned had bad dress sense down to an art form. Wrinkled black dress-suit, open-necked stained white shirt. He looked more like a drunken best man than a staid undertaker. But it was his physical features that had truly earned him his nickname. A bulb-shaped head, a protruding jaw, and deathly white complexion made him look more like a corpse than the ones that he tended.

He was also renowned for his meanness. There were no lengths to which he wouldn't go to beat his local rival to any business that came available from time to time. He had, however, jumped the gun on a number of occasions.

Jack Hegarty often recalled the time he had received a call from an elderly man who had locked himself into his house. Hegarty had rushed down to the end of the village and had been attempting to break down the elderly man's door when, whether by coincidence or not, the black death carrier, with Ned Hennessy at the wheel, pulled up beside the path just as Hegarty had broken in the door and freed the old man.

'Everything all right?' Ned had enquired of the two men who were standing in the doorway. The old man had raised his fist defiantly and shouted after the departing hearse.

'I'm not ready for you yet, you miserable bastard.'

Superintendent Murray gave the uniformed men some brief instructions, directing one to travel with the corpse in the hearse and advising the remainder to stagger their meal breaks and not to allow any unauthorised persons near the scene.

Pleased with his morning's work, he sat into the patrol car that was to accompany the hearse to the morgue. The events of the day so far had gone according to plan. Even his mistake of not summoning a clergyman to administer spiritual assistance to the deceased had been covered up successfully. His encounter with the media, albeit a short one, had gone off without a hitch. He was getting the feel of the investigation now. His confidence was high.

'Follow that hearse,' he said in an authoritative tone to the driver, who looked curiously back at him. It would be another story for the canteen.

Picking the radio microphone from the dashboard, he held it, his lips pursed, pondering his next line.

'Victor . . .'

He stopped and turned to the man beside him.

'What's our call sign?'

'Victor eight five, Super,' replied the guard, putting the car in first gear as the hearse in front of them began to move off.

Murray cleared his throat.

'Victor eight five to Chief Superintendent Brosnan. Come in.'

'Yeah,' came the reply on the radio speaker.

'Superintendent Murray here, the body is on its way to the morgue by hearse and should be ready for identification by the relative in about two hours . . . Over.'

'Very good, Superintendent,' Brosnan's voice crackled. 'We'll see you at the hospital in two hours then. By the way, how did your press interview go?'

'Very well sir. I told them nothing.'

'Well done, Superintendent. You'd have made a great prisoner of war.'

Before the radio message finished, Murray could hear Hegarty's loud laughter in the background. The guard beside him looked out the driver's window in a vain attempt to hide his smile, but Murray had seen him.

'Do you find something amusing?' he asked, about to take his wrath at Brosnan's comment out on the driver.

'No, sir,' replied the guard, gulping back the laughter.

'Very well then,' said Murray curtly, replacing the radio mike on its catch. 'Let's keep our minds on the job in hand, shall we?'

Flann O'Neill was a man of simple pleasures. His entire existence was centred on Gaelic sport and he had followed it with a passion ever since he was a youngster some seventy years ago. He was known locally as 'The Scoremaster' because of his vast knowledge of every football and hurling match that was ever played. From inter-county matches to the lowliest junior game, if a result was required, then Flann was the man to ask. He had attended every senior All-Ireland football and hurling final since his father had taken him to his first, at the tender age of eight. His prized possession was a black and white photograph of Christy Ring accepting the McCarthy Cup, and in the background, Flann himself, watching the proceedings.

'All the greats are gone now,' he would sigh regretfully, puffing his pipe beside the marble fireplace in Clancy's bar. He was always inconsolable whenever the county team were knocked out of the championship.

'I remember when football was football and those who played it were men,' he would announce to those who would join him at the fireplace for his words of wisdom. 'There are young fellas playing for the county now that couldn't catch a bale of hay if it were kicked out to them. Ah well . . . shagged for another year.'

Flann was cracking an egg into his blackened frying pan when he heard the loud knocking. He waited for the egg white to set before taking it off the hot ring and going to the front door.

'By God, you're up early this morning, Flann,' said Hegarty. 'This is Chief Superintendent Pat Brosnan from Dublin. Now, I don't know if you've heard yet . . . Can we come in?'

'Of course, Jack, come on,' replied Flann leading them into the kitchen. 'I was just getting the breakfast. Will ye have a drop of tea?'

'Yerra, why not?' said Hegarty, sitting himself down beside the Formica-covered table and pushing another of the chairs towards Brosnan.

'It's about John Burns, Flann. His body was found down by the river yesterday evening. Maybe you've heard?'

'Oh Jesus Mary and Joseph, I had not,' gasped

Flann, filling the kettle at the tap. 'How did it happen at all?'

Brosnan glanced across at Hegarty and gave a quick shake of his head.

'Well, we're not sure yet, Flann. Well . . . actually we *do* know. I mean . . . we know that he was murdered . . .' faltered Hegarty.

He was glad that it was not his job to announce the facts in front of the television cameras. He did not envy Superintendent Eamon Murray his task, trying hard not to give too much away and at the same time trying not to appear incompetent.

Hegarty decided to get a grip on the conversation.

'Flann, the real reason we're here is to ask you if you saw anything that you might have found strange.'

'Murdered!' whispered the old man incredulously.

'Sit down here, Flann,' said Brosnan softly, rising to offer his chair. 'I want to ask you a few simple questions.' He removed the copybook and pen from his inside pocket. 'You own the field behind this house, don't you?'

'Ye-es.'

Brosnan quickly reached under the table and pulled out a *sugán* stool and sat down, facing the old man.

'Now, Flann,' he continued, 'think hard. Did you see anything suspicious yesterday, any stranger on the road, anyone in your field or fields near by that you mightn't have known . . . or *anyone* for that matter?'

The old man sat back on the chair and rubbed

the side of his face, deep in thought. Silently, as if in a trance, he rose and moved across the kitchen and switched off the kettle. The officers' eyes followed him. He continued to rub the side of his face, his forehead deeply furrowed in thought. The tension in the room was palpable. Brosnan stared hard, willing him to speak. Suddenly, the old man clicked his fingers.

'There was a car . . . two men in a car . . .'

'What colour, Flann?' asked Brosnan, trying hard to contain his excitement.

Hegarty raised his hand to speak. Brosnan glared at him and shook his head. He knew from the past that a different interviewing technique had to be used on older people. They should not be interrupted, be allowed to speak, but not to wander. Most importantly, the questions should be short and to the point.

'Two men in a car,' mused the old man. 'It parked down the road a ways . . . didn't know them. It's a great river for salmon, ya know.'

'Flann, what colour was the car?' repeated Brosnan.

Again, Hegarty raised his hand. 'Excuse me, Chief,' he started.

Brosnan bared his teeth at him. 'Guard Hegarty,' he said, as calmly as he could, 'the kettle is boiled. Why don't we all have a cup of tea?' He gave a fake smile and pointed at the kitchen dresser.

Flann began to rise from the stool.

'No, no,' said Brosnan, taking him by the arm and sitting him back down. 'I hear that Jack makes a storming cuppa.'

'Fair enough . . . You know where the pot is, Jack,' said Flann.

Hegarty slapped his thighs and smiled as he rose from the chair. Brosnan gave him the thumbs up, pleased that his old friend had not taken his exclusion from the interview to heart.

'I'll let you at it, so, Chief,' said Hegarty with a grin.

'Now then, Flann,' started Brosnan and slapped his hands gently. 'Can you tell me the colour of the car you say you saw?'

The old man looked at him. His shoulders drooped in disappointment.

'No, indeed I cannot,' he said quietly.

Brosnan placed the copybook on the table and stood up. Scratching his head in frustration, he paced back and forth across the small kitchen floor.

Hegarty placed the lid on the teapot and then leaned back against the sink with his arms folded.

Brosnan sat back down beside Flann.

'Let me get this straight now. You tell us that you saw a car with two men in it. What time was this?'

'It was about half-three. I went out to feed my dog.'

'OK, so you saw a parked car down the road. Did you get a good look at it?'

'I saw it in the distance. I couldn't say what make it was,' gulped the old man, suddenly getting nervous of the situation and looking at Hegarty for consolation.

'Did you get a look at the two men in the car?'

continued Brosnan, oblivious to Flann's discomfiture.

'No. They were in the distance as well. Like I told you, I thought they were fishermen.'

Brosnan clasped his hands together and rubbed them slowly. He had the lead that he was looking for, but he wanted more.

He looked up and straight at Flann.

'The colour of the car,' he said softly.

Flann smiled weakly.

'If it was parked here in the kitchen, I couldn't tell you what colour it was.'

'What do you mean?'

'I mean that I'm one in a hundred thousand.'

Brosnan's face fell.

'What?'

'One in a hundred thousand of the male population suffers from monochromatism, Chief Superintendent.'

Brosnan turned back to look at Hegarty who stood grinning at the sink.

'What the hell is he talking about, Jack?' he asked.

Without warning, Hegarty laughed out loud. 'Don't ask me, Pat. I'm only making the tea.'

When Brosnan turned back, the old man had moved his face closer until their noses almost touched.

'I'm colour-blind, boy,' Flann all but shouted into Brosnan's face.

Brosnan closed his eyes for a moment before looking back at Hegarty and giving a nod of apology.

'Well now, Jack,' said Flann cheerfully, 'that tea must be ready for pouring.'

Mike Daly yawned loudly as he went through the door of Dunsheerin Garda station. The detective who sat behind the desk in the investigation room looked up and nodded a greeting.

'You're late. It's half past ten,' he said casually.

Daly was in no form for correction. 'Ah, good man,' he said. 'Isn't it a great thing to be able to tell the time.'

The detective did not reply but flicked through the pages of the grey book in front of him. 'Name?' he asked abruptly.

'Garda Michael Daly of the Traffic Corps, present and correct for duty.'

The detective fingered through the list of names and then stopped.

'Yes. Mike Daly. Well it looks like you're on questionnaires, Daly.' He leaned across the desk and handed over a pile of paper sheets. 'Have you done this before?' he asked.

Daly shook his head.

'Well it's simple enough. Just follow the questions on those sheets. Here's your list of premises and houses. Do the pubs first before they get busy at lunch time.'

Daly read down through the list of questions.

'Seems easy enough,' he said as he left.

'Only if they're done properly,' called the detective after him.

Daly went to his car, took out his empty clipboard and attached his handful of questionnaires to it, then put on his cap. He straightened it on his head and set off down the village. His first port of call would be Conroy's bar.

Big Madge Conroy rested her plump folded arms in front of her on the counter as he walked in.

'Good morning to you, Guard,' she said with a smile.

Daly smiled back and nodded. He surveyed the bar as he made his way slowly to the counter. All the various bric-à-brac that hung from the blackened rafters. Old horse collars and tackling for donkeys. Painted milk churns, blackthorn sticks and a giant stuffed leprechaun. He smiled to himself as he removed his cap and placed it with the clipboard down on the counter. He pulled out one of the high stools and sat on it.

'Now so,' he said as he held his pen up and clicked it open, 'what's your name, Madam?'

'Madge Conroy,' she said softly. 'But you can call me Margaret if you like,' she added dreamily.

Daly gave a nervous cough and started to write. Big Madge leaned closer and sniffed at him.

'That's a lovely smell you have,' she purred, studying his strong facial features as he wrote. 'Ye're getting younger by the day.' She smiled coyly. 'I remember when I was a child, all the guards looked old. 'Tis good to see a handsome buck like yourself in uniform.'

Daly was beginning to feel uneasy. He could handle anything except the unwanted advances of big, elderly women. Not even his sharp humour could save him now. He lifted the clipboard and held it for protection against his chest.

'God,' she heaved, lifting her ample breasts with her folded arms, 'if only I were a few years younger, you'd have your work cut out for you.'

Without warning, she all but threw herself on the counter towards him.

'Miss Conroy . . .' he protested, hoping that his officious tone might act as a deterrent to her making any more free with him.

'It's Mrs, actually.' Madge's voice lowered to a confidential tone. 'My husband is in the hospital at the moment . . . bit of liver trouble . . . you know what I mean.'

Daly leaned back further on the bar-stool as her head neared. She turned to survey the array of bottled spirits in the shelves behind her.

'Still . . . the place is beginning to show a profit since they took him.'

'Mrs Conroy. I'm here to ask you a few questions about John Burns. You've heard the news, I take it?'

'Oh yes, craythur, I have,' she moaned in a tone of exaggerated sorrow.

Madge, like many others in the village, had disliked Burns. His lack of community spirit, his failure to salute her on the street and, most important, the fact that he refused to drink in her pub, ensured that Madge held no flag for the recently deceased Mr Burns. Still though, common decency would call for some expression of sympathy.

'Poor John,' she sighed, 'wouldn't hurt a fly. Who would do such a thing?'

'That's what we're trying to find out,' replied

Daly, not fooled by her magnified sorrow.

'When did you last see John Burns?' he asked.

'Last Sunday at Mass, with his wife. Poor Claire. She must be going through a terrible time of it.'

'Has there been anyone strange in your premises in the last few days? Strangers?'

Madge leaned forward and patted Daly's hand. He withdrew it as if she had scalded him.

'My dear young man,' she continued, unruffled. 'This is Dunsheerin, one of the most popular tourist areas of the country and you ask me if I've seen any strangers. Germans, Africans, Americans . . . we get them all.'

'And under-age drinkers as well, I see,' added Daly, nodding in the direction of the two youngsters who were downing pints at the pool table.

'They told me that they were eighteen,' Madge replied nervously, leaning back from the counter.

It had done the trick. Daly sighed inwardly. Big Madge's advances were quickly disposed of. He had her full attention now.

'When I say "strangers", Mrs Conroy, I'm talking about people who don't look like tourists. Irish people. A person, or persons, who may have looked suspicious to you.'

Madge pulled herself up straight and listened to the question. For a moment, she considered making up a story about how a gang of dangerous-looking men had sat huddled in the corner all afternoon, and that she had felt that they were up to no good. But she knew that such a story could have serious consequences for her when it was revealed to be untrue. So instead she began to call up in her mind the faces of the day before. The ten-strong group of elderly American tourists who had bought two pints of 'Guy-niss' between them, commenting on how 'really Irish' her pub was.

'Two pints and ten pisses,' Paddy Larkin had laughed. Yes . . . Paddy Larkin. He was here as well. Then there was the group of youngsters on the first day of their long-awaited summer holidays. They had crowded in front of the television to watch a newly released horror film on the video. The ruck-sacked Australians, Quilter and Hickey, the other men . . . all local. After tea, locals again and a tall American man with his wife.

'No,' announced Madge in a decisive tone.

Daly clicked his pen closed and replaced it in his shirt pocket. He placed his cap on his head and gave it a couple of gentle taps to settle it.

'Well that's it so,' he said.

'Will you have a drink, Guard? A glass of lemonade maybe?'

It was the only consolation that she could offer him.

'No, thank you,' replied Daly, rising from the stool and replacing it underneath the counter. 'Thank you for your time.'

'Are there many guards in town?' Madge called out as he made his way to the door.

Daly shrugged.

'I'm not sure. Why do you ask?'

Madge thought of the amount of ham and cheese that was stored in the fridge in the kitchen. She would have to get more.

'You might tell them that there's tea and sandwiches for them here if they want it . . . on the house.'

Daly smiled as he glanced over in the direction of the under-aged drinkers, then back to Madge.

'Don't worry, Guard,' she said quickly, lifting the leaf of the counter and moving outside the bar. 'This won't happen again.'

'Very good, Mrs Conroy. I'll tell the lads about your generous offer. I'm sure they'll take you up on it.'

'Oh . . . one other thing, Guard . . .'

'Yes?'

'I'd appreciate it if you wouldn't make a mention of . . .', she nodded towards the pool table, 'this, to Jack Hegarty.'

'Not a word,' replied Daly.

'God bless your handsome heart,' exclaimed Madge and raced towards him, her arms outstretched. Daly, not wishing to revive her earlier passions, turned and opened the door.

'Don't mention it,' he said quickly.

He could sense her getting nearer. He was almost out. But not quite. Her hand gripped on his left buttock and gave it a gentle squeeze.

'My Jesus, but you're only gorgeous,' she squealed behind him.

He freed himself and ran out into the street. Madge waved at him from the doorway.

She smiled with pleasure as she made her way back behind the bar, and from there into the kitchen. She opened the door of the fridge and stood for a moment, surveying the plate of thick slices of ham. She lifted one out for inspection and sniffed at it, holding it between her thumb and forefinger. Its freshness was indeed questionable.

'Iffy ham indeed . . .' she thought, but the guards wouldn't complain. Anyhow, a dollop of strong mustard would do the trick.

Her thoughts were interrupted by the sound of a coin being tapped loudly on the bar counter. Madge replaced the slice of ham carefully on the plate and walked back into the bar, rubbing the brine from her fingers onto the sleeve of her blouse.

The young man was nodding in rhythm with a rock song that was playing on the jukebox.

'Change for the pool table, Madge. And the same again.'

Her response was not as he had expected.

'Get outta here, the two of you,' she roared, waving an arm in the direction of the door. 'Have ye no respect for the law?'

Flann O'Neill lit a match and held it over the bowl of his pipe.

'Down there,' he nodded, sucking hard, trying to bring the tobacco to life. Satisfied that the job was done, he quenched the match. 'C'mon . . . I'll show ye,' he said, moving quickly ahead of Hegarty and Brosnan.

As he moved to go, he looked up at the warm sun. 'A sporting morning to be alive, men.' They walked together for a short distance before Flann stopped and pointed. 'Right about here . . .'

Brosnan bent down to examine the roadside, running his hand through the grassy verge, hoping for some clue. He knew that it was hopeless. Even if a car had parked for a considerable time on the edge of the road, it would not have left a print. The earth had been turned almost to dust by the weeks of hot sunshine. None the less, he would have Sullivan examine it. Flann watched him as he moved his hands around the ground, like a wizard conjuring up a spell. To break the silence he turned to Hegarty.

'It's gone now though . . .' he sighed heavily.

'Not to matter, Flann,' replied Hegarty, smiling at the innocence of the old man. 'It may have left some tracks.'

Brosnan stood up and removed his jacket. The heat was getting too much for him.

'Are you sure it was here the car parked, Flann?' he asked, throwing the jacket over his shoulder.

'I am indeed sure,' replied the old man, a flash of temper in his eyes. 'Amn't I after saying it? I might be colour-blind, but I can see as far as any man. I mean . . . look over there.' He pointed in the direction of the field where Sullivan and the two guards were searching. 'They're your men, aren't they?'

Hegarty positioned himself behind the old man and squinted, barely able to make out the black dots in the distance.

'Jay . . .sus, that's the guts of a hundred and fifty yards away. Pat . . . can you see them?'

'Flann,' asked Brosnan, 'what age would you say they are?'

The old man puffed pensively on his pipe.

'Well, the two lads in grey are in their late twenties, and the fella in the middle . . . is he a prisoner?'

'No, Flann, he's not. What age do you think he is?'

'I'd say he's around forty, there or thereabouts.'

'What ages were the two men you saw yesterday, Flann?' continued Brosnan casually, continuing to look into the field, his excitement rising.

'About thirty, the two of them.'

Brosnan turned, rubbing his hand impatiently through his hair. He stood in front of the old man.

'Why didn't you tell us that already? I asked you in the house if you had got a good look at them and you said that you didn't. Now you tell me that you know what ages they were. How is that?'

'You upset me with your question about the colour of the car. I thought that was all you wanted to know.' He spat sideways into the grass. 'Well, I'm fine and relaxed now, so you can ask me what you like.'

Brosnan looked wild-eyed at Hegarty, who grinned back at him. He deftly removed the copybook from his pocket and clicked the pen into action.

'What height were they?'

'Well, one was about five foot ten, the other . . . he got out of the passenger side . . . he was about six two or so.'

Brosnan scribbled frantically, aware that the old man was on a roll.

'Hair . . . hair colour, no, . . . what kind of hair styles had they?'

'Both had their hair cut short, well cropped at the back . . . like the guards.' He smiled.

'Dressed? What were they wearing?'

Flann inhaled deeply from the pipe.

'The big fella was wearing a dark jacket, like a fishing jacket, hip length . . . trousers and a light coloured T-shirt.'

'I thought you couldn't see colour, Flann?' interrupted Hegarty.

'I can't, but it looked light. It's either black or white with me, Jack, but I can tell if it's dark or light.'

'The smaller man,' continued Brosnan quickly, 'what did he wear?'

'Mmm . . . T-shirt and trousers.' The old man raised a hand of caution. 'I couldn't swear to that now though.'

'I see . . .' mused Brosnan closing the copybook and tapping it lightly on his chin. 'How long were you looking at these men?'

'About thirty seconds . . . no more than that. The dog doesn't like me standing over him when he's eating.'

Brosnan waved the book in front of the old man.

'And you can tell me all this from looking at two men who were nearly . . .' – he turned back to judge the distance they had walked from Flann's house – ' . . . nearly a hundred and fifty yards away?'

'Thirty seconds is a long time,' said Flann, patting at his trouser leg for his matches. Having found them he proceeded to set about re-lighting the pipe. He spoke through pursed lips.

'I remember one Munster Final with that exact amount of time to play . . . one point in it. A high ball dropped into the square, goalie came out . . .'

'Listen, Flann,' interrupted Brosnan, cutting short the heroic story, much to Hegarty's dismay, 'I have one other question for you, and I want you to answer it truthfully. How could you tell the ages of the two men from that distance?'

Flann removed the pipe from his mouth and pushed the tobacco from the edges down the bowl with a blackened thumb, then looked up at Brosnan.

'From the way they moved,' he said quietly.

Brosnan turned to Hegarty and threw his eyes up to heaven.

Flann continued.

'I've been watching sport all my life, and I could tell you to within a couple of years what age a player was by watching him from the far end of the field. The young lad in his teens is loose and gangly, fast on his feet but awkward. The fella in his twenties has it all, speed and co-ordination, everything moving together. From thirty on they start to lose it.'

Brosnan took his jacket back from Hegarty and signalled his intentions with a single nod in the direction of the patrol car. Flann walked slowly behind them outlining his theories.

'Ah yes, they lose it in the thirties, like that big fella yesterday. Quick enough on his feet but awkward enough climbing my new gate.'

Brosnan turned on his heel, the jacket over his shoulder swinging around and striking Hegarty on the side of the face.

'What did you say?' he said, holding his arm out to stall the old man. Flann looked up at him, trying to recall his last sentence.

'Ah yes . . . fellas in their thirties,' he continued, happier now that the big man had finally shown an interest in his knowledge of the growth and decline of physical ability on the playing field.

'Did I hear you say that one of the men climbed a gate into your field?'

'Yes,' replied Flann, disappointed that the conversation had once again turned. 'The big fella climbed my gate. The dog growled at me then, so I went inside.'

'Where's the gate?'

'About fifty yards on the right,' replied Flann, pointing back in the direction from which they had come. Brosnan looked wildly towards the gate and sprinted off in its direction. Hegarty made a move to follow him.

'What age would you think he is, Flann?' he asked, pointing ahead to the racing chief superintendent.

'Just gone sixty,' replied the old man and began to follow on.

When Hegarty approached him, Brosnan was bent at the waist and panting heavily, the trickles of sweat breaking loose from his side locks.

'Isn't she a beauty, Jack . . .' he gasped, holding a hand out to the white-painted aluminium farm gate.

'There she is,' said Flann, arriving. 'Bought her from the knackers last March . . . cost me forty pounds. Hung her and all for me they did. She's perfectly balanced . . . watch this . . .'

'Don't touch it!' screamed Brosnan.

The old man took fright and quickly retreated behind Hegarty. Brosnan's voice had resounded so loudly that the guards in the distant field had looked up from their work.

'I'm sorry, Flann,' he said to the shaken old man, reaching around Hegarty and taking the old man by the arm. 'You see,' he continued softly, pointing to the gate, 'This could have fingerprints on it . . . evidence. Do you understand? I'm sorry. I didn't mean to shout. Are you all right?'

'Never better,' replied Flann heartily, his heart pounding in his chest.

He was still not sure what Brosnan meant, but he knew that it wasn't the time to ask for a further explanation. He flinched as the big man roared again.

'Finbarr! Finbarr, get over here.'

The plain-clothes man in the middle of the group stood up and looked in their direction. Brosnan beckoned to him with exaggerated waving of his arms.

'You were always a great man for traffic control,' laughed Hegarty, looking at him.

Brosnan continued to wave, laughing at Hegarty's comment. When he saw Sullivan break free from the line, he stopped waving, turned and looked straight at Flann and extended his hand.

'Thanks for all your help, Flann. Again, sorry for upsetting you by shouting. I'll be sending one of my lads around later to take a statement. Will you be there at about half two?'

'Yes I will. Oh, tell him to mind the dog. He doesn't like strangers.'

'Fair enough, Flann. I'll warn him,' replied Brosnan, releasing the old man's hand. 'His name is Detective Ger Hanahoe.'

'Any relation of . . .?'

'No, Flann. But he's a fanatic on Dublin football all the same.'

'Dublin football! Hah! I'll tell him a few things about the game,' said Flann with a toss of his head. 'That's of course if the dog doesn't ate him first.'

No sooner had Flann left than Sullivan arrived on the scene. He was following his own advice, advice that he had given to numerous uniformed men whose job it was to protect a crime scene. Keep your hands in your pockets to stop yourself touching anything.

He addressed Brosnan from across the top of the farm gate.

'What's up, Chief? We heard someone roaring like a bullock a few minutes ago. Thought there was another murder to solve. Are you all right, Chief?' he asked, examining his officer from the distance between them.

Brosnan's face was flushed, the red glow on his cheeks brought on by the sudden exertion of the sprint to the gate.

'Actually,' joked Hegarty, 'he's just beaten the shite out of a seventy-year-old man. As you can see, I was holding his coat.'

Brosnan turned and smiled, swiping the jacket from Hegarty's arm.

'You see this shining jewel before you, Finbarr?' asked Brosnan, pointing to the gate that stood between them. 'Our killer was seen climbing this yesterday. Well, he may have been our killer. Fingerprint it. If he was wearing gloves, then we're back to square one. If not . . .' he clenched his fist and glanced from Sullivan to Hegarty, ' . . .then we've got him by the balls.'

CHAPTER FIFTEEN

Liam McCann sat alone beside the window in the corner booth of the popular city-centre coffee shop, an English tabloid newspaper opened out on the table in front of him. He was not reading it. Now and then he would look impatiently at his watch and then glance out at the busy city street, with its contrast of shadows and bright sunshine, people going cheerfully about their daily business.

Liam liked Dublin, especially in the summer. It was a big change from the Creggan area of Derry where he was born and had spent eighteen years of his life before his petty criminal activities and a punishment knee-capping by the Provisionals had forced him to leave. His elder brother Michael, however, had not been so lucky. He was found face down in a patch of waste ground near the Bogside, his hands tied behind his back, a victim of quick justice. Although Liam had left it all behind him some ten years ago, his limp would always serve as a reminder.

'You've been a troublesome wee shite again, Liam lad!'

He remembered the voice from behind the black hood, the smell of cordite after the .45 Colt automatic had fired. It was a deafening sound, his own screaming drowning out the ringing in his ears.

'Don't do it again, Liam!'

He had rolled over on the ground clutching his left knee, the searing pain being eased only by his lapse into unconsciousness.

Yes, Liam liked the summer. The pain was always worse in the cold weather.

He lifted the small coffee cup and drank the last lukewarm mouthful. Over the rim, his eyes watched as a middle-aged woman, puffing under the weight of four plastic shopping bags approached the table and set them down at the edge of the booth.

He looked out the window and spoke in his soft northern tone: 'It's taken.'

She looked at him and then at the empty booth. Her mouth was about to open in protestation.

'I said, it's taken.' His voice was steely cold.

He waited for her response. There was none. The woman bent down and quickly grasped the twisted necks of her shopping bags and shuffled away.

'Gurrier,' she muttered.

Liam smiled and resumed his watch onto the street. Then there came a shout from the doorway,
    'Oi, boy-o!'

Two men approached and settled themselves in the seat opposite, the larger of the two edging himself towards the window.

'Where the *fuck* have you two morons been? I've been waiting here almost half an hour.'

'Sorry, Liam,' said Seanie apologetically and turned to grimace at Tony. He had known that Liam would be upset by their lateness.

'Had a bit of a night on the town . . . couldn't resist it,' he offered by way of explanation.

Liam raised a pointed finger in Tony's direction.

'Is this your wheels man?'

'Yeah . . . the best fella I ever seen behind a wheel,' said Seanie with a smile, twisting himself in the confined space of the seat to give the man beside him a friendly punch.

Liam leaned forward across the table. His voice lowered.

'Mr Carroll said to say well done. He'd like to be here himself, but as you know, he doesn't talk to the staff.'

Seanie laughed.

Tony disliked the remark. 'Where's our money,' he asked. 'The two grand?'

'First things first, wheels man,' said Liam, holding out his hand, almost touching Tony's chin. 'Where's the map I gave you?'

'Oh yeah, the map.'

Seanie patted the pockets down the front of his

army jacket and, reaching into the top one, he removed a folded piece of blue paper.

'No problems, I take it,' said Liam, slipping the paper gently from Seanie's hand.

'We did exactly as you said,' began Seanie, and stopped as Liam signalled across the table.

'Shh . . . keep yer fuckin' voice down.'

'Sorry,' whispered Seanie. 'Well, we arrived there as planned and parked the car on the side road that was marked on the map. We had to wait a while, though, the old guy was nearly an hour in the middle of the river. Then there was a fella talking to him for a while. After that he came out, sat down and bam! Gone. Then back out before anyone knew what had happened.'

'So you got away clean then,' said Liam.

Seanie nodded. 'No problem. No problem at all.'

'What about the bar?' asked Liam.

'Dropped it in the canal.'

'The car?' he continued.

'Wiped clean and dumped.'

Seanie was ready with all the answers.

'Gloves?'

'Gloves . . .,' repeated Seanie, as he thought for a moment.

'Didn't need them,' he said, brushing the question aside. 'We were in the middle of the sticks. There was nothing to touch. Besides, Tony and I decided that it would look a bit stupid to be wearing gloves on the hottest day of the year, if we were seen that is . . . which we weren't.'

Liam sat back and thought about the logic of what the other man had said.

'Yeah, okay,' he nodded, and lifted the edge of his newspaper to reveal a brown envelope. 'Take it. There's an extra ton for each of yiz, compliments of Mr Carroll.'

Seanie moved his hand slowly down and fingered the envelope along the table towards him. He weighed it in his hand for moment, before slipping it inside his jacket, then turned and winked at Tony.

Liam leaned across the table and, looking from one man to the other, he whispered: 'If what you've told me is true, then this was a job well done. However . . . if either of you fucked up and the cops are on to it, then you're on your own. Mention me or Mr Carroll and you're both dead. There won't be a safe place on this earth to hide.'

Tony's eyes narrowed in anger. 'I'm no rat,' he said. Seanie looked at him and nodded in agreement.

Liam leaned back and smiled at them before edging himself out of the seat. 'Good day, gentlemen,' he said with a grin, and limped to the door.

Claire Burns stood outside the front door of her house, fingering a ball of damp tissue paper, occasionally patting her reddened eyes. Beside her stood a defiant Jenny, holding her arm.

Their preparation for the journey to the morgue and identification of the body of John Burns had been interrupted by the arrival of Councillor Bill Jennings.

Having offered his condolences, he volunteered, much to their dismay, to stand by Claire in her hour of need. Their pleas of wishing to be left alone were brushed aside. Jennings would have none of it.

This murder of a prominent businessman and the subsequent comforting of his weeping widow would be the ideal opportunity to change his political image from that of a self-centred, egotistical megalomaniac to that of an unselfish and caring public representative. It was after all, only a year to the elections.

And so, as the patrol car drove up to the steps, Bill Jennings pulled the front door closed behind them.

'Wait here a moment, ladies,' he said as he started hurriedly down the steps to intercept Brosnan who was just getting out of the passenger side of the car.

'Is this absolutely necessary?' he inquired in an annoyed tone. 'I mean . . . can't you see that the woman is going through enough at the moment?'

Brosnan looked down at the round moustachioed face of the man who stood in front of him. He disliked him instantly.

'Who are *you*?' he asked abruptly.

Hegarty was standing at the opposite side of the car, leaning on the roof, looking across at both men. He was going to enjoy this.

'Actually, I'm Bill Jennings, a local politician,' came the indignant reply.

'Ah . . .' said Brosnan, glancing across at Hegarty and nodding in the affirmative, 'another fella getting expenses for dressing up and talking.' He stared down again at the small man. 'Well now, Mr Jennings, my name is Chief Superintendent Pat

Brosnan, and unlike you, I have a job to do. So keep out of my way like a good man.'

Hegarty smiled and looked at the ground. He never liked to see a man being humiliated, but there were exceptions to every rule.

Jennings's bottom lip trembled with anger. For a moment he was lost for words as he watched Brosnan pass, making his way towards the steps. The attitude of this senior policeman was beyond contemplation, more so because the affront was made in the presence of a guard, who would as a rule recognise his standing in the community by way of a salute whenever they met. This was the way particularly with the younger guards. It was the way things should be. The attitude of this senior policeman, on the other hand, was not the way things should be.

'One moment, Chief Superintendent.'

Brosnan stopped his ascent of the steps as Jennings walked slowly up to meet him, taking one step up from Brosnan's so as he could look him in the eye.

'I think it's only fair to warn you that I'm a personal friend of your boss-man. Actually, we went to school together. Now don't get me wrong, Chief Superintendent . . . I know that you've a job to do, and far be it from me to interfere with your investigation, but I'd like you to know who you're dealing with . . . Understand?'

Jennings moved away and, without waiting for a reply, started down the steps.

'Mr Jennings?' called Brosnan, beckoning with his hand for the councillor to return.

'Yes, Chief Superintendent?' Jennings did not make a move to approach.

'We . . . well, it's just that I've never had to say this to a politician before,' said Brosnan, lowering his head, his voice seeming to waver in apology.

'It can't be that difficult for you,' said Jennings, giving the chief a wry smile as he moved back up to him.

'Well, actually it is,' muttered Brosnan. 'You see, I've never been in this position before. In all my years as a policeman, I've never had to . . .'

'Very well,' said Jennings consoling him. 'I promise that I won't tell a soul. It will be our little secret.'

'Do you mean that?' asked Brosnan with childish innocence, his face lighting up in relief.

Jennings was feeling magnanimous in victory. 'My word is my bond,' he announced in a judicial tone. He inclined his head, awaiting the policeman's repentance.

Brosnan bent towards his ear, his voice rasped in anger.

'Firstly, I don't give a shite who you went to school with, boy... Secondly, and this is the part you should pay attention to, if you get in my way again I'll tear that little mouse from under your nose and shove it up into your arse. Good man.'

Jennings's mouth fell open. He moved down two steps and looked at Hegarty.

'Did you hear what this man just said to me, Guard?' he panted in shock.

Hegarty shook his head slowly. 'You said that it was a secret so I didn't listen, Bill,' he smiled back.

Brosnan turned and approached the two women.

'When you're ready, ladies . . .'

Brosnan led Claire and Jenny down the steps towards the patrol car. Jennings spoke softly to them as they passed.

'I'll see you at the hospital, my dear . . . Look after her, Jenny.'

The women sat into the car and the door was closed gently by Hegarty. Jennings turned to Brosnan.

'You haven't heard the end of this, Chief Superintendent,' he hissed, 'I've never been so insulted in all my life!'

'Then perhaps you should get out more often,' quipped Brosnan as he lowered himself into the passenger seat. 'Oh . . . and by the way, like any true politician . . . your word is your bond.'

The car accelerated and drove off down the driveway, leaving the dumbstruck politician to wipe the dust from his black suit.

'We'll try to make this as quick as possible, Claire,' said Hegarty as they drove out on the main road. She sniffed loudly in response and Jenny handed her a fresh tissue.

'Th . . . thank you, Jack,' she whispered. ' I . . . I hope I'm up to it. I don't feel so well.'

'You'll be fine, Mrs Burns,' said Brosnan. He was sitting bolt upright, his arms folded, his face blanked in deep thought as he stared straight ahead.

His encounter with Councillor Jennings had annoyed him, but his mind was beyond that now. He had long since given up being nice to people he didn't like. Especially politicians, the majority of whom he considered to be nothing but a bunch of idle slackers living off the fat of the tax-payer. And slackness was the one thing that he could not tolerate.

In conversation the previous week with a newly promoted superintendent, he had made his views on this well known. Handing the officer a shiny Sam Browne belt, which was to fit smartly over his tunic, he had said, 'Many before you thought that respect came with this piece of leather. Just remember, it's made of the same stuff as a donkey's winkers and carries the same clout. You must *earn* the respect of your men. Do not be hard on the policeman who fails having tried his best. Encourage him. As for the slacker, help him along too, by booting him up the arse every chance you get.'

Hegarty gave a quiet sigh of relief as the tall white pillars of the hospital came into view. His face was flushed, even though he was in his shirt-sleeves and the window was rolled down. The journey had drained him mentally, his attempts at idle chit-chat with the sobbing widow and her silent friend in the back seat having failed miserably.

The superintendent met the sombre party at the door to the morgue.

'Well, Superintendent Murray?' said Brosnan as they approached.

'Everything is arranged, Chief,' he replied holding open the aluminium framed door, nodding his condolences to the two women as they entered the lobby.

'Last door on the left . . .'

The party moved along the darkened hallway, the sound of their footsteps on the red stone tiles echoing off the cold walls.

In the mortuary, the body of John Burns lay on a hospital trolley covered by a single white sheet.

Brosnan and Murray moved solemnly to one side while Claire, Jenny and Hegarty took up position on the other. Brosnan turned to the morgue assistant and gave a curt nod. The man moved forward to the head of the trolley and lifted back the sheet to reveal the face to all present.

Claire Burns stared down at her husband, the pale, bluish face of her dead tormentor. She wished that she could reach out and slap it as hard as she could. She wanted to beat at his body as he had done to her for so long.

She'd said to Jenny that she was afraid she might not be able to cope with the strain of identification, but she had been wrong. She felt nothing now but hatred. She hated him for the years lost to fear and physical pain, years that could not be retrieved. But at least it was over now.

She closed her eyes again.

'Is this your husband, Mrs Burns?' asked Brosnan, in a low, respectful tone.

Claire did not reply.

'Mrs Burns?' Brosnan raised his voice slightly.

Claire opened her eyes and looked across blankly at Brosnan.

'Yes, Chief Superintendent, that's my husband, John Burns.'

'Thank you, Mrs Burns. I know that was difficult for you.'

The morgue assistant moved forward to replace the sheet. Claire reached out her hand to stop him and looked at Hegarty.

'Do you think we could have a minute alone with him, Jack?'

'Of course, Claire. Take as long as you like.'

The heavy door groaned behind the policemen, leaving the women alone with the corpse. Claire released her grip on Jenny's arm and moved closer to the body. She touched the face and then flinched back suddenly.

'What the hell are you doing?' gasped Jenny, pulling her friend's hand away and looking in a panic at the door.

'Shh . . . just making sure,' said Claire, and moved forward again. She lifted the sheet to reveal the grey pudgy arm and grasped it with both hands, squeezing as hard as she could. Jenny raised her hands to her mouth in shock.

'That's how it felt, you bastard,' whispered Claire, standing back and throwing the sheet back over the body in disgust. She turned and looked at her friend. The tears streamed from Jenny's eyes down over her hands which she still held to her face.

'Why the hell are we crying?' said Claire stoutly. 'My problems are *over*.'

Outside, Brosnan stood with his back to the other men. He rummaged through a large plastic evidence bag, which held the personal effects of John Burns. After a moment, he turned to the superintendent.

'Has anyone examined this yet?' he asked.

Superintendent Murray shook his head. 'No,' he replied. 'Anyway it doesn't look as if there's anything of evidential value.'

Brosnan turned around and placed the bag back on the vacant trolley. 'I'll decide what evidence is of value and what isn't,' he said curtly. 'Do you understand, Superintendent!' he said, glaring at him, his raised voice echoing in the corridor.

Murray furrowed his brow and stared back angrily. He glanced sideways at Hegarty and the morgue assistant and then back at Brosnan.

'Might I have a quiet word with you, Chief?' he whispered through his teeth.

Brosnan nodded and they both moved to the end of the hall.

'What is it?' said Brosnan abruptly. 'Have you forgotten to contact someone else, like a priest, or maybe it's the state pathologist this time.'

Murray gave a short sneer. 'So I forgot to get a priest for a dead man. That's what all the abuse is about? I thought it was that you just didn't like the fact that I had reached this rank.'

'That too,' nodded Brosnan. 'Let's get one thing straight for the record,' he continued, his voice lowered. 'I never liked you as a guard, because you never *were* one. And now that you're a super, I dislike you even more.' He eyed him up and down. 'You're one of those fellas who never made a decent arrest in his life but can feel at home sitting around a big table, making elaborate plans for the job with some other shower of gobshites who never walked the beat. You're just a recruit in an officer's uniform.'

Murray smiled back.

'You never moved with the times, did you, Chief?' he said. 'All these years and you're still caught in that policing time-warp. You still think that a good policeman is one who pounds the beat and kicks gougers up the backside.' He gave a shake of his head. 'Not any more. We have moved into the age of technology, Chief.'

Brosnan eyed him with disdain. He hadn't changed a bit.

'You're still the same arrogant little prick that you always were,' he said. 'Well, let me tell you, all the technology in Japan couldn't make up for an incompetent like you. A computer is only as smart as the brain that works it. And if that brain is yours, then we're *all* in the shit.'

Murray fumed inside. Outwardly he was a portrait of calmness.

'When are you retiring, Chief?' he asked casually. 'I feel like jumping another rank.'

Brosnan snorted a laugh as he turned around.

'You should have no problem. There's always a few arses that need kissing. What time is the PM set for?' he asked, changing the subject.

'Two o'clock.'

'Good. Stay here and find out what you can, and keep a *real* guard with you to take any notes so you don't bollocks it up. And,' he added as he walked towards Hegarty, 'I want them on a sheet of paper like the good old days, and not on some smart-arsed computer.'

The door opened.

'Thank you, gentlemen,' said Jenny. 'We'd like

to get home as soon as possible. Claire isn't feeling very well.'

As they walked towards the front door, Claire stumbled forward slightly, then regained her balance by reaching out with her hand to the wall. Hegarty rushed forward.

'Are you all right, Claire?'

Claire nodded weakly.

'I'll be fine now, Jack,' she sighed.

The return journey was made in silence. On arrival at the Burns residence Brosnan turned back to Claire.

'I'll need to talk to you when you're feeling a bit better, nothing to worry about . . . just a few things I want to clear up.'

The two women got out of the car and stood at the foot of the steps. Brosnan wound down the window.

'Shall we say seven o'clock this evening? Is that okay?'

'That'll be fine, Chief Superintendent,' replied Claire. 'See you both at seven.'

They watched the patrol car drive away.

As it exited from the gate, Jenny turned to Claire. 'I wonder if you're a suspect?' she asked.

Claire gave a short laugh. 'Don't be ridiculous,' she said. 'Why ever would he think that?'

CHAPTER SIXTEEN

Costigan leaned on the pillar outside Dunsheerin Garda station with a broad grin on his face. He watched as Daly ambled towards him with an expression of total dejection and fatigue, the trickles of sweat breaking from his shaven sidelocks.

'Bollocks to this for a crack,' was Daly's greeting to Costigan. 'I shouldn't be here at all, you know. The Traffic Corps don't get involved in this kind of thing.'

He struggled to remove his tie, overheated by his temper and the hot sun.

'Maybe it's because you're such an all-round policeman,' smiled Costigan, leaning back against the low wall.

'Yeah, fierce smart, Costigan.'

Daly was in no mood for messing. He grunted with annoyance as he removed his cap and flung it through the open window of his car where it bounced on the passenger seat and fell on the floor.

'Hey you,' he said to the detective who stood in the doorway. 'Add them to the pile.'

The detective smiled as he took the completed questionnaires. 'They're great fun aren't they,' he said and went back inside.

Costigan looked at his watch. 'C'mon, Grumpy, we have time for a coffee in Conroy's . . . my treat.'

Daly's face softened. 'Why that's very kind of you, Kieran, and perhaps your generosity might stretch to a sandwich?'

'Don't push it, Daly,' came the quick reply.

'You'll have to do the ordering,' said Daly. 'I think the big one who owns the bar is a bit of a nympho.'

Costigan burst into laughter. 'Did she grab your arse?'

Daly joined in the laughter. 'Grab my arse! Jesus, she nearly sexually assaulted me.'

'Big Madge does that to everyone,' explained Costigan. 'Sure, Jack is lucky to have a bit of an arse left at all.'

As they walked towards Conroy's bar, Hegarty pulled up alongside them in the patrol car. Brosnan nodded in greeting from the passenger seat.

'Are ye goin' for a cuppa, lads?' called Hegarty.

'We're just on our way to Madge's now, Jack,' replied Costigan.

'Will we go for one?' asked Hegarty turning to Brosnan. The big man looked at his watch.

'We have half an hour . . . why not?'

'Right so, lads,' called Hegarty, 'See ye below.'

The patrol car continued down the road and parked outside Conroy's.

'That's all I need to make complete shite of my day,' grunted Daly as he watched the two men entering the bar ahead of him. 'Afternoon tea with a thick guard and Ireland's answer to Sherlock Holmes.'

Costigan laughed. Even when Daly was upset, he had the ability to bring out humour in his anger.

Inside the bar, Madge handed large plates of roughly cut ham sandwiches across the counter, which in turn were passed around the crowd. She looked up as the guards came through the door, raising and lowering her eyebrows quickly at Daly, who looked down at the floor, only looking up when he felt that her attention had turned back to the business at hand.

'Which one of you lads ordered the Guinness?' she called out, giving the tap a final pull.

A hand holding a ten-pound note appeared from between two shoulders. She took it quickly and replaced it with the overflowing glass. The thirsty recipient waited for his change, then squeezed himself around in the confined space and into the chest of Pat Brosnan. He looked up.

'Don't drink too much of that stuff, Bill,' said Brosnan as he moved past the open-mouthed detective.

'Over here, Pat,' called Hegarty indicating a

table with two empty stools. 'Madge, pot of tea and two sandwiches.'

The big woman smiled in acknowledgement. Her open invitation to the handsome Guard Daly had obviously been accepted by all. However, what she had not counted on were the locals, who were also availing of the free lunch.

'They're for the guards, ya tramp ya,' she snapped, whisking the plate from in front of Tadhg Barrett.

'My uncle was a guard, Madge,' he protested, a brown crust hanging from the side of his mouth.

'Yerra, will you get out of it!'

Rearranging the sandwiches on the plate, she left the shouting crowd for the silence of her back kitchen where she hurriedly filled a pot of tea.

On returning to the counter, Madge was astonished to find that the calls for porter and lager that had been coming earlier were now changed to requests for coffee and minerals.

She handed the tea and sandwiches on a small tray over the heads to Hegarty.

'Who's that fella with you?' she enquired.

'It's the Chief,' he shouted back.

So that was the reason.

'Tell him he's barred,' she called to the laughing Hegarty. 'He's bad for business.'

Brosnan stirred his tea slowly and leaned over to Hegarty.

'Jack. Tell me about Claire Burns. She comes across as a very quiet, private sort of woman.'

'Well there's not much to tell,' replied Hegarty. 'She is a native of the village. Her father was a blacksmith by trade. I knew him well. A decent man. Burns and herself were in their late twenties when they married.'

He shook his head. 'By God, Pat, you should have seen the wedding. 'Twas like something out of a child's storybook. A black horse-drawn carriage led by two white horses. The whole village was invited to it. Sure the reception in the hotel went on into the small hours.'

Brosnan was not interested. None the less he could not bring himself to spoil the story.

'The village street was like a Patrick's Day parade,' continued Hegarty, smiling to himself as he recalled the day. 'People lining the footpaths and cheering. By God, Pat, what a day.'

The smile faded. 'How did it all end up like this?' he muttered.

'No happily-ever-after in that story, Jack,' said Brosnan.

'No indeed then,' agreed Hegarty, leaning forward for his cup.

'These beatings that Burns gave her,' said Brosnan. 'How long did you say that they were going on for?'

'Ten years,' replied Hegarty. 'At least that's what Jenny Maguire said.'

Brosnan picked up a beer-mat from the small table and tapped it methodically on his fingers.

'I wonder . . .' said Brosnan as if to himself. 'What makes a man do something like that to a quiet woman like Claire Burns?'

Hegarty leaned towards him. 'Well, there was a rumour going around that she couldn't have children. I suppose that could have played on Burns's mind.'

Brosnan turned to him and smiled. 'I'd say that Dunsheerin is a great place for the rumours,' he said.

'You can say that again,' said Hegarty with a short laugh. 'About three years ago, the super was putting fierce pressure on me to get a few offences for the local court. There was mayhem in the village. They all thought I'd gone stone mad. You know yourself, now. "Keraisht, Hegarty is doing another checkpoint."'

Brosnan sniggered. 'Did you catch many?'

'Yerra, 'twas like shooting fish in a barrel,' replied Hegarty. 'I gave most of them a caution and they straightened things out. But the few smart-alecs I brought to court put out the rumour that I was giving Madge there a bit on the side.'

'Good Jesus.' Brosnan gave a short laugh as he looked up at the big woman behind the counter. 'And were you?' he said, looking back.

Hegarty frowned at him, wondering if it was a serious question. It was hard to know what the chief was thinking at the best of times.

'I remember a time, Jack, when you'd get up on a cracked plate.'

Hegarty hushed him to silence with his hand. 'Well, not since I got married,' he whispered.

'Good man. Glad to hear it. Just another rumour then.'

'If you want to know what's going on in the village,' said Hegarty, ignoring his sarcasm, 'then look no further than your landlady, Rose Scully.'

'Yeah, I've experienced her interrogation technique already,' smiled Brosnan. 'She's a true professional. Anyway Jack, that's enough about her. We're still searching for a motive here. I want you to have a discreet word with the local doctor about Claire Burns. See if he's treated her in the past for any cuts or bruises. And if so, when and how many times. Do think he'll help?'

'I doubt it. He's a raving alco. And a right grumpy one at that. Besides, Pat, isn't all that doctor-patient stuff confidential?'

Brosnan turned to him and raised an eyebrow.

Hegarty understood. 'I'll wait till he's drunk.'

'Good man, you're beginning to sound like the old Jack Hegarty I used to know.'

He took a bite from the sandwich and spoke through the chewing.

'What about the friend, Jenny Maguire? What's the story with her? I'd say that she was a right gamey bird in her time.'

'Gamey would be a very tame description of her, Pat,' smiled Hegarty. 'As the fella says, the only thing she didn't ride in her early twenties was a Grand National winner.'

Hegarty did not get the response to the joke that he had anticipated.

Brosnan frowned. 'That's a terrible thing to say about any woman, Jack,' he said. 'I'd have to say that a statement like that was very politically incorrect, more so coming from the mouth of a senior guard.'

Hegarty leaned back in surprise on the low stool and stirred his tea slowly.

'By Jesus, but you're getting very sober in your old age, Chief,' he said.

He waited for a moment as he watched the side of Brosnan's face. The jowls wrinkled back as the grin broke, the shoulders beginning to shudder with the silent laughter.

'Aw shite,' smiled Hegarty as he replaced the cup on the saucer and watched Brosnan's face redden. 'Yeah, yeah, very good, you got me,' he muttered.

Daly and Costigan stood just inside the door, grappling with their cups of coffee in the crowd.

'Thanks very much for this wonderful treat, Costigan,' said Daly, as he lifted his cup under his chin to allow someone to pass. 'I now owe you a slap-up feed in the Shelbourne,' he added with sarcasm.

'Ah well, at least we don't have to join in the crime-busters' conversation,' replied Costigan, nodding in the direction of the small table where Hegarty and Brosnan sat.

Suddenly, out of the corner of his eye he caught sight of a multi-coloured shirt and turned to the shiny, tanned face of the wearer, a tall, middle-aged American.

'Hi there, Officer.'

As Daly was the only guard present who wasn't wearing a civvy jumper, he assumed that the drawling Yank was addressing him.

'How are things?' nodded Daly.

'Things?' repeated the puzzled American. 'Oh yeah,' he said clicking his fingers in sudden realisation of what Daly had meant. 'Things are great. I'm a cop myself,' he continued, reaching into his back trousers pocket and removing a bulging black wallet from which he took a shiny identification badge. He held it up in front of Daly for inspection.

'Very nice,' Daly nodded. He turned to Costigan and raised his eyebrows.

'Say . . . Tigue over there tells me that you've got a homicide on your hands.'

'That's right . . . only over here we call it murder,' said Daly, going heavy on the r's.

'You're pretty small for a cop, ain't ya?' The tall frame of the American loomed over Daly. Costigan grinned and turned away.

'What do you mean by that?' protested Daly. 'I'm no smaller than any of the other guards around here.'

Daly was indignant. The American looked around the bar at the other men.

'Yeah, sure. But in the States all our cops are six feet or over. Not too many big guys here. As a matter of fact I'd say that you were all pretty small.'

'Agreed,' said Daly, finishing the last of his coffee and placing the empty cup on a table nearby. 'But there's a specific reason for that difference,' he continued. 'You see, in the States as you call it . . . ye only measure your prospective cops from hair to heel, whereas here in Ireland we like to measure them from ear to ear first. Good luck now, and enjoy the rest of your holiday,' he finished with a grin.

Brosnan and Hegarty finished their lunch and rose to their feet. The chief clapped his hands loudly.

'I want to see you men in the station in ten minutes,' he announced.

'Does that mean me as well?' called Tadhg Barrett, downing his fourth ham sandwich since Madge's back was turned.

'No thanks,' smiled Brosnan when the laughter had died down. 'I have enough comedians on the staff at the moment. Ten minutes.'

No sooner had he left than Madge was inundated with shouts for quick pints.

'See you lads tonight,' Madge reminded the crowd as they filtered out the door, having downed their quick pints.

'Now that's more like it,' she chuckled to Tadhg.

CHAPTER SEVENTEEN

Finbarr Sullivan held his breath as he peeled back the tape from the silver-painted gate. Although the black charcoal powder, which he had dusted on moments earlier, had clearly revealed a set of palm-and fingerprints, the surface of the gate was making them difficult to lift. His first attempt had smudged. Sullivan knew that such a print would be rejected by the Bureau computer. He pulled the tape back slowly, a millimetre at a time, checking and rechecking its surface and that of the gate.

Behind him stood a uniformed guard holding a single white card onto which the vital evidence, if obtained, would be stuck. He stood motionless, watching Sullivan's every move as if he was assisting him in the defusing of a nuclear weapon.

Sullivan turned slowly, holding the tape nimbly between his fingers, and, without speaking, held out his other hand for the card.

Cautiously, he pressed the tape down with his index finger, running it over and back across the card, then held it up for examination.

He sighed heavily. The uniformed man shook his head as he moved for the first time in ten minutes.

Sullivan looked up at him and smiled widely. 'Got him by the balls I think is the expression used,' he exclaimed and turned the card to show him. 'Lovely, isn't it?'

Having placed the card carefully in an evidence bag, Sullivan began to dust at the gate with the charcoal powder once more. One print would narrow down the suspects to a maximum of twenty; another two good prints would leave the print computer in no doubt as to who had climbed the gate the previous day – if the culprit had been previously printed, of course.

Their success moments earlier had eased the tension now and, although Sullivan was as cautious as ever, the uniformed man felt more relaxed.

'Tell me, Finbarr,' he asked, looking for an answer to a question that had been something of a puzzle to him for some years. 'Can a print be got from human skin?'

It was a mistake. Sullivan lifted his head and, without looking back, spoke into the field. His reply was a low murmur of anger. Anger at the guard's apparent lack of crime investigative knowledge, and anger that this ignorance had been the cause of breaking his intense concentration.

'Why, Guard,' he asked. 'Do you want me to dust your wife?'

Brosnan rested his hand on top of the large pile of questionnaires. In the silence of the room, he picked one up and glanced through it.

'Garda Mike Daly, where are you?' he asked without lifting his head.

There was a murmur in the crowd at the back of the room.

'Garda Mike Daly, sir,' he said as he moved forward through the crowd.

Brosnan raised his eyes and looked across the table at Daly who stood there, his hands clasped together nervously in front of him.

'What in the divine Christ is this, Daly?' asked Brosnan, holding the sheet out at arm's length.

Daly moved forward a step and took the paper. He glanced through it and looked down at Brosnan in puzzlement and shrugged his shoulders.

'It's a questionnaire . . . one of mine, sir.'

Brosnan leaned over the table and snapped the paper back.

'I know that, smart-arse, but look at the way it's filled out. This one alone has four blanks on it. Perhaps you didn't feel that they were important enough questions to ask. Maybe you feel that the men who thought up these questionnaires were just wasting good paper.' He pointed down at the sheet.

'Look at this for an answer. "I don't remember."
It's your job to make them remember, Guard.'

He raised a cautioning finger. 'You're not in the
Traffic Corps now, Daly,' he growled, 'standing at
the side of the road scratching your balls with a
speed-gun. This is a murder investigation, boy.'

Daly blushed crimson and looked down at the
floor. He could feel the eyes of the entire room on
him.

'Yes, sir,' he muttered as he took a step backwards into the safety of the crowd.

'And as for the rest of you,' continued Brosnan,
looking around the small room, 'some of you fellas
are treating this as a bit of a joke, an opportunity
to make a few bob and drink porter. Well let me tell
ye this now, I don't tolerate that type of carry-on.
There are school children who would make a better job of filling these out.' He slammed the palm
of his hand down on the pile of questionnaires. 'So
now, gentlemen, we begin again. Get cracking.'

The assembled detectives rose and as they left
the room, whispered amongst each other, their
heads nodding in agreement.

'Yes . . . I *am* a thick bollocks,' Brosnan called
after them, 'and don't forget it!'

He turned to Hegarty, who was standing in
silence, his arms folded.

'I know, Jack, don't say it. This is not a place for
slackers, the sooner some of those fellas realise that
the better.'

Why he was justifying his outburst to a man
who held a rank four places below his own,
Brosnan could not understand. The expression on

Hegarty's face had somehow demanded an explanation.

'Call that Daly fella back, maybe I was a bit rough on him,' sighed Brosnan.

Hegarty went to the door, calling out the name, and a few seconds later returned with Daly at his side.

Brosnan looked up at him from behind the desk.

'I hear that you're a good traffic policeman, em . . . Michael, is it?'

'Yes, sir,' replied Daly.

'Well, Michael, I know that this is all new to you. I also know that you're capable of much better than this,' said Brosnan, holding up the questionnaire he had taken from the top of the pile. 'Be more specific in your questioning from now on. The questions here are set down only as a guideline for you. Don't stick rigidly to them. If you feel you have a different question to ask, then ask it.'

'I will, sir.'

'Good man, Michael, that's all.' Daly turned and looked at Hegarty who gave him a knowing wink.

When Daly had left, Hegarty looked down at the big man who was examining the other papers on the desk.

'That was quite an apology, Pat.'

'Mmm . . . I wonder if he'll be at my retirement party,' mused Brosnan.

'I doubt it,' laughed Hegarty.

The door of the small room swung wide open and a breathless Finbarr Sullivan stood before them like a three-card-trick man, holding a number of white cards in his hand.

'Pick a card, any card,' he panted.

Brosnan rose slowly from behind the table and took all three. Holding them up at arm's length, he examined each carefully in turn. When he was finished, he handed them to Hegarty and turned to Sullivan. 'From the gate?'

Sullivan nodded.

'How long will it take?' asked Brosnan.

Sullivan was still panting. 'If I get them up straight away, I'd say tea time this evening, maybe sooner. The cast of the print will take a bit longer.'

Brosnan took him by the shoulders. 'You have a foot-print as well,' he said excitedly.

Sullivan nodded. 'Partial. Got it in the centre of the field.'

'Then what are you waiting for? Get going,' beamed Brosnan, taking the fingerprint cards from Hegarty and handing them back to Sullivan.

'As soon as you know, ring me,' he shouted as the detective raced from the room.

He clapped his hands loudly.

'Things are looking up, Jack,' he smiled, taking the copybook from his jacket pocket. 'Now let's see, we have two men seen by a witness, colour-blind or not, approaching the scene of the crime yesterday. That ties in with the time of death given by Frank Long. Burns was last seen alive by your man . . .' He snapped his fingers, trying to recall the name.

'Jim Quilter,' prompted Hegarty.

'Yes, Jim Quilter . . . at around a quarter past twelve, and now these prints taken from the gate which was used by one of the two men. Things are coming together nicely, Jack.'

'What if there's no match on file for the prints?'

The implication of Hegarty's question stopped Brosnan in his tracks. But he was not going to be deterred.

'The man who did this, it wasn't his first time, Jack. Only a certain breed of animal can sneak up behind a man and beat him to death. Our culprit may not have actually killed anyone before this, but it wasn't the first time that he used violence against someone. I'd stake my reputation on it.'

He closed the copybook, rolled it and tapped it against the palm of his hand.

It would be a long four hours before Sullivan returned to Dublin and got a result from the print computer. There was still a lot of work to be done.

CHAPTER EIGHTEEN

Michael Carroll sat behind the leather-topped desk in his office, leafing through several sheets of paper, signing each one in turn.

The peace of the room was broken only by the tap-tap of the silver ball bearings of a desktop toy colliding with each other at regular intervals.

Carroll lifted his head.

'Put that back,' he snapped at a man who was slouched in the armchair beside the door.

Liam McCann placed his finger in between the swinging silver balls, limped across the room and replaced the toy on the desk.

'A little touchy today, aren't we, Michael,' he grinned and went to resume his position on the chair.

Carroll ignored the comment.

When he was finished he shuffled the ream of paper, tapping the ends on the table top, and replaced them in a neat pile on the corner of his desk.

He was about to address McCann when the telephone rang. On the third ring he picked up the receiver.

'Hello, Michael Carroll Motors.'

McCann sniggered.

'Jesus, what kept you? Why the fuck didn't you ring me sooner?' exclaimed Carroll, pointing to the door with his free hand.

McCann rose to his feet and stood in front of the chair. Carroll covered the mouthpiece of the receiver with his hand.

'Wait outside,' he ordered, and watched as the man limped from the room, closing the door behind him.

Carroll ran his hand through his hair. 'What the hell is going on down there?' he said, and leaned back on the chair, raising his heels up on the table as he listened.

'So the cops suspect nothing. Yeah, I heard the news this morning.'

The person on the other side spoke.

'Brosnan,' replied Carroll. 'Sure I've heard of him, who hasn't?'

'It's as simple as this,' he said calmly, to the next outburst. 'If you keep your mouth shut, then no one will suspect you.'

His voice rose in anger. 'For Christ's sake, you're the last one they would suspect. He's just another dumb cop who has nothing to go on. Say nothing and he'll stay that way.'

He shook his head slowly. 'Forget it. This one is on the house. You can owe me.'

He replaced the receiver with a bang and looked towards the door.

'McCann!'

The door was opened almost immediately.

'Hear enough, did you?'

McCann limped across the room and pulled a chair in front of the desk. He jokingly raised one of his eyebrows.

'Tut, tut, problems,' he smiled.

Carroll swung his heels from the desk, rose to his feet and walked around to McCann. Grasping him by the lapels of his jacket, he pulled him from the chair with one hand.

'Listen, you northern fucker,' he spat, the spittle from his mouth peppering his henchman's face, 'You keep that smart shit for the other scum. When you're in my presence you'll show some respect. Understood?'

He released his grip on McCann by throwing him back on the chair, and watched him as he painfully regained his balance by stretching out his left leg for support.

'Now then, Liam,' continued Carroll as he ran his hand down along his silk tie, his voice calm, 'tell me about this job again. I know you've told me already, but just one more time for the record.'

McCann nervously straightened the front of his jacket.

'Well, Mr Carroll, Seanie and his driver went down to Dunsheerin, did the business without being seen, and came back that evening just like you instructed. I spoke with them this morning and made the pay-off. The weapon has been dumped and the car they used was cleaned of any prints. I got the map back from them. All ties have been cut.'

He took out a piece of blue paper from the inside pocket of his jacket and placed it on the table.

'Then we don't have a problem, do we, Liam?' asked Carroll.

'No we don't. Look it, I picked Seanie for the job myself, you have nothing to worry about. I've used him before, he's a professional. I can trust him.'

McCann got up from the chair.

'Fair enough, Liam,' said Carroll. 'You've always been loyal to me, ever since you joined us eight years ago. I'm a man who appreciates loyalty. You know that, don't you?'

'Indeed I do,' smiled McCann. He was beginning to relax.

Carroll walked over to the door and held it open. He nodded as McCann limped past him then held his hand out in front of him. 'By the way,' he asked 'Who was the wheels man?'

'A fella by the name of Tony Kearns. He's all right. He's no rat.'

Carroll dropped his arm from in front of McCann and signalled to him to leave.

'Thank you for calling, Liam,' he said. 'It's good to know that everything went according to plan.'

Daly rested his hands against the coolness of the low stone wall. Tilting his cap back, he massaged the red line on his forehead, rubbing the sweat away with the palm of his hand. He had walked a considerable distance from the village, calling to each isolated house in turn in an attempt to get at least one piece of vital information that would put him back in the good books of the chief superintendent.

His efforts had come to nothing. The best he had come up with were three invitations to tea and sweet cake and a request from a local farmer to help him bring in the hay, 'fine strong *garsún*' that he was.

Seating himself on the wall, he looked into the recently cut field and smiled as he watched what was going on there.

Under a low, unsteady goal-post made from rough timber stood a small boy, no more than four years of age, his blond flyaway hair rising gently in the afternoon breeze, feet together, arms outstretched, a look of deep concentration and fear on his browned cherubic face. The light-coloured T-shirt and short pants that he wore were dusty from previous attacks on his goal mouth. Standing motionless in his low-cut wellies, he followed every movement of the oncoming striker.

In the middle of the field, an older boy approached, dribbling the ball in front of him along the stubbled ground, encouraging himself by shouting loud match commentary as he ran.

'It's McGrath to Quinn, Quinn to Aldridge, to Houghton . . . Houghton shoots!'

He let fly.

The ball soared into the air and came back down at speed, the small goalkeeper moving slightly, chest out, arms outstretched, as he squinted up at the bright sun. By the time he closed his arms, it was too late. The plastic football had rebounded off his forehead sending him down on his backside, the hay dust rising round him. The older boy turned, his hands on his hips, spitting, then cursing at the ground, imitating his idol.

Daly swung his legs over the wall and ran to where the small boy sat on the ground. He hunkered down in front of him and stretched out his arms to pick him up. The small face peered up at him, the eyes blinking with tears, the bottom lip quivering.

'Mighty save,' smiled Daly. He heard the whipping sound of running wellingtons behind him.

'Is he okay?' inquired the older boy anxiously.

Daly stood up. 'Yeah . . . but he's a bit on the small side for goalkeeping, isn't he?'

'Not at all, Guard,' called the boy, running to where the football had come to a halt. 'That's how my dad trained me.'

Daly grinned down at the small boy and stretched out his hand. It was readily accepted.

'Is that so?' he replied. 'Well, what do you say I try a few shots on you?'

The challenge was readily accepted and the ball was thrown into mid-field.

'Do your best,' the boy called out.

'What's your name, by the way?' enquired Daly, letting the small boy's hand go and running gingerly towards the ball.

'I'm Seamus, and he's Padraig my brother,' replied the boy stepping back between the posts and spitting on his hands like a man getting ready for battle.

'Well, Seamus, I'm going to give you a taste of your own medicine,' shouted Daly.

The small boy ran beside Daly and laughed up at him as he exaggerated the jog to the ball by lifting and dropping his shoulders.

'Ready?' he shouted.

'Give it your best, Guard,' said Seamus who stood in the goalmouth, legs apart, hands resting on his knees.

Daly took two steps forward, then drop-kicked the ball towards the goal. Seamus reached out and with one hand, stopped it and threw it back out.

'Is that the best you can do?' he laughed.

Daly ran to the ball and flicked it up with the toe of his polished shoe.

'Just a warm-up,' he warned.

The second and third shots were palmed away easily by Seamus, the fourth being pushed around the side of the upright by a spectacular dive. Daly increased the ferocity of his kicks, moving closer to the goal to increase his chances.

Seamus laughed loudly as he fisted another attempt over the crossbar.

'The curse a' Jaysus on it,' whispered Daly to himself as he ran to collect the ball, the sweat of his back and armpits turning his light blue shirt a darker shade. The small boy smiled as he watched him, sniffing loudly and rubbing his arm across his nose.

'What age are you, Seamus?' Daly panted.

'Eleven,' he replied, never taking his eyes from the ball.

'Well, I have a few questions to ask you so. After this shot, okay?'

'Right you are, Guard.'

Daly ran towards the ball for the last time, stumbling on the spikes of hay that had been left there after cutting.

'By the way,' he shouted, 'Your wellies are open.'

Seamus looked down and lifted one of his legs up for a quick inspection. The ball whizzed past him.

The small boy jumped up and down excitedly beside Daly.

'Goal! . . .Goal!'

'That's cheating, Guard,' shouted Seamus angrily as he turned to run to retrieve the ball.

Daly bent down to pick up his hat and clipboard, his legs already beginning to stiffen from the unexpected exercise.

'No, lad,' he said, 'That's life.'

The three of them adjourned to the low wall, Seamus and Daly panting loudly, their faces reddened from the exertion, the small boy smiling in admiration at the guard who had conquered his brother.

'What's your name?' he asked excitedly.

'Jack Charlton,' replied Daly.

'You are *not*,' squealed the small boy with laughter.

Daly laughed and turned his attention to the older boy.

'You're quite a goalkeeeper, Seamus,' he said pulling at the dark uniform trousers, which had begun to stick to his shins.

'What questions do you want to ask me?' muttered Seamus. He was still upset about the tactics that had been used to ruin his previously unblemished record.

'Well, you know about the death of John Burns . . .'

'What?' interrupted Seamus, suddenly interested, his eyes open wide. 'I heard my mother and father talking about it this morning. Was it a murder? Are you the investigator? You want to ask *me* questions about it? See if *I* can help? Hey!'

His voice was rising with excitement, the goal from trickery now forgotten. He smiled down at Padraig, but then changed it to a look of disappointment as the realisation dawned. His four-year-old brother was not much of a witness to the fact that he was now helping the full-scale manhunt. Would his pals believe him? How he wished that Big Brian, the bully in sixth class, was here now.

'I just want to know if you saw anything yesterday that might be of help,' said Daly, 'anything unusual in the area.'

Seamus rubbed his face hard, his grubby fingers leaving streaks of sweat and dust across his cheeks. 'I wasn't in the village yesterday,' he said. 'I spent the evening training Padraig. The two of us were in this field from after dinner yesterday until nearly tea-time.'

Daly nodded. He had guessed that the young lads probably knew nothing. He turned and looked at the small boy who leaned against him for balance. Lifting him down from the wall, he looked back up at Seamus.

'Take it easy on him from now on,' he said

sternly. 'You're only frightening him by blasting shots at the goal, and mind him on that road, the traffic can be very heavy there at times.'

Seamus jumped down from the wall in panic and tugged at Daly's shirtsleeve. 'Is there nothing else you want to ask me, Guard?' he asked breathlessly. 'I mean . . . I mean, I want to help.'

Daly looked at him for a moment and smiled. He reached into his shirt pocket and removed one of his small blue calling cards with his name, telephone number and the crest of An Garda Síochána, and held it out to the open-mouthed youngster. 'You are to contact me immediately if you think of anything,' he said with authority.

Seamus took the card and cupped it in his hand, his eyes fixed on the crest. Wait until Big Brian saw this.

Daly placed his leg on the wall. 'Mind yerselves on this road,' he said. 'The traffic can be very heavy here at times.'

Seamus looked up from the calling card. 'You're right there, Guard,' he said casually. 'I was nearly knocked down myself yesterday.'

'What happened?' asked Daly, his interest in traffic violations aroused.

'Banana shot,' sniffed Seamus. 'I was trying to swerve one around Padraig, but I caught it wrong and out on the road it went. I got over the wall and was just crossing to get it out of the ditch when this car came screaming down the road. It skeeted a bit, I got over just in time. The fella in the passenger seat was fierce thick.'

'What time was this?'

'Dunno, after dinner. Why?'

'How many were in the car?' continued Daly.

'Two, two men.'

Daly could feel his heart beginning to thump in his chest. He strained to disguise the excitement in his voice.

'What colour was the car?'

'Dark red. Will I get into trouble for this?'

'No. No, you won't. What did they look like, these men?'

'Well, I didn't get a look at the driver but I did see the fella in the passenger seat. They slowed down as they passed and yer man shouted out the window at me.'

Daly fumbled with the paper on the clipboard as he wrote down everything that the young boy was saying.

'What did he shout at you?'

'Well,' said Seamus, kicking at the ground, an injured look on his face as he recalled the incident. 'He stuck his head out the window and shouted "Get in off the road ya little bollocks, ya."'

Padraig peered up at his brother and the funny guard, his head moving from side to side, tennis-match fashion, back and forth with each question and answer.

'What did he look like?' asked Daly.

'Well, I only saw the top half of him. He looked big, bigger than you.'

'What age would you say he was?' asked Daly.

Seamus gave a quick shrug of his shoulders. 'Emmm . . . fiff . . . no, forty.'

Daly stopped writing and stood up straight to

attention. Both youngsters laughed.

'Tell you what, Seamus,' he said. 'I'll give you a pound if you can tell me what age I am. Think hard about the man yesterday as well. Would I be older or younger than him? If you say that he was forty, than what would that make me?'

Seamus closed his eyes tightly for a few seconds. 'He would be a small bit younger than you,' he said slowly, ' so that would make you . . . forty-five?'

He opened his eyes and looked at Daly for a response. Daly smiled to himself as he wrote 'Late twenties/early thirties' on the sheet.

'Well, was I right?' enquired Seamus.

Daly fumbled in his pocket for some change and selected a fifty-pence coin. 'Nearly,' he replied as he held the coin out.

Seamus took it and placed it on top of the calling card in his hand. Two trophies.

'What colour hair had he?' continued Daly.

'Emm, short brown hair, like a skinhead at the back, a bit longer at the top, fattish face.'

'Did he have a moustache or beard?'

'No, but his face was a bit hairy, like my Dad's in the morning,' said Seamus.

'Did you see what he was wearing?'

'Only his jacket. It was green, like the ones the soldiers wear.'

'A combat jacket you mean,' suggested Daly, writing furiously, afraid that at any moment the young boy's memory would blank.

'Yeah,' said Seamus. 'Listen, Guard, am I going to get into trouble for this? My Dad says he'll take the football away if he hears that I was out on the road.'

'I've told you already, Seamus, don't worry, but I will have to see your parents about this. It might have something to do with what happened to John Burns. Where do you live?'

Seamus leaned over the wall and pointed down the road at a yellow, two-storey house. Daly had called there already – it was one of the places where he had declined an offer of hospitality. He jumped the wall and reached inside to lift the small boy out.

'C'mon, Seamus,' he groaned, as Padraig grasped him around the neck.

'Maybe I'll have that tea and sweet cake after all.'

Johnson sat back from the blue computer screen, threw his silver-rimmed spectacles on the desk and massaged the red patch on the bridge of his nose. He leaned back and took the three finger-print cards from an impatient Finbarr Sullivan. He sighed heavily as he replaced his glasses and carefully examined the each card in turn.

'Well, Bob,' asked Sullivan, 'what do you think?'

Johnson shook his head.

'I've seen better. I don't know, Finbarr, I have my doubts.'

Sullivan fidgeted with his hands. Things were not going at the pace he wanted. Johnson's blasé attitude was beginning to annoy him. He had driven like a man possessed from the village of

Dunsheerin to Headquarters and then sprinted the short distance to the finger-print section.

He leaned over, resting one hand on the desk, the other on the back of Johnson's chair.

'Listen, Bob,' he said, patting the top of the computer monitor, 'with all due respect, I couldn't give a tinker's curse what you think. It's this thing's opinion I'm interested in.'

'Easy there, Finbarr,' cautioned Johnson, moving Sullivan's hand away. 'This is a delicate instrument. Like any good-looking woman, if you treat her right she'll come up with the goods.'

Sullivan straightened himself and arched his back.

'Look, Bob, just cut the crap and see if there's a match on file for those prints, okay? I'm on a bit of a tight schedule at the moment. The sooner you get it done the sooner you can get back to playing space invaders. All right!'

Johnson moved his chair closer to the monitor and tapped out a code on the keyboard, then inserted one of the cards into an aperture at the front of the drive. Leaning back on the chair, he pressed the Enter key and smiled at Sullivan, twiddling his thumbs and whistling loudly.

'You want a printout, I take it.'

Sullivan nodded. Both men waited as the computer whirred in front of them. After fifteen minutes, the printer finally buzzed into action.

'Whoops! Here we go,' said Johnson, leaning across to watch as the first name appeared. 'Looks like you're in luck.'

Sullivan's heart hammered.

When the printer stopped, Johnson tore the

paper from it, gave it a quick glance, and then handed it over his shoulder.

'Well, that narrows the field down a bit,' he said.

Sullivan looked down at the names. There were ten of them.

'Do the other two,' he said. 'They should give us the common denominator of the three lists.'

Johnson repeated the process with the remaining two fingerprint cards, tearing out each list of names in turn and laying them on the desk in front of Sullivan.

'What you want is the same name in all three lists,' he suggested, leaning on Sullivan's shoulder.

'Thank God you're here, Bob,' said Sullivan. 'I'd never have figured that one out on my own!'

He ran his pen down through each sheet of paper in turn.

'There y'are, ya good thing,' he exclaimed, circling the same name 'Seanie Hughes'.

'Amazing piece of technology this,' commented Johnson sitting back down and adjusting the screen in front of him. 'Pity we didn't get it a bit sooner, then half the search teams wouldn't be gone blind from looking through magnifying glasses all day. What's the number beside that fella's name?'

He tapped it in as quickly as Sullivan dictated it from the printout sheet.

'There you are. Name, address and all his previous convictions. My my. He has been a naughty boy, hasn't he?'

Sullivan read down through it.

'GBH, assault with a deadly weapon, common assault, larceny, extortion . . .'

He folded all the papers together and looked down at Johnson.

'Do it all again – with the prints, one more time.'

'C'mon, Finbarr, I told you this is an honest woman, she doesn't tell lies.'

'Let me put it this way, Bob. Either you do it again or you can phone Brosnan yourself and swear to him that you've got the right man.'

Johnson slipped the first card into the terminal.

'Point taken,' he muttered.

Jenny moved quickly across the large hall to answer the ring of the front door bell. Her evening had been spent like that. Answering the telephone calls of concerned villagers, assuring them that Claire was making a recovery from her ordeal, albeit a slow one. She had cut the media interview short, retreating from the sound of snapping cameras and the persistent questioning of reporters holding small tape machines at arm's length.

She checked her appearance in the hall mirror and then opened the front door.

'Why, Chief Superintendent Brosnan, we weren't expecting you until seven,' she said glancing back at the hall clock. 'It's only five now.'

'Well, Mrs Maguire,' said Brosnan walking inside, 'there are a couple of things that I have to ask. The sooner I get them cleared up the better. I hope you understand.'

Jenny shivered as she closed the door. She rubbed her arms vigorously.

'Getting cold, isn't it, Mrs Maguire?' said Brosnan watching her.

'Yes, indeed it is.'

She motioned with her hand to the sitting-room.

'If you'd just like to wait in there, Chief Superintendent, I'll go and get Claire. She's been up in bed resting for a while.'

'Thank you, Mrs Maguire,' said Brosnan, opening the door.

She stopped in the middle of the hall and turned, saying, 'I don't want to hear any more of this *Mrs* Maguire business. Call me Jenny, please.'

'Very well then, *Jenny*,' said Brosnan pleasantly, and went inside, closing the door behind him.

Jenny smiled to herself as she made her way quickly up the stairs to the master bedroom. Claire sat at the built-in dressing table patting her face with a small make-up sponge.

'It's that Brosnan,' whispered Jenny. 'Says he couldn't wait until seven . . . he's got a few questions that he wants to ask.'

'A few questions?' said Claire in confusion. 'What could he possibly want to ask me?'

'Don't know,' shrugged Jenny. 'Let's go and find out.'

Claire stood up and checked her appearance in the mirror.

'Maybe they've caught someone for it already,' she said as they left the room.

Brosnan was sitting on the large sofa, drumming

his fingers on the armrest. He rose to his feet as the women entered.

'Mrs Burns, sorry to have called a bit earlier than planned, but as I've explained to Jenny here, there are a few things I'd like to straighten out.'

'No problem at all, Chief Superintendent,' said Claire, sitting down in an armchair and straightening her dress with her hands.

Jenny sat in the other armchair, opposite Brosnan, watching him closely as he resumed his seat.

'Now,' he said, taking out his copybook and pen, 'tell me, Mrs Burns, you last saw your husband at what time?'

'At around half past ten. That's when he went fishing.'

'I see,' said Brosnan, noting the time in his copybook.

She took a deep breath and exhaled loudly.

'It's okay, Claire,' said Jenny softly, leaving her seat to move over beside her friend.

'Did he go fishing often?' asked Brosnan.

'Yes, he loved fishing,' said Claire as Jenny rubbed at her hand. 'Every Thursday and Friday without fail.'

'And where would he go to fish?' continued Brosnan, not raising his eyes from his writing.

'Always to the same spot on the river.'

'Beside the footbridge you mean,' prompted Brosnan, looking at her.

'Yes, he always said it was the best place in the country for salmon fishing.'

She turned and looked at Jenny who continued to stroke her hand.

'And you were at home all day yesterday, Mrs Burns?'

The women looked at each other.

'Why do you ask that?' asked Jenny casually.

'It's leading up to my next question,' smiled Brosnan. 'Were you?'

'Yes! I never left the house,' replied Claire. 'Why do you . . .?'

'So there were no callers, I take it. No one that you didn't recognise, that is,' he continued.

Claire gave him a confused look.

'I don't know what you mean, Chief Superintendent,' she said.

Brosnan moved to the edge of the armchair and rested his elbows on his knees.

'What I mean is this. Did any stranger call to the house while you were here yesterday?'

'Oh, I see what you mean,' said Claire, relaxing as she realised the innocence of the question. 'No. No one called.'

Brosnan nodded and rested back in the armchair and jotted down her answer

'And you, Mrs Maguire – sorry, Jenny – what time did you arrive here at?'

Jenny put her finger to her lips and thought for a moment. Brosnan glanced at the ticking clock.

'Let me see, I'd have come over here at around . . . what?' she mused, looking at Claire, ' . . . about half past eleven.'

Both women nodded in agreement.

'I call to Claire every day. We're the best of friends, Chief Superintendent.'

'Yes, I've heard that,' said Brosnan, eyeing the two women. 'It's a great village for gossip, isn't it?'

Jenny rose up from her seat and strolled to the window. She looked out at the driveway.

'Did you not bring that nice Jack Hegarty with you?' she asked.

Brosnan turned around to reply to her question.

'No, Jack is off on a different mission at the moment.'

'Pity,' she smiled. 'He's a real charmer. Have you many more questions to ask, Chief Superintendent? Anything else that we can help you with?'

Brosnan closed the copybook and stood up, moving over near the mantelpiece to examine the clock.

'That's a very nice ornament,' he said, running his fingers down the smooth black marble form.

He stood for a moment, his back to the women, admiring the craftsmanship. Jenny glanced quickly at Claire and threw her eyes up to heaven. Claire covered her mouth with her hand in an attempt to stifle a smile.

'It's Venetian, Chief Superintendent,' she said with a cough, standing up and pointing to the inscription on the face. 'We got it on our holidays.'

'Very nice it is too,' said Brosnan turning and looking from one woman to the other and back again.

'Is there something else you want to know?' asked Jenny as she stood beside the window. 'Perhaps you'd like a cup of tea . . . or something stronger?'

Brosnan folded the copybook in half and put it inside his jacket. 'No. No thank you,' he said, as he made his way slowly towards the door.

'I've got what I wanted for the moment,' he said, turning the handle. 'I'll call again if I think of anything further.'

Jenny crossed the room quickly to follow him. He turned back as he left.

'Thank you for your time, ladies.'

'I'll show you out, Chief Superintendent,' said Jenny, brushing out past him and opening the front door.

'Thank you, Jenny,' said Brosnan, 'And please . . .' He paused on the first step and looked back at her. 'Call me Pat.'

Hegarty rested his legs on the dayroom table as he read through the evening paper's version of the events in Dunsheerin. More important worldly happenings had relegated the story of John Burns' murder to the second page. He smiled as he looked at the black and white photograph, the caption of which read, 'Local farmer Jim Quilter points to the spot where he found the body.'

He folded the paper and turned it around to Costigan, who was sitting across from him.

'Would ya look at the big sad head on that,' he laughed.

Costigan glanced at it and smiled.

'Isn't that Hickey behind him?' he said, pointing to the onlooker who stood a short distance away facing the camera.

Hegarty narrowed his eyes and squinted at the photograph.

'Jaysus,' he said softly, 'I hope they haven't done any television interviews. There's no self-respecting tourist would come within a hundred miles of the place if they saw either of those two planks on the telly.'

Costigan laughed.

He had seen Hegarty kick Myles Hickey's arse more times than he could remember, seen him drag a struggling Jim Quilter into the patrol car and drive him home to his rundown house. But there was never any malice in the punishment he dealt out to them.

'You have a choice now, Hickey,' he would roar. 'The District Court or Hegarty's court.'

'W-what's the d-d-difference, Guard?' Hickey would ask, stumbling against the patrol car.

'The only difference,' Hegarty would shout, taking the drunk by the shoulder and running him out in front, 'is that I don't have to take the oath and there'll be no warrant for this.' Then his shoe would connect with Hickey's rear end. 'Now get home before I change my mind,' he'd shout after him.

At first, Costigan used to question Hegarty's methods of dealing in such a summary manner with the two of them.

'They both need to see an alcohol counsellor, Jack.'

Hegarty would be amused at his innocence.

'The longer you're in this job, lad, the sooner you'll realise that the best therapy of all is the toe of a strong boot.'

The phone rang, startling Costigan out of his musing. He lifted the receiver.

'Yeah – hold on a minute.'

He handed the receiver to Hegarty, who listened and rummaged on the desk for a blank sheet of paper.

'Yeah, go ahead now. No, he's not here at the moment, he should be back shortly.' He scribbled at speed for a few seconds, then stopped suddenly and leaned back on the chair. 'Yeah, I'll tell him. I'm sure he will.'

Hegarty replaced the receiver.

'They've got a match for the prints,' he said, sitting upright. 'A Dublin gouger.'

Hegarty was relieved. The thought that the perpetrator of such a terrible crime could have been a local had been a great worry to him. Now it was an ease to know that the cause had stemmed from the anonymous anarchy of the big city, and not from the peaceful hinterland of his own beat.

Costigan looked puzzled. 'Dublin, did you say, Jack? Why would a Dublin gouger kill a local businessman like John Burns? It doesn't make any sense.'

Hegarty leaned back on the chair, placing his hands behind his head. He did not have the answer. 'Nothing in this entire case makes any sense, Kieran,' he said.

'Anyway,' said Costigan, picking up the paper, 'that's what Brosnan is getting the big bucks for.'

'Speaking of Brosnan . . .' said Hegarty.

Costigan turned and looked out the window.

'Oh Christ!' he cursed, throwing the newspaper down and grabbing his walkie-talkie. 'The meal-break is over.'

'Evening, sir,' he said as he passed the Chief Superintendent on the narrow path. Brosnan nodded in acknowledgement.

'Any news for me, Jack?' he asked as he entered the dayroom.

'Well,' said Hegarty, 'which would you like to hear first, the good news or the good news?'

'That makes a pleasant change,' said Brosnan. 'Let's hear it.'

Hegarty leaned forward on the desk.

'Well, I talked to the local doc. A complete waste of time if you ask me. He says that Claire has only been to see him twice in the last year. He gave her a tetanus shot. Says he never saw any marks on her until the ones he saw last night when he visited the house.'

'Is that it?' asked Brosnan.

'Afraid so. Oh no, one other thing,' smiled Hegarty. 'Sullivan phoned.'

'And?' said Brosnan expectantly, leaning his knuckles on the desk.

'He's got a match. Dublin gow by the name of Seanie Hughes.'

Brosnan straightened.

'Is he positive?'

'Absolutely positive.'

Brosnan slapped his hands together, beaming with satisfaction. 'No time to lose then.'

'By the way,' asked Hegarty, 'how did you get on at the Burns house?'

'Well, Jack, let's just say that I'm putting it on the back burner for the moment.'

Hegarty picked up a completed questionnaire from the desk.

'One other thing, Pat, Traffic Corps Daly has a very interesting piece of information here. Well . . . it might be.' He handed the questionnaire to Brosnan. 'It appears,' he continued, 'that one of the young Healy lads saw a car yesterday with two strange heads in it and his description of one of them is not unlike Flann's.'

Brosnan read carefully through the questionnaire, then folded it and put it in his pocket.

'And it looks like he isn't colour-blind, Jack. Listen, I have to go, I'll give you a ring to let you know how things are progressing.'

Hegarty watched Brosnan with a wistful look as he made his way quickly to the front door. He thought for a moment and decided to follow him out. After all, there was no harm in asking. Brosnan was opening the door of his car.

'Pat,' he called. 'I want to ask a favour.'

Brosnan looked up and closed the driver's door and walked back to where Hegarty was standing.

'What is it, Jack?' he asked curiously.

Hegarty put his hands in his pocket and shuffled his feet.

'It's a fairly unusual request, Pat.'

Brosnan shrugged.

'If it's in my power, Jack . . . name it,' he said.

'I want to be there when this gouger is picked up,' said Hegarty.

Brosnan looked at him for a moment, then glanced down at his watch. 'You've got fifteen minutes,' he said. 'And then I'll be gone without you.'

CHAPTER NINETEEN

Superintendent Murray stood outside the door of the morgue, sucking in the fresh air. The Angelus bell of the hospital church rang. He checked his watch and again breathed deeply. Even the smell of the newly mown grass of the hospital lawn could not shift the stench of body parts from his nostrils. He shivered as he thought of the post-mortem of John Burns, the sharp knife moving from neck to gullet, the bone saw following the thin incision and the pulling apart of the ribcage. The uniformed man had stood beside him, scribbling down the snappy dictation of Frank Long.

'A very small quantity of water in the lungs . . .,' Long had mused. 'Certainly not enough to drown a man. Wouldn't you agree, Superintendent?'

'Whatever you say yourself,' Murray had croaked in response, limply placing a cigarette between his lips.

'Don't even think of lighting that in here,' warned Long, pointing a bloodied glove in Murray's direction. 'As a colleague of mine once said, "If you smoke, I cannot smell what I want to smell . . ."'

'Jesus, Frank, why would you *want* to smell this? Why the hell don't you get some of those fancy air fresheners in here?'

Murray pulled up a chair to rest his weakening legs.

'It's a pathologist's thing,' smirked Long as he turned to the uniformed man.

'Now take this down, Guard. There are no other apparent injuries to the lower body . . . bruising to the upper body, left arm and back . . . stomach and lung samples have been retained for further tests . . . That's it.'

The bone saw buzzed into life once more as Long moved to the head of the body. Starting at the forehead, he cut in a perfect circle around the skull, stopping where the incisions met. He eased the top of the head off slowly.

Murray watched from the chair, his arms and legs tingling. The voices around him were fading.

'Guard . . .,' said Long, nodding towards the ashen superintendent. 'Take him out and put his head between his knees. He'll be fine.'

The aluminium doors swung open and Frank Long walked out into the bright evening sunshine.

'It's all over, Superintendent, you missed the best part. First post-mortem, was it?'

'Certainly not,' replied an indignant Murray. 'I . . . I just haven't been feeling well of late.'

'Ah yes, indeed,' nodded Long sympathetically. 'It's that summer flu, I expect, nasty dose. You'd want to be careful with that. Anyhow, to *cut* a long story short – eh, forgive the pun – your Mr Burns died as a result of a number of blows to the back of the head, possibly three . . . and with a heavy, rounded instrument, like a lead pipe. To give it its correct term, he died of cerebral haemorrhage. Anyway, your man has all the details. I'll send my preliminary report to your chief in a couple of days.' He gave Murray a friendly pat on the shoulder. 'Everything okay now, Superintendent?'

'Never better,' replied Murray.

The two men shook hands and Murray watched Long making his way to the car, whistling as he went. His thoughts were interrupted by the approach of the guard, notebook in hand.

'Feeling better now, sir? By God, you're heavier than you look. I thought we'd never get you back on the chair.'

'Tell me, Guard,' asked Murray casually, walking towards the car, 'have you ever done a stint in one of the border stations?'

'No, sir. Why do you ask?'

Murray turned suddenly, almost colliding with the uniformed man.

'Because if I hear one word of what happened back there from anyone else, you can get your suitcase packed. Do we understand each other?'

'Don't worry, Super,' grinned the younger man, unlocking the car door. 'It'll be our little secret.'

CHAPTER TWENTY

The early morning sun squinted out from behind a tall office building, its single yellow beam breaking through the gap in the curtains of Seanie Hughes's two-roomed flat.

He turned slowly under the blankets. His eyes blinked open. His weak and sickened state had been brought on by the previous night's over-indulgence in drink and chicken curry. His temples throbbed. The foul taste in his mouth made his stomach churn. He wondered why he had woken so early. The question was answered by a loud persistent knocking on the door of his flat.

'Who is it?' he croaked, his voice dried from alcohol.

'It's me . . . Tony,' came the reply. 'Let me in.'

Seanie heaved himself out of the bed and muttered to himself as he staggered forward and unlatched the door chain.

'Kearns, ya bollocks, have you any idea what time it is? You better have a good reason for this.'

He threw himself back on the bed, scratching himself into wakefulness. Tony stood grinning at the sight of his accomplice suffering from an almighty hangover.

'Rough night, was it?'

'Not at all *no* . . . What do you think? What are you grinning at, ya smart bollocks?'

Seanie held his temples. The exertion of all this talking wasn't helping his head.

'Jesus . . . I'm going to stick to the black stuff from now on. That cheap lager is like cat's piss . . . 'twould rip the guts outta ya.'

'Well, I've got something that'll cheer you up,' smiled Tony, jangling a set of car keys in front of Seanie's face.

'Got us a motor. She's old but she's high-powered, two point eight . . . goes like a fuckin' rocket.' He clenched the keys in his fist and punched the air in front of him.

'Well that beats all,' said Seanie shaking his head. 'The best car thief in the city goes off and buys himself a friggin' car.'

He lifted a shirt from where it lay in a crumpled heap on the floor.

'I need a coffee,' he yawned, brushing past Tony who was looking thoughtfully at the car keys in his hand.

'R–right . . . I'll wait for you below. I'm still trying to tune the stereo in her.'

Tony was glad to escape the smell of sweat and stale drink that hung in the room.

Seanie stuck his head out of the kitchen.

'Yeah . . . Go ahead and get her warmed up. We'll go to Limerick for the day.'

Tony admired his car from the doorway. Its low-profile tyres on alloy wheels, long-nosed bonnet and tinted glass gleamed bright in the new day's sun. He felt very satisfied. The eight hundred pounds for the twelve-year-old car had been well worth it. Nobody wanted big-engine cars any more, he thought. People just couldn't handle the awesome power. But Tony could.

Above in his flat, Seanie was pouring boiling water on to the granules that rested at the bottom of his brown-stained mug. He grimaced as he took the first unsweetened mouthful, then made his way back to the small bedroom where he rested the mug on a makeshift bedside table. Dressing himself slowly, he mused on how stupid it had been for Tony to waste his money on a second-hand petrol guzzler. He tied his laces and reached under the mattress and took out the roll of bank notes that were bound tightly together by an elastic band. He peeled four fifties from it, and replaced the roll in the hiding place. Taking his coat from the back of the chair, he took a last gulp of coffee.

A loud knock stopped him in his tracks. He cursed loudly as he turned the knob. 'Christ . . . I said I'd follow you down.'

The force of the door being burst open pushed him back into the room. Seanie was grasped around the throat by a large plain-clothes policeman, while the other pulled a set of silver handcuffs from his belt.

'Gotcha, ya bastard,' one of them shouted.

Although Seanie's eyes widened at the initial shock, he was quick to regain his bearings. Bop! His forehead came up squarely on the bridge of the large man's nose, his boot rising to catch the other detective, not connecting with the groin as intended, but in the stomach. The effect was the same. In the few seconds that it took them to recover, Seanie was free of their grasp and running towards the door of the flat. He knew that if he could make it to the street, they could never catch him. He swung himself around the jamb of the door that led to the corridor and stopped dead in his tracks. His heart pounded.

Something was wrong.

The hall, which was usually lit by a dim, unshaded bulb, was now in darkness, except for the light from the opened door of his flat. Taking a deep breath, he pull-started himself from the door, striding into the blackness of the long corridor.

There was movement from a doorway, and before he could react, a fist caught him directly under the chin, the force of the blow sending him reeling backwards. The two detectives, now recovered, were on him and the cuffs were snapped behind his back.

Pat Brosnan stepped out of the shadows. 'Going somewhere, Mr Hughes?' he said coolly. 'Bring him along, gentlemen.'

Down in the street, Tony was beginning to get impatient. He pressed angrily at the broken buttons of the car stereo, listening to the persistent whine of radio static. He glanced at his watch and cursed loudly.

'For Christ's sake, Seanie . . . are you givin' yourself a fuckin' home perm or what?'

He heard a shout from outside and sat bolt upright in the seat.

Seanie, his hands behind his back, was being forcibly dragged to an awaiting car, a man with a bloodied face straining to keep him upright.

In the doorway of the flats stood a tall, older man, his hands in the pockets of his dark overcoat. He looked around and then started to follow.

Tony looked down at the door panel and pressed an electric switch. It buzzed as the window opened slightly.

The detective pushed Seanie's head downwards in an attempt to get him into the back seat of the unmarked police car. He twisted and turned his head and stood upright, looking wildly around the street, and on seeing Tony, stared across at him.

Tony turned his head away, avoiding eye contact with Seanie.

'You ratted me out!' Seanie roared as he struggled between the two detectives. 'You're fuckin' dead, ya scumbag, d'ya hear?"

Brosnan looked in the direction of the object of Seanie's anger. The young man in the large silver car sat still at the driver's seat. Even at that distance, Brosnan could see his shoulders rise and fall in panic breathing. Brosnan edged towards the kerb of the footpath.

'Tony Kearns,' said Brosnan softly, then watched for a moment as the man struggled with the ignition before the engine roared into life. The car scraped loudly against the car in front as it screeched out on to the street.

With a wave of his hand, Brosnan beckoned to a second unmarked car that had been parked at the end of the street and signalled it to follow the car that had sped away. Hegarty joined him at the edge of the footpath and they watched as the two cars drove at high speed towards the four-street junction, the one in front shaving the sharp corner, the car in pursuit doing likewise, its two-tone siren howling in the distance.

Tony sat back in the driver's bucket seat, holding the steering wheel at arm's length, his chin almost touching his chest, eyes firmly focused on the road ahead. There would be no need to use his rear mirror. He knew they were following. He could see the people ahead on the footpath turning to gape open-mouthed, watching him as he passed, then back to look at the pursuing Garda car. He could barely make out the sound of the siren above the roar of his own fuel-injected engine. Grinding his teeth, he rounded another corner, the back of the car being pulled out of the skid as he pressed his foot down on the accelerator, pulling away once again from the lower-powered car behind him.

He knew, however, that although the car he was driving was capable of much higher speed, the winding city streets would prevent him from using it to its full potential. He would have to reach the dual carriageway before he could leave the unmarked car in his wake.

Suddenly, he realised that he was going the wrong way.

He waited for a wider stretch on the road and, shifting the car into a lower gear, he swung the wheel around, at the same time pulling up hard on the hand-brake. The car spun, the tyres screeching and raising smoke, and faced the direction from which it had just come, facing the unmarked car. He drove at speed towards it. There would be just enough room to squeeze past on the other side when the driver would swerve to avoid him. He had done it before.

'None of the cops like a head-on,' he had laughed with his pals. 'It scares them shitless.'

Quickly he changed gear, the entire car vibrating with the high revs of the engine as he made straight for them. The arm of the speedometer rose quickly.

'Nought to sixty in seven seconds . . . come and get it, fuckers,' he shouted, and laughed as he saw the passenger in the unmarked car raise his arms to shield himself from the impact, the driver straining to turn the car towards the kerb.

The accelerator touched the floor. The long nose of the bonnet rose with the sudden surge of power. He braced himself back against the seat.

'Eee . . . haa,' he squealed as the cars swept past each other, the front of his colliding with the rear wing of the unmarked patrol car, tearing it from the rest of the body.

The impact threw Tony sideways on the seat, his hand pulling down on the steering wheel, the front left tyre bursting loudly as the car mounted the footpath, followed by the deafening grating of metal on concrete as it tore against the low wall. He wrenched at the wheel to bring the car back on to the street. It was too late to brake.

The windscreen and driver's window exploded in a hail of glass as the car struck a parked lorry on the other side, the speed at which he was travelling forcing the car under the rear of the truck. The roof support on the driver's side bent and snapped, the force of the crash throwing him forward. Then came the groaning of metal, followed by silence.

The smell of oil and burnt rubber filled his nostrils. He breathed deeply through his mouth. His throat gurgled. He could not move. His eyes followed the broken roof arm from the corner of the windscreen to where it was impaled in his chest.

He heard the loud shouting for ambulances and the sound of footsteps as they ran to his aid. He relaxed his grip on the steering wheel and his hands fell limply on to his lap.

He closed his eyes.

Seanie struggled between the two detectives in the rear of the car, his hands still cuffed behind his back, the bigger man pushing his head down to his knees.

Brosnan and Hegarty stood outside on the footpath.

'Did you see the head driving that car, Jack?' asked Brosnan.

Hegarty folded the green army jacket over his arm and shook his head. 'No, I wasn't down in time. Do you know him?'

Brosnan took Hegarty by the sleeve and spoke in a low voice. 'Yeah, his name is Tony Kearns. A string of convictions for car theft. He went alibi for a fella two years ago accused of knocking down and killing a woman on the dual carriageway while driving a stolen car. Turns out it was bullshit . . . Listen, Jack, I don't want you to say anything in the car . . . Let the talking to me, okay? You drive.'

Hegarty nodded.

Seanie struggled in the back seat. 'What the fuck is goin' on . . . tell me now or I'll kill the lot o' yiz.'

Brosnan turned round and gave a faint smile. He spoke in a low, calm voice. 'You know perfectly well what's going on, Seanie. You should choose your friends more carefully.'

Seanie threw himself against the back seat, looking up at the ceiling of the car. 'I don't give a shite what that fella told yiz . . . I'm not saying nothing 'till I see my brief.'

Brosnan reached back and patted Seanie's knee. 'Good man. We don't want you to say anything . . . In fact, we don't *need* you to say anything.'

He turned back in his seat and frowned an inquiry at Hegarty. 'So you have all the arrangements made to meet that man later for his statement, Guard?'

Seanie looked perplexed.

Hegarty nodded as he drove quickly through the winding streets. 'It's all arranged, Chief.'

It was a good feeling to be back. He needed no directions from Brosnan. He had travelled the same route to the station many times in the past.

'Just like the good old days,' said Brosnan, looking across at Hegarty as if reading his thoughts.

Seanie sneered in the back seat. 'Yiz haven't got a thing on me,' he muttered.

The car pulled up at the station door.

'Now then, Mr Hughes,' said Brosnan, reaching back to open the door. Seanie attempted to break free of the grip of the two detectives and shoved his face forward at Brosnan as he wriggled.

'I want a solicitor, ya old bollocks.'

Brosnan caught Seanie's face in his hand, squeezing hard on the man's cheeks, wrenching him forward between the two front seats. Seanie's eyes watered with pain.

'Listen, gouger,' whispered Brosnan through clenched teeth, 'you're the prisoner here, and I don't want another word from you until I ask you a question. Am I making myself clear?'

His large hand closed tighter on Seanie's face as he waited for a reply. The two detectives looked away into the distance.

'Yes.'

Brosnan released his grip and pushed back Seanie's reddened face.

'Good man.'

Seanie was led up the steps flanked by the two burly detectives. 'That fella's a fuckin' psycho.' He looked from one to the other, waiting to see if either concurred with his opinion. There was no reaction. 'Ahh, yiz are all the fuckin' same.'

The door eased itself shut behind them.

Hegarty leaned with folded arms against the side of the car. 'I'm glad to see that you haven't lost the human touch, Pat,' he said with a smile.

'No then, Jack, that'll be the last thing to go.'

Brosnan fell silent for a moment before looking again at Hegarty. 'Tell me, Jack,' he said, 'why did you want to be part of the capture? I mean, it wasn't that big a deal.'

Hegarty looked up at the station door. He had walked many prisoners through it during his service in the DMA.

'I suppose, Pat, I wanted to prove to you that I hadn't lost my touch . . . and to prove to myself that I can still mix with the best.'

Brosnan walked up the steps, laughing as he went. 'You certainly made a believer out of me, Jack. I thought that the uppercut you gave Hughes had closed the case.' He stopped at the door. 'Listen . . . This gurrier thinks he's been grassed by Tony Kearns, so we'll set one off against the other and then move in for statements . . . that's if they can get Kearns. He's one hell of a driver, I'm told.'

Hegarty followed Brosnan into the station, stopping for a moment to inhale the smell of the place and to listen to the barrage of complaints being hurled across the counter at the young station-orderly.

Brosnan stood beside Seanie and the two detectives, watching the station sergeant filling out the record of detention.

'Reason for arrest?'

'Murder,' said Brosnan with relish.

'Tut tut, Seanie,' said the sergeant as he wrote, 'looks like you finally made it into the big time. We always knew you'd graduate from beating up old ladies.'

One of the detectives moved behind him and unlocked the handcuffs. Seanie massaged each wrist in turn and leaned forward on the desk, towering over the sergeant.

'Listen, flat-foot . . . I'm entitled to a solicitor and I want one right fuckin' now.'

The sergeant glanced at Brosnan who gave a brief shake of his head. He got the message.

'All in good time, Seanie. I take it you want to have a little chat with him, Chief?'

'What?' asked Seanie incredulously and pointed a finger at Brosnan. 'You mean to say that this old fart's a chief?'

The sergeant did not reply, but lowered his head and continued to fill out the form. The two detectives moved aside. Brosnan put his hand on Seanie's shoulder and squeezed, gripping cloth and flesh. Seanie bared his teeth with the pain and shouted in protest as he was frog-marched down the corridor.

The sergeant looked up at the detectives who stood and watched. 'Well lads, either that Seanie's got a lot of guts or else he doesn't have a brain in his head.'

Hegarty was waiting at the door of the interview room. He watched as the chief approached, accompanied by a lopsided Seanie.

'Cool yer arse in there for a minute,' said an

angry Brosnan, pushing him into the room and pulled the door shut.

Taking Hegarty by the arm, he moved him along a short distance from the door.

Brosnan whispered: 'Listen, Jack, it's going to be a real bluff job with this fella. I'm going to take a few risks in there. All I want you to do is to sit back and give the occasional nod.'

Hegarty understood. 'You mean you want me to look like I know exactly what's going on, when in fact I haven't got a shaggin' clue?'

'Something like that.' Brosnan smiled at him.

As they approached the door of the interview room, their attention was caught by the sergeant beckoning frantically to them from the end of the corridor.

'What is it?' asked Brosnan as they approached.

'It's your other man, Kearns,' replied the sergeant.

'What . . . did they get him?'

'They got him all right . . . he was killed in the chase. I just got the call.'

Hegarty gave a sharp puff of dismay. 'Well, that fucks that!' he exclaimed.

A momentary silence followed. Brosnan looked thoughtful.

'Give me a minute to get myself together, lads,' he said, walking slowly down the corridor.

The two men watched the chief superintendent walk to the end of the hall, and lean against the windowsill.

'Looks like the old brain is going into over-drive,' commented the sergeant.

Brosnan leafed through his green copybook, pausing occasionally to rub his chin pensively. He took out the questionnaire that had been filled out by Guard Daly and read through it for the second time. He looked up and signalled to Hegarty.

'Have a quick read of that,' he said, holding out the sheet of paper as Hegarty approached. 'It's where you'll come in. Nothing has changed, Jack. We'll stick to plan A.'

'Ready when you are, Pat.'

Brosnan clenched his fists and took a deep breath.

'This is it, Jack . . . here we go.'

He opened the door.

Seanie was leaning back on the plastic chair, resting his feet on the table. He swung them down quickly and jumped up, about to voice his protest when the two policemen entered the room. Brosnan got in first.

'Seanie, me oul' stock,' he smiled, 'sit back down there for yourself like a good lad.'

Seanie reluctantly returned to his seat and watched as Brosnan slid open the table drawer and remove several white paper sheets.

'You must think I've got a lot to say,' said Seanie. 'Well, don't waste your time cop . . . I don't make statements.'

'Statement?' Brosnan repeated the word in a quizzical tone. 'No, no, Seanie. This paper is for my memoirs. I'm writing them at the moment. As a matter of fact, I'm getting very close to the end.'

Brosnan took the gold pen from his breast pocket and leaned forward on the paper, shielding what he was writing from Seanie, like a schoolboy who didn't want to have his answers copied by a classmate. He spoke slowly as he wrote.

' . . . and then Seanie Hughes was charged with the murder of John Burns and all the guards went to the pub to celebrate the fact that one of the biggest scumbags in Dublin had been put away for life.'

He exaggerated the full stop and replaced the pen in his pocket.

'Don't worry, Seanie, I'll send you a copy of it when you're in the 'Joy. After all, you'll have twenty-five years to read it.'

Seanie was unruffled by what was being said. He glanced from Hegarty to Brosnan and calmly rocked himself to and fro on the chair, eyeing the two men in the silence of the room as he weighed up the situation. Finally he spoke, his voice a sneer: 'You've got nothing. I know a bullshit job when I see it and I'm looking at one now. If you're going to charge me then do it . . . if not, let me out.'

Brosnan sat back in the chair. He stared at Seanie.

'You know, Seanie, for a fella who has been in the system for the last eighteen years, you really haven't got a clue how it works, do you? Do you really think that I'd bring a gouger like you in here on a murder charge if I didn't have all the evidence backed up by . . .'

He hesitated and gave Seanie a knowing smile.

Seanie shifted uneasily in his chair, searching the big man's eyes for a sign of deceit. He could find none.

He thought about his short friendship with Tony Kearns and the possible motives he could have for ratting him out. He had doubted Kearns's guts for the job, his panic in the car on the journey home. Still though, he would need more convincing. Seanie leaned forward, resting his elbows on the table.

'Tell me, cop, exactly what do you know?'

Brosnan reached inside his jacket and took out the green copybook. His heart pounded as he licked his thumb and flicked through the pages. He hoped that Hegarty was ready.

'Ah yes, here we are,' he smiled. 'Chapter three.'

He fingered his way down through the page and over to the second one, giving himself time to think. Then he began.

'Two men sit into a car and drive down to the village of Dunsheerin, arriving there in the early afternoon. They drive up a narrow lane and park the car. One of the men – that's you, Seanie – goes a short distance away and climbs a gate into a field. The other man remains with the car. The first man crosses the field and lies in wait for his victim who is fishing. He sneaks up behind the aforementioned fisherman while he is sitting at the bank of the river and hits him a number of times on the back of the head. The fisherman falls into the river and the first man – that's you again, Seanie – runs like a hare back to the awaiting car, concealing the weapon under his green army jacket. They drive back to Dublin like the hammers of hell . . .'

'But . . .' interrupted Hegarty, 'not before near-ly knocking down a young footballer on the road.

You really shouldn't curse at small boys, Seanie, it sets a bad example for them.'

Brosnan and Hegarty grinned happily at each other.

'So now, Seanie, what do you think of that for a bluff?'

The two policemen watched with bated breath as Seanie's face whitened, the colour disappearing from his cheeks as the reality of the accusations set in. He chewed for a second on his thumbnail. His shoulders slumped and then, without warning, he jumped up in anger, knocking the plastic chair against the wall.

'That *fucker* . . .,' he yelled. He leaned across the table towards Brosnan. His voice lowered. Hegarty moved cautiously towards him. Seanie pointed a shaking finger at him.

'What's in it for Kearns?' he snapped. 'I mean what kind of a deal have you made with the fucker?'

Brosnan shrugged his shoulders. Hegarty took Seanie by the arm and sat him back on his chair.

'Deal?' Brosnan smiled with calm pleasure. 'What deal are you talking about, Mr Hughes?'

'Don't bullshit *me*,' warned Seanie. 'What did you promise him? He drove the car. You know that. So what's the story with him?'

Brosnan rolled back his sleeve and glanced at his watch. He leaned forward on the table and whispered, as if taking Seanie into his confidence: 'As of an hour ago, your friend became immune from prosecution.'

Seanie's brow furrowed in confusion. 'What the fuck are you talking about?'

'The law works in mysterious ways,' smiled Hegarty, leaning back against the wall.

'Never mind Tony Kearns for the moment, Seanie,' added Brosnan. 'Your main concern is to look after number one. Am I right?'

Seanie looked at the floor. 'I don't suppose you'll give me the same treatment as Kearns?'

Brosnan drummed his fingers on the table and looked at Hegarty.

'Believe you me, boy, much as I'd like to give you the same treatment, I don't think the law would allow it.'

'So what's in it for me if I co-operate?'

Brosnan shook his head. 'You know the score, lad. I can't promise you anything. All I can say is that if you help us, it'll be mentioned in court.'

Seanie grunted in disgust. 'Huh! Fuck that for a game of cowboys.'

Brosnan pointed to the door. 'Fair enough so, lad. Jack, go and get this gentleman a solicitor and bring back the charge sheet when you're coming.'

Hegarty placed his hand on the knob of the door.

'Hold it a minute,' called Seanie. 'Just give me a minute to think, all right? Can I have my jacket? My fags are in the pocket.'

'Oh . . . which reminds me, Seanie, we'll be needing that jacket for technical examination. Who knows what those busy little boys in the forensic lab will come up with.'

He looked down at Seanie's black runners. 'Did you know that you left a lovely print of your big crube in the field as well?'

He turned with a look of mock enquiry to Hegarty and pointed to Seanie's runners. 'Guard, I wonder if it will match the footwear currently being worn by the prisoner?'

Hegarty moved forward and looked down at Seanie's feet. 'By God then, Chief, but there's always that possibility,' he agreed and moved back to the wall.

Seanie glanced from one to the other. Brosnan raised his eyebrows then suddenly snapped his fingers.

'Oh my God, I nearly forgot,' he blurted out, then tapped at his head as if punishing his forgetfulness. 'Your flat will be turned upside down as well for anything that you might have overlooked yourself.'

Hegarty handed the cigarettes to Seanie. As he lit up, he remembered the large roll of money under the mattress. He would have some explaining to do. His thoughts were interrupted by Brosnan's voice.

'Are they the clothes you wore yesterday?'

Seanie nodded dumbly.

'Well, we'll need to take them. Don't worry, you won't be left bollocks-naked in the cell, the sergeant always has some trendy gear lying around for such occasions.'

Seanie inhaled the smoke deep into his lungs and held it there for a few seconds before exhaling with a defeated breath.

Brosnan watched his every expression and decided to speed things up. He stood up and began to replace the half sheets in the drawer.

'Go ahead, Jack . . .' He nodded towards the door.

Hegarty made as if to leave, followed by Brosnan.

Seanie looked at them wild-eyed. 'For *fuck* sake, wait a minute . . .'

His mind went into overdrive as he contemplated the consequences of telling the truth. The consequences of ratting out Liam McCann, and worse still, Michael Carroll. Against that, there was the thought of going alone. Why should he take the rap? After all, a problem shared is a problem halved, or in this case, divided in three. Anyway, he wasn't the one who caused all this. Kearns was the cause of all of this. He was the rat. He had told the cops everything. What harm would it do now for him to talk and help *himself*?

'What do you want me to say?' he asked finally.

'Tell you what, Seanie,' said Brosnan calmly as his heart pounded, 'we'll play it like this. You tell me what you know and I'll tell you whether you're lying or not.' He raised a cautioning finger. 'The first lie I hear out of your mouth,' he warned, 'I'm out that door and you're in the shit up to your neck. Understand?'

Seanie gave a nod of defeat and eased himself back on the chair. Both men watched him in the silence of the room as he took a few moments to compose himself.

Then he started.

Brosnan wrote furiously.

Jack Hegarty listened in disbelief to the story. Seanie Hughes and the late Tony Kearns had received payment of two thousand pounds through Liam McCann to kill John Burns. Life had got very cheap in the city. Seanie had not even asked the reason why the man was to be killed. When asked why not, he calmly stated that he didn't care. Why should he? It was just another job to do. McCann was the go-between for Michael Carroll. Maybe he knew the reason.

Brosnan clarified some points of the statement before spinning the sheet of paper around to Seanie. 'Read it through. Tell me if it's correct and then sign,' he said, hiding his disgust.

He glanced over at Hegarty and gave a quick wink. Seanie had sung a sweet song.

Seanie's head rose up from the paper and held out his hand. Brosnan rolled his gold pen between his fingers before reaching inside his jacket and withdrawing a plastic biro. Seanie eyed the gold pen with contempt.

'A present.' Brosnan eased his curiosity. 'From the parents of a teenage murder victim. You'll no doubt get to meet with her killer when you're put away.' Brosnan stared coldly.

Seanie broke free of the look and back at the statement. He leaned down heavily on the biro and awkwardly signed his name.

Brosnan palmed the sheet towards himself to check the signature. 'Very good. Now I'll arrange for your clothes and shoes to be taken for examination and you'll get replacements. I take it you don't want a solicitor?'

'What's the fucking point now?' grunted Seanie, lighting up another cigarette.

'That's just it, lad. You did it, why complicate things?'

Brosnan left the room, followed by Hegarty, and made his way up to the sergeant's desk.

'I want all his clothes taken and bagged . . . this as well,' he said, taking the jacket from Hegarty's arm. 'Note that he has waived his right to a solicitor. Another thing. I don't want him to hear about Kearns. I'll tell him when the time's right.'

'Got it, Chief,' replied the sergeant. 'By the way . . . any luck?'

Brosnan grinned.

'It's funny you should say that, Sergeant, because that's all it was. But we have a result, if that's what you're asking.'

Hegarty was still stunned by the disclosures in the interview room. 'I can't believe it.'

'We only have a small piece of the puzzle solved yet, Jack. Wait until you see the full picture.'

Hegarty stood thinking.

Brosnan leaned over the counter and beckoned to a young guard. 'Get me a line out please, lad,' he said as he lifted the receiver.

CHAPTER TWENTY-ONE

In the hour that followed, twenty hand-picked detectives were summoned from every district in the city. Their booming voices filled the dayroom of Pearse Street station. They wondered why they had been called, but the sergeant refused to answer the barrage of questions being hurled at him from all directions.

The internal phone rang.

'Yes, sir . . . straight away.'

Manoeuvring his way into the midst of the chattering group, Sergeant Joyce raised his hands.

'Gentlemen . . . will you all please *shut up* for a moment,' he shouted.

The room fell silent apart from a low murmuring

from the back. He waited while those in front turned to admonish the two offending detectives by cursing them to silence.

'Now then, an incident room has been set up, top of the stairs, first door on the right. Chief Superintendent Pat Brosnan awaits your company. And may I say, I've seen him in better form.'

Cigarettes were stamped out and the group moved quickly down the hall and up the stairs. The first man through the door was forced forward by the heave of the men behind him. The chairs rattled to silence. The man standing next to Brosnan was familiar to the elderly detectives.

'Jack! How are things, Jack?' rose up in a shout from the group.

Hegarty looked around and located the source of the greeting. He acknowledged it with a friendly nod.

'How's life in the country treating you?' enquired another.

Brosnan raised his hand.

'All right . . . that's enough of that crack,' he shouted. 'You can buy him all the drink you want when the job is done. Speed is of the essence, gentlemen. The sooner we wrap this one up, the sooner we can resume the important work, like sitting outside some politician's house.'

The men groaned loudly.

'Now,' continued Brosnan, 'many of you have spent hours of back-breaking surveillance watching our good friend, Michael Carroll. Well lads, our hour has come.'

Excited chatter filled the room as the details of

the connection between Hughes and Carroll emerged. Brosnan was pleased with the reaction. He felt that this morale boost was coming at a good time, when the fight against major crime was proving to be an increasingly difficult up-hill battle.

He outlined the plan.

Dividing the twenty men into teams, he gave each of them their directions. One to locate the car that had been used by Hughes and to preserve it for examination. The next to find the murder weapon by following the directions given by Hughes in his statement. A further team to search the flat. And finally a team to carry out surveillance on Michael Carroll.

Brosnan watched the disappointed look on the faces of the final team.

'I'd rather dive into the canal and search for Seanie's iron bar than follow that bastard around for the day,' whispered a fair-haired young detective to the man beside him.

There was a short burst of laughter.

Although Brosnan gave a withering stare at the red-faced young man, he knew that the young detective had good reason to feel the way he did. Surveillance duty was a monotonous, uncomfortable and quite often fruitless undertaking, particularly in the case of Carroll, who had been followed for the past eight months with negative results. But still, that did not excuse insubordination. Brosnan switched one of the men from the search teams to replace the young detective.

'So you don't like surveillance work, Detective?' he said. 'Well, don't worry. I've got a very special assignment for you. You'll really enjoy it.'

The young man looked panicky. Brosnan diverted his attention to the rest of the group.

'I want everything done within the next hour, especially the flat. I want you in and out of there in double quick time. When that's done, I want the word to go out on the street that Seanie Hughes has been detained for questioning in connection with a murder down the country. Tell it to everyone you know.'

The chair legs once again rattled to a crescendo as the men left the room, fuelled with a sense of urgency. Clipped exchanges had now replaced the banter of their arrival. The door was closed. The room was silent.

The young but strongly built fair-haired detective walked slowly towards Brosnan's desk. He was in trepidation, like a child kept after school for giving the teacher a back answer.

'You look like a man who can handle himself,' said Brosnan looking up at him. 'Here's what I want you to do . . .'

Hegarty watched as Brosnan spoke in low intense tones to the young detective, who nodded eagerly. The conversation finished with Brosnan pointing a cautionary finger.

'You do exactly as I've told you. Got that?'

'Yes, sir,' replied the younger man and left the room quickly.

'What's next, Pat?' enquired Hegarty as Brosnan gathered the papers from the table.

'Well, Jack,' replied Brosnan, 'I think it's time to let the hare sit.'

Michael Carroll looked around the carpeted show-room from his office doorway. He watched as the elderly, well-dressed man in the double-breasted suit examined the interior of one of the high-priced models, his hands cupped around his face in an attempt to inspect the interior.

Carroll looked towards his secretary. 'What the hell am I paying that salesman for?' he hissed furiously.

She shrugged and continued to type.

'Well I suppose,' he guffawed, 'I can hardly expect any comment from you. since you're riding him.'

Straightening his tie, he approached the potential customer.

'I see you've got an eye for beauty,' he said with a smile.

The man stood upright and nodded in agreement. 'I must admit to having a weakness for the finer things in life,' he said and then frowned. 'The price tag is a bit hefty though.'

'Ignore that,' replied Carroll, deftly removing the plastic card from the windscreen. 'This just serves to keep the riffraff away.'

They both laughed.

'At my dealership, everything is negotiable.'

Carroll took the man by the arm and began to lead him to his office.

'Are we talking about a trade-in or straight cash?' Carroll enquired in a casual tone.

'BMW seven series . . . two years old,' came the reply.

Carroll rubbed his chin and sucked air through his teeth.

'A difficult motor to re-sell, you know.'

A disappointed look swept over the man's face.

'C'mon,' said Carroll enthusiastically. ' Let's see if we can work something out. I can see you've your heart set on her.'

Just then the salesman crossed the showroom towards them, throwing his eyes to heaven.

'Sorry, Michael,' he said. 'There was a problem with the order for the turbo model, but I've got it sorted now.'

Carroll held up his hand to cut him short.

'It's okay, Brian,' he smiled, 'I'll handle this.'

Inside the office, Carroll pulled a chair in front of his desk.

'Sit yourself down here, Mr . . . eh?'

'Bishop . . . Jonathan Bishop.'

'What line of business are you in, Mr Bishop, if I may be so bold?' asked Carroll, taking a set of forms out of his desk drawer.

'I'm managing director of a pharmaceutical company,' replied Bishop. 'You might have heard of the Japanese Ytiro factory on the south side? Well, that's us.'

'I have indeed, Mr Bishop, a prosperous company it is too,' lied Carroll as he removed a pen from his breast pocket. 'I don't think that that money should be a problem for the managing director of such a successful company.'

Bishop looked embarrassed. Carroll silently cursed himself for being so crass.

There was a quick knock and the secretary popped her head around the door.

'I'm off now, Michael,' she said cheerfully.

She did not wait for a reply before closing the door again.

'My word, is it that time already?' said a surprised Carroll, glancing at his watch.

'The day passes quickly for a busy man,' smiled Bishop.

'Indeed it does, Mr Bishop, indeed it does.'

Carroll fingered the calculator on the desk as he added and subtracted figures. Then he turned the calculator to the customer.

'That's with the BMW taken into consideration, you understand, and I haven't even seen that yet.'

Bishop noted the amount and turned the calculator back to Carroll.

'I think that you are being more than fair,' he smiled. 'Shall we shake on it, Mr Carroll?'

Both men stood up and extended their hands. A satisfied air pervaded the room.

Without warning, the door behind them swung open and a panting Liam McCann rushed into the office. He walked shakily up to the desk, then eased his breathing when he saw the face of the stranger.

'C–can I see you outside for a minute, Mr Carroll?' he asked, his voice stricken with panic.

'Are you all right, young man?' enquired a concerned Bishop, reaching out his hand to steady McCann. 'You appear to have hurt your leg.'

'Excuse me for a moment, Mr Bishop,' said Carroll in an apologetic tone. 'I had better see what's the matter with this chap.' He picked up a brochure from the table. 'Why don't you have a look at the list of optional extras while you're waiting?'

Outside he gripped McCann by the arm.

'What the *fuck* is the matter with you?' he spat. 'Can't you see I've a fish on the line in there?'

McCann held his hands out helplessly. 'They've got Hughes,' he gasped, trying to catch his breath. 'Picked him up early this morning. The driver is dead . . . died in a chase from the house.'

Carroll paled.

'Don't worry,' McCann continued, seeing the alarm on his boss's face, 'Seanie won't talk. Besides, there's nothing that can lead it back to us.'

Carroll was not convinced. His heart began to pound in his chest.

'B–but how? How did they find out that it was Hughes? Wait here a minute.'

Carroll went back into the office and smiled at Bishop, who had by now seated himself back down at the desk. He flicked casually through the brochure.

'I'm sorry about this,' said Carroll in an apologetic tone, 'but I'm going to have to postpone the sale. Something rather urgent has cropped up, I'm afraid.'

'No problem at all,' replied Bishop with a good-humoured smile. 'I can always wait until tomorrow to surprise the wife.'

Carroll escorted Mr Bishop to the glass front door of the showroom. A meeting was arranged for the following day.

'Tomorrow at four then . . .,' Carroll called out before returning quickly to McCann.

'Is there anything that ties us to that fucking moron?' he asked urgently, as soon as Bishop was safely out of earshot.

McCann thought for a moment.

'I got the map back from him,' he said, counting the single task on his finger like a child learning his sums.

'What about the money? What about the . . .,' Carroll began.

'All used bills like you said. All untraceable.'

Carroll put his hands up to his face and spoke through them.

'I suppose you counted it along with the extra hundred before you paid them off?'

McCann looked perplexed.

'Of course I did.'

Carroll dropped his hands and grabbed McCann by the lapels of his black leather jacket, shaking him violently and shouting hysterically into his face.

'With your *fuckin'* gloves on I suppose . . .? You *didn't* wear gloves . . . did you?'

Liam's eyes widened as he gave a single nervous shake of his head.

'D–don't worry, Mr Carroll,' he said, his voice trembling. 'I'll fix it. J–just leave it to me.'

Carroll reached out for McCann's cheek and pinched it until the lump of flesh was distorted and reddened between his thumb and forefinger.

He spoke in a calm voice. 'You'd better, Liam. Because if this shit comes back on my doorstep, the only thing they'll find belonging to you is that peg leg of yours sailing down the Liffey.'

Carroll smiled and released his grip, then slapped McCann's face back into shape and walked slowly back to his office.

McCann left the showroom quickly, nursing his smarting cheek, a plan building in his head.

Jonathan Bishop had by this time walked smartly back to his car. He sat in and loosened his tie.

'I nearly bought a motor for thirty-three thousand big ones.' He exhaled slowly. 'I even had the cheek to shake on it.'

The man in the passenger seat smiled. 'Overtime must be pretty good on the north side. All I was able to afford was a bottom-of-the-heap model that does seventy miles to the gallon.'

The detective in the back seat edged forward, resting his elbows on the shoulders of the two front seats. 'Ah sure, he was always a man for the high-powered cars. Who did you pretend to be? A high-class pimp?'

Detective Sergeant O'Donnell was struggling in the driver's seat to remove the jacket of his double-breasted suit. 'Blast it to hell. I'm burning up in this thing.'

Having finally negotiated both sleeves he handed the jacket to the man in the back seat.

'There you go, Gerry, put that next to you. And be careful with it. It's the only decent suit I have.'

He settled himself into a comfortable position.

'McCann came in while I was there. He didn't look too happy.'

'I wonder why,' grinned the detective in the passenger seat. 'He left just after yourself. Looked like he was in a hurry. I can't understand why Brosnan doesn't have surveillance on him. Why the hell don't we just pick up the whole lot of them?'

There was no answer to his enquiry.

'Ah well . . .' he sighed, 'Ours not to reason why.'

The man in the back seat suddenly punched the older detective on the shoulder.

'C'mon, tell us,' he urged. 'Who did you pretend to be?'

The older detective raised his chin and pursed his lips.

'My name is Jonathan Bishop,' he said in a haughty voice. 'Well actually, Mr Carroll, I am the managing director of the Japanese firm, Ytiro, on the south side.'

His two colleagues laughed loudly. The detective dropped the accent.

'The little shite-hawk even had the balls to say that he'd heard of it.'

'Ytiro,' guffawed the detective in the back seat. 'Where did you come up with that one?'

'It's a shorter version of something,' came the reply. He looked and grinned at the two confused detectives. 'It stands for Your Time Is Running Out.'

Liam McCann stood at the entrance to Seanie's flat. He pressed the doorbell and waited. Nothing. He pressed it again, this time with more insistence. Nobody home. He looked up and down the street once more, before entering the dilapidated building. The stairs was lit by a single bare bulb. He knocked on the door of the flat and waited. No reply. Reaching inside his jacket, he removed a shortened jemmy bar, which he deftly forced between the jamb and the door itself. He pulled back on it and there was a single loud crack. The door swung open slowly.

McCann checked the stairs and then stepped cautiously inside. The room looked empty, though its contents had been disturbed. A chest of drawers, he noticed, had not been replaced in its original position. Down the length of its side, the thin strip of bright paint was preserved in its original colour by lack of exposure to the light. McCann knew the signs. He had plenty of experience. His flat had been searched many times by the RUC.

Even though he knew that it was too late he went inside, still hoping that they had missed it, that Seanie had hidden it so well that not even the most qualified search team would find it. He closed the door and replaced the jemmy in his jacket pocket. He began with the drawers, pulling each one out in turn, reaching under the unit skeleton, feeling around the base of it with his hand. Nothing.

He turned his attention to the wardrobe. Inside, Seanie's clothes lay in a dirty and untidy pile. He examined each garment in turn, feeling the material through. He squeezed the dirty denims and the hardened socks. Nothing.

He sat down on the bed and began to panic inwardly as he contemplated his predicament. He punched the pillow in anger and then in a frenzy he picked it up and searched through it. He pulled back the darkened sheets and blankets, shaking each one out in turn, and threw them on the floor.

He knelt down to examine the sides of the mattress for signs of recent repair. His leg hurt as he tried to pull the mattress from its base. He stopped until the pain eased. Then, keeping his left leg straight and resting his weight on his bent right leg, he reached between the mattress and the base and groped frantically underneath. His breathing quickened. His index finger brushed against something. He reached deeper, closing his fist around it and took it out.

'Dear Jesus, thank you,' he exclaimed as he smacked his lips on the bundle of rolled bank notes. He hurriedly stuffed the roll into his inside pocket and paused momentarily to contemplate his good fortune.

'How the hell did they miss it?' he asked out loud.

'We didn't,' came the reply.

An open-mouthed and pale McCann swung around to see the fair-haired young detective standing in the doorway accompanied by three uniformed gardaí.

'Thank you for taking the bait, Liam. It makes our job so much easier.'

The door was pushed open further as they moved into the room.

Liam raised his hands. One of the uniformed men pulled them down behind his back and cuffed him. McCann looked up at the detective.

'I didn't think you needed such a crowd to catch a simple burglar,' he sneered.

The young detective walked towards him.

'Liam McCann . . . I am arresting you for conspiracy to murder. You do not have to say anything unless you wish to do so, but whatever you say will be taken down in writing and may be given in evidence.'

'What the *fuck* are you talking about, man?' shouted McCann as he was pushed towards the door. 'I was trying to make a few quick pounds. What's this fucking *murder* crack about?'

He shouted his protests all the way down the stairs, interspersing them with whispered curses of incredulity. A hand was placed on his head as he was lowered into the unmarked car.

'You're making a big mistake here, lads,' he threatened. 'A *very* big mistake.'

The detective sat in to the back seat beside him and smiled.

'Not this time, Liam,' he whispered to McCann. 'Not this time.'

TWENTY-TWO

Hegarty and Brosnan sat in the large station canteen in silence. Hegarty watched the chief as he scribbled in the copybook, pausing now and then to scratch his head in deep thought.

'Why don't you get yourself a decent notebook like everyone else, Pat?' he asked.

Brosnan looked up and stopped writing. He held up the copybook and turned it around in his hand, examining it. 'Dunno,' he shrugged. 'I got into the habit of it.'

He gave a smile as if at a private joke. 'Would you believe that the first case that I was in charge of, I went to the prime witness and when she started to talk I discovered that I didn't have a thing to write on.

I took the statement on her child's copybook that she gave me and tore out the pages. Jaysus, that young lad was cross,' he laughed, recalling the day. 'I remember I had to give him twenty pence to stop him crying.'

Hegarty smiled as he pictured the scene in his mind. The giant Brosnan in a copybook tug-of-war with the protesting youngster.

'So,' finished Brosnan as he opened the copybook, 'that's why I always use them. I suppose it's for luck.'

His explanation given, he resumed writing. Hegarty stood up and went to the canteen fridge. He opened it and peered in at the scant contents. A half-finished yoghurt and a milk carton. He picked up the carton and shook it. It was almost empty.

'Well it's good to see that things haven't changed in the big city,' he muttered to himself and replaced it in the fridge. He slapped gently at his stomach. 'When are we going to eat?' he asked. 'Or are we going to starve to death until this thing is finished?'

Brosnan smiled as he wrote. 'There'll be time enough to eat later,' he replied.

Hegarty sighed with despair and made his way to one of the windows. He looked down from the second-storey window at the bustling city below. 'You know, I really don't miss this at all,' he said. He turned around quickly to Brosnan. 'Don't get me wrong,' he added quickly. 'I wouldn't have missed that arrest for the world.'

He looked out the window and thought about Dunsheerin. The peace and quiet of the small country village, crime-free up to now. Poor Jim Quilter, he thought to himself with a smile. How easy it would have been to wrong him if Seanie Hughes's fingerprints had not been found on Flann O'Neill's shiny gate. He was glad now that he had met him on the village street before leaving with Brosnan for Dublin. Glad he had told him that he was in the clear but would be required later to make a full statement. He turned around to Brosnan as his thoughts changed.

'Why would a Dublin criminal arrange the killing of a country businessman like John Burns?' he asked.

Brosnan threw the copybook and pen on the table in front of him.

'Could be any number of things,' he replied. 'Money and business spring to mind. Who knows what people like Burns are involved in?'

'Ah now, Pat,' said Hegarty in mild protest. 'I think I'd have a fair idea if I had a crime-lord in the village.'

Brosnan gave him a sharp glance. 'And would you know if he was beating his wife, Jack?'

It was neither a put-down nor really a question. Merely a comment on how much can be going on behind closed doors, even in a small country village like Dunsheerin.

Hegarty nodded in acknowledgement. 'I see what you mean,' he said in a low voice.

Brosnan, beginning to regret what he had said, slapped his hands to change the mood. 'Anyway, as a magician would say, all will be revealed shortly.'

The door suddenly opened violently and slammed against the wall. The sergeant pointed to the phone on the counter. 'I've been looking for ye for the past half hour. Is that thing not working?' He continued without waiting for an answer: 'The lads have Liam McCann downstairs. Caught him in Hughes's flat.'

Brosnan clenched his fist and grabbed the copy-book and pen from the table. The sergeant stood back as Brosnan and Hegarty brushed out past him.

The fair-haired detective turned at the approach of Brosnan. 'Happened just as you said, Chief,' he said. There was admiration in his voice. 'He's in the interview room with his solicitor. I've got every-thing set up as you planned.'

Brosnan smiled and slapped the young man on both shoulders. 'Great stuff, young fella,' he smiled. 'Have you the results from the fingerprint section?'

'Got them just now.'

'Then what are you waiting for, boy?' said Brosnan. 'Go get him.'

The solicitor snapped open his black briefcase on the table and looked up as the detective entered the room.

'I assume, Detective, that my client has been advised of his rights?'

'Yes, he was advised of his rights directly after arrest.'

The solicitor withdrew a handful of papers and arranged them on the table before him.

'My client seems to be under the impression that he has been wrongfully arrested for some part or other in a murder, when in fact the only crime committed was burglary. Perhaps you can clarify this, Detective?'

He stared across the table, pen poised for note-taking. The young detective rolled his back into the chair, attempting to assume a more comfortable position. The delay in responding annoyed the solicitor who tapped irritably on the desk.

'Well . . .?'

McCann, who sat beside his brief, looked down at his hands, rubbing his fingers which were stained black from fingerprinting.

The detective spoke in a relaxed confident tone. 'We have in custody one Seanie Hughes, who states that he and another man, Tony Kearns, received two thousand pounds in payment from your client on behalf of a third party to murder John Burns of Dunsheerin. He also states that it was your client who gave him the orders and the map with directions.'

The solicitor stopped writing and smiled across the table. 'And you have this map, Detective?'

'No we don't. But we do have the money. And we have fingerprint evidence to show that your client handled it. In any case, Mr Hughes has been very thorough in his statement. He outlines times, places . . . the whole shebang in fact. Now, we know that your client was merely the messenger boy for someone else. We know who that third party is. But we'd prefer to hear it from your client.'

The solicitor looked incredulously at the detective and gave a dismissive wave of his hand.

'Hold on there a moment. You appear to be jumping the gun. All you have at the moment is the statement of another man. A man, by all accounts, with a serious criminal record, convicted many times in the past for violent crimes.'

He pointed his pen to the roll of money on the table.

'And this . . . evidence, my client tells me, was obtained using shall we say . . . unusual methods?'

McCann giggled. The detective and the solicitor looked at him as his giggle broke into a laugh, which continued for a few moments before he stopped and looked at the two men with an air of mock seriousness.

'Is there something amusing about all of this?' asked the detective. 'If you have a joke, I'd appreciate it if you'd share it with us.'

'The joke's on you, copper,' McCann snorted. 'Of course you've got my prints on the money, I counted it all when I found it in the flat. Even if I did handle it before I made the pay-off to Hughes, that evidence is useless now.' His voice rose in triumph. 'You've got nothing, pig. Now charge me with burglary and let me the fuck out of here.'

The solicitor turned quickly to McCann and held up a cautionary hand.

'As your legal advisor, I must advise that you say nothing further.'

He turned back.

'Is this true, Detective? Did my client handle this money during the course of the *trap* that you set for him?'

The detective nodded slowly.

'Without gloves?' pressed the solicitor.

The detective looked from McCann to the money. 'Yes . . . without gloves.'

The solicitor eased back in the chair and threw out his hands dramatically.

'Well then, Detective . . . it's no big surprise that you found his fingerprints all over it. Is it?' The solicitor waited. 'Is it any surprise?' he insisted.

The detective sighed and rubbed his forehead. 'No . . . it's no surprise.'

McCann snorted a laugh and sneered across the table. The solicitor made to speak, but was stopped in his tracks by the detective, who leaned forward with a wide grin.

'But it's a massive surprise that they were found on this!'

He reached down into the side pocket of his jacket and withdrew a small plastic evidence bag, which contained a roll of money.

'You see, Mr McCann, we replaced the money we found under the mattress with that roll there,' he explained, pointing to the money on the table. 'Which reminds me, I mustn't forget to give back that cash to the lads. They'd be very upset if their porter pot went missing.'

He rose slowly from the chair.

'Tell you what, gentlemen, why don't I go and have a cup of coffee for a few minutes and leave the two of you alone to have a chat?'

He looked back at McCann as he walked to the door.

'"Even if I had handled it before I made the pay-off to Hughes." That's a very interesting statement you made, Mr McCann. We must talk further about that later on. Oh, I nearly forgot . . .'

He tiptoed back gingerly to the table.

'Better not leave this lying around,' he smiled, taking the roll of money 'You never know when a burglar might strike.'

He stepped quickly out into the corridor and moved towards Brosnan and Hegarty who stood talking to the sergeant at his desk. Brosnan rose to his feet expectantly.

'Well, how did it go?' he asked hurriedly.

The detective shook his head. 'Well, he fell for the money roll,' he said. 'But I'm not sure if he's going to talk. He didn't look that worried about it when I left.'

Brosnan took him by the arm and led him a short distance away. 'Never mind how the gouger looked, young fella,' he whispered. 'How did his solicitor look?'

The detective thought about the question for a moment. His face broke into a confident smile as he realised its relevance.

'Yeah, Chief!' he exclaimed. 'He didn't look a bit pleased at all.'

Brosnan winked at the detective, then turned and beckoned to Hegarty.

'Right then, men,' he addressed the huddle. 'We're going to give them a few more minutes then the three of us are going in.' He prodded the detective in the chest. 'You're in charge of this interview,' he added. 'Jack and I are there strictly as observers unless you need a hand.' He looked from one to the other and waited for them to acknowledge.

They paused in the corridor for a few minutes and then entered the room. Brosnan and Hegarty stood just inside the door with their backs to the wall.

'This is Detective Chief Superintendent Pat Brosnan and Garda Jack Hegarty,' announced the detective, as he moved towards the table.

The solicitor looked the two big men up and down, then cleared his throat. The detective eyed him, waiting for him to speak.

'I have discussed the situation with my client and he is prepared to co-operate. However, with regard to the money on which his fingerprints were found, he says that he did not know at the time that it was payment for a killing. He tells me that he was asked to make a payment to this Hughes person for a punishment beating. He is merely the middle-man, you understand. Also, he strongly denies the allegation that he provided the map and other instructions. He is willing to make a full statement to this effect.'

The detective looked at Brosnan and then to McCann.

'Who were you delivering the money for?' he asked.

There was a short silence as McCann hesitated. The solicitor turned to face him.

'Liam?' he asked expectantly.

McCann raised his eyes.

'Michael Carroll.'

'Why did you go to Hughes's flat to get the money back if you didn't think it was payment for a killing? You panicked, didn't you?'

McCann, not knowing what to reply, glanced nervously at the solicitor who nodded.

'Tell the detective the reason.'

'It's like I told you before,' said McCann. 'I knew that he had the money and I just went there to steal it.'

The detective sighed heavily and took a few sheets of paper from the drawer.

'So that's your story and you're sticking to it, I suppose.'

Brosnan gave a short intentional cough.

The solicitor glanced at him. 'You have something to add, Chief Superintendent?' he asked.

Brosnan moved forward from the wall and placed his hands in his pockets as he looked down at McCann. 'So you expect us to believe that you took money from Michael Carroll which you gave to Seanie Hughes and Tony Kearns in payment for a punishment beating.' His voice rose with incredulity. 'A punishment beating on whom? This was no drug dealer who had been short on his repayments or some innocent shopkeeper who pays scum like you and Carroll for so-called protection.'

The solicitor held up his hand. 'Chief Superintendent, I must protest.'

Brosnan was unshaken by the objection. 'This was an innocent businessman from down the country,' he continued, his voice rising. 'This was a planned killing. What we want to know is *why*. Why would a scumbag like you be interested in killing an innocent businessman from down the country?'

Brosnan was almost shouting. McCann looked up at him with fear in his eyes.

The solicitor stood up and slammed his brief-case down on the table. 'Chief *Superintendent*,' he roared.

'Why?' Brosnan roared louder at the flinching prisoner.

McCann held his hands up. His answer was in a barely audible whisper like that of a scared child. 'It was done for a . . .' He stopped and hesitated.

'For what? What was it done for?' shouted Brosnan above the solicitor's loud protests. He was at the finishing line and he knew it. That familiar smell of victory filled his nostrils. '*Answer the question.*'

The booming voice rang around the room.

Hegarty held his breath as Brosnan moved closer. The young detective narrowed his eyes and waited. Brosnan and the solicitor panted in the silence.

McCann raised his frightened face and looked at each of them in turn, before settling his gaze on the reddened face of the chief superintendent.

'It was done for . . .' he started.

The solicitor pointed down at him. 'Mr McCann, before you speak, I must urge you to think very carefully. Do not be intimidated by . . .'

Brosnan hammered his fist down on the table, at the same time moving the solicitor out of the way with his free arm. He leaned forward. McCann raised his hands as Brosnan neared. 'Now, you listen to me, you little bastard,' he hissed. 'And not to this smart suit who'll be drinking champagne in the Gresham while you'll be watching your arse in the prison shower for the next twenty-five years.'

'I wish to make an official complaint, Detective,' announced the solicitor. 'About this officer's behaviour. Do not be intimidated, Mr McCann,' he continued, hidden from the prisoner's view by the towering chief.

'Oh, be intimidated . . . be very intimidated,' said Brosnan. 'Because you took money from Michael Carroll and gave it to two others, knowing that it was for the killing of John Burns.' His voice lowered to a barely audible whisper. 'Last chance, Willie, boy. Why was it done?'

McCann slowly lowered his hands, his expression one of calm understanding.

'For a woman,' he said. 'It was done for a woman.'

Brosnan gave him a nod and straightened up. He looked back to Hegarty. The village guard's eyes were shut tight, his hand held over his mouth. When he opened them he looked up and gave a weary shake of his head.

Brosnan turned back to McCann. 'Name?' he demanded.

CHAPTER TWENTY-THREE

Claire Burns stood at the verge of the back patio, scattering breadcrumbs of bread on to the lawn. The gathering of small birds fluttered in excitement each time she raised her arm to pepper the ground.

Claire dusted the remaining crumbs from her hands and sat down on a white plastic chair to watch the birds enjoying the feast. Jenny had left an hour earlier with the promise of returning that evening.

'I'd better go home and feed Gerald,' she had attempted to joke. 'Although he might as well be dead too, for all the good he is.'

Claire had winced inwardly at the comment. When she remembered her pain and suffering at

John Burns's hands, she believed she was glad that he was dead. And yet, she had a nagging ache of sorrow in her heart.

She quickly brushed this feeling aside. There could be no more sadness. The joy of release far outweighed any nagging doubts. She could now come and sit on the patio whenever she liked and feed her birds. For the first time in many years she felt as free as they were. As this realisation dawned on her she began to cry.

She had shed many tears during the unhappy years of her marriage, but these tears were different. They were tears of overwhelming release.

The sobbing stopped as quickly as it had begun. Claire suddenly felt awash with ease and wiped the last drop from the corner of her eye.

The sound of footsteps on the stone patio sent the small birds flitting across the lawn. Claire stood up to greet her visitor.

'My dear Claire,' cried Bill Jennings, walking towards her, arms outstretched. 'Are you all right? I tried the door but there was no answer.' He leaned forward and kissed her on the cheek.

Kissing came naturally to Councillor Jennings. The object of his affection was irrelevant – babies with congealed snot, young children with cold sores, old ladies with dermatitis. So long as it provided a photo opportunity, Jennings would run the risk of putting his immune system to the test. 'A vote is a vote,' he would be heard to say, wiping his lips on his white linen handkerchief.

Claire sniffled and backed away from him. 'I'm fine, Bill. You didn't have to call. To tell you the truth, the pain abates when I'm on my own.'

Jennings eased Claire back into her seat before sitting down himself. 'I know exactly what you mean, Claire. My brother-in-law died in California last year. Naturally we were all devastated. But that's enough of my hardship,' he continued. 'I just came to tell you that I have made the arrangements for the burial. I know what a terrible time this must be for you, so I took the liberty. You don't mind?'

Claire smiled weakly. 'Of course not, Bill. It was very thoughtful of you.'

Jennings was pleased.

Although Claire was grateful for his help, she could not bring herself to prolong his visit with an offer of refreshment. A silence hung over the patio, broken only by the excited high-pitched whistles of the small birds, who were tentatively returning to their feeding.

'So,' said Jennings finally, slapping his knee, 'I'd better be off then. Leave the arrangements to me, Claire. I'll see John right, God rest him.' He rose to his feet. 'I'll pick you up on Monday morning.'

Claire stood up, shaking her head in confusion. She could not understand his concern.

'What do you mean, Bill?' she asked.

He was already at the verge of the patio. He did not answer, but waved a departing hand and smiled as he disappeared from view. She sighed gently and sat back on the chair, resigning herself to the fact that Bill Jennings had, as of that moment, taken charge of all the funeral arrangements. She reached into the small bowl on the patio table and took out another handful of crumbs. The small birds chattered excitedly as she threw the bread in a semi-circle. It landed on the ground in a perfectly formed arc. The birds exclaimed their pleasure in loud whistling and descended.

The setting sun shone down on Claire, and she lifted her face to it, closing her eyes and basking in its warm rays. She opened her eyes and smiled down at the chirping birds, watching in quiet pleasure as they finished the last of the crumbs.

Suddenly, they flew away. One remained behind, hopping across the feeding area as it searched for a morsel that had eluded his companions. Having found it, he flew away to join the others in the nearby bushes.

Claire relaxed on the chair and closed her eyes. Soon she was asleep. Her father walked towards her in great sweeping steps, his hands outstretched, a wide grin of pride on his face.

'How's my little angel?' he exclaimed as he picked her up and wrapped his strong arms around her, his unshaven face rubbing a kiss against her cheek, the strong smell of pipe tobacco from his breath. 'My little angel,' he repeated as he placed her back on the ground and looked down at her little friend.

'And you, young Jenny,' he smiled. 'I hope you girls have made something nice for my tea.' He had a mock frown as he leaned down to examine the plastic tea-set.

'Cakes,' Jenny smiled up at him. 'We're having tea and cakes.'

The adult rubbed his hands together and knelt

down beside them. 'Oh I do love tea and cakes,' he thundered as he picked up one of the small plastic cups and lifted it to his lips.

They shrieked with laughter. 'But it's only pretend,' squealed Jenny as she took the cup from him.

'Claire,' called a voice in the distance. 'Wake up, Claire!'

She opened her eyes. The sun had set. She felt a sudden chill. A reddening darkness had descended on the garden. Jenny stood above her, smiling.

'My God, girl. What are you doing out here?' she asked in surprise.

Claire shivered and stood up. She turned to her friend and smiled. Without warning, she threw her arms around Jenny and hugged her.

Jenny laughed as she patted Claire gently on the back. 'You haven't been at the brandy again, have you?' she joked. 'Get inside before you catch your death,' she said as she turned them towards the door.

Claire looked back at the lawn. 'I was just feeding the birds,' she explained. 'I must have fallen asleep'.

Jenny laughed. 'It must have been a pleasant dream,' she said. 'I could see you smiling the minute I came around the corner.'

Claire stopped at the patio door of the house. 'It was a *very* pleasant dream, Jenny,' she said. 'The first in many years.'

Jack Hegarty lifted his finger from the steering wheel and pointed to a petrol station a short distance up the road.

'I'm pulling in here, Pat. I need to get something.'

The car pulled into the large tarmacadam forecourt of the garage and Brosnan waited, watching Hegarty as he entered the shop, patting the pockets of his trousers.

The car was warm. Brosnan rubbed at his bare arms, which had turned from a pale grey to a salmon pink from his time in the country sunshine. He recalled the look on Hegarty's face when McCann had answered the final question, his uncharacteristic silence in the car, the distant look and the odd shake of his head as he rolled the facts over and over in his mind.

Brosnan knew that the case was closed. Solving it had not been difficult. No longer was there honour amongst the criminal fraternity. Much as they would boast about their loyalty to each other, very few of them were prepared to take the rap on their own when caught. Although it was this very weakness that Brosnan and all other dedicated policemen like him preyed on, he felt a hidden disgust for those who betrayed their accomplices to save their own hides.

His thoughts turned back to the job at hand. Soon he would be returning to the near normality of headquarters. But as for Hegarty, he would be returning to a community that had been rocked to the very core by an incident from which it would never recover, an incident that would be spoken of in hushed tones for many years to come.

Inside, Hegarty had gathered a handful of chocolate bars and placed them on the counter.

The young female assistant gave a broad welcoming smile before tapping the prices into the cash register.

'Will that be all?' she asked cheerfully.

Hegarty, about to answer, halted for a moment and glanced quickly at the shelf behind the young assistant. He felt like a man who had come into a chemist shop with the purpose of buying a packet of condoms and was leaving with a bottle of shampoo.

His mind was made up.

'Give me the strongest packet of pipe tobacco you have,' he said with authority.

The assistant looked curiously at him before reaching back and removing a selection of packs from the shelf. Hegarty examined each one in turn.

'I'll take this one,' he said finally, holding up a red tartan packet.

Once outside, Hegarty tore the plastic wrapping from it and held the open pouch up to his face like an oxygen mask. He inhaled the sweet aroma and nodded to himself with calm pleasure.

'Are we right so?' asked Brosnan as Hegarty got into the car.

'Grand altogether.'

Inside the shop, the female assistant had watched the goings-on through the heavy glass window. She had been joined by a male colleague who leaned across her to get a better view. 'Who the hell was that fella?' he asked as the car pulled out of the forecourt.

'Don't know,' she shrugged, pushing him away

with her elbow. She flicked through the glossy pages of a women's magazine. 'Just another spacer from the country I suppose.'

Michael Carroll stood in front of the oval bathroom mirror patting the cold after-shave lightly on his face. He turned from side to side, checking his appearance, then returned to the bedroom and took his tuxedo from the bed where it was lying. His wife sat in front of the dressing table, applying her blusher with light strokes of her powder brush.

'Are you going to be long more at that?' grunted Carroll as he hurriedly swung his arm into the jacket. 'I told them we'd be there at eight.'

She watched him in the mirror as he straightened his bow tie. She snapped on a pair of gold earrings with pearl detail and then took a slim chain from its suede box and held it up to her neck.

'What do you think? Does it go with the dress?' she asked in a casual tone.

Carroll did not reply. He patted his pockets and turned to take his wallet from the bedside locker. His mind was elsewhere. He thought about Liam McCann, wondering what solution to the problem his right-hand man had come up with.

Although Carroll had never met Seanie Hughes, he felt confident that his reputation for dealing harshly with anyone who crossed him would ensure that the cops would not be in the know. As Carroll well knew, the last person to cross Seanie

Hughes was still searching for the fingers of his right hand. He sniggered at the thought of it.

His wife noticed the laugh.

'What's so funny?'

'Nothing. Here let me at it . . .'

He moved quickly behind her, fumbling with the necklace clip underneath her hair.

'There, that's fine. What the hell are you so dressed up for anyway?' he asked. 'You've never taken as long to get ready.'

She palmed at her hair, still eyeing him through his reflection in the mirror.

'Now, now, Michael,' she purred, 'you know how I like to look my best when I'm meeting all your girl friends.'

He glared at her. His neck reddened as he tightened his fist.

'Just don't make a show of yourself like you did the last time.'

She stood up and straightened her dress.

'Will they be impressed with these shoes do you think, or should I wear something a little bit classier?'

He grabbed her bolero-length mink jacket and flung it in her direction. It landed at her feet.

'*Fuck you*,' he shouted as he stormed towards the door, 'If you don't want to come, then stay the *fuck* at home.'

She smiled to herself as she put on the coat. One of her few pleasures in life was seeing him like this.

'Wait for me, darling,' she called out in fake distress, as she made her way down the stairs a distance behind him.

In the hallway she waited as he fingered in the code on the control box of the house alarm. It beeped the thirty-second warning as he took her roughly by the arm and led her out the front door. He jumped with shock as he placed the key in the door.

'Michael Carroll,' said a voice. He turned quickly, releasing his grip on his wife.

Four men stood at the bottom of the steps.

'Who wants to know?'

'Well, Mr Carroll, my name is Detective Sergeant Kenny.'

Carroll's face paled as he waited for the next sentence. He closed his eyes as he listened.

'I'm arresting you for conspiracy in the murder of one John Burns.'

Carroll's eyes scanned the faces of the other three men. They were all familiar to him. One in particular.

'Jonathan Bishop,' he said softly, shaking his head in disbelief as he searched the face of the older detective.

'It's O'Donnell, actually,' the detective sergeant smiled. 'And I was right . . . your time *was* running out.'

Carroll looked puzzled. He reached into his jacket pocket and fumbled for a moment. The four men moved quickly up the steps. He took his hand out of his pocket and held up a small black diary in front of them.

'Jesus, relax,' he exclaimed, holding up his other hand in surrender.

He flicked the book from his hand in the direction of his wife. It fell at her feet.

'Contact my solicitor,' he ordered, as he descended the steps, two detectives in front, two behind. 'Tell him what's going on.'

The car drove off. It was well out of sight before she turned to unlock the front door. Once inside, she sat on the bottom step of the stairs and searched through the black notebook. She found the solicitor's name and began to dial the number. Her mind raced with a combination of shock and exhilaration. She paused for a moment and quickly replaced the receiver.

Picking up the book again, her scarlet nails flicked through the leaves as she read the many names of her husband's 'secretaries'. Her eyes never left the pages as she lowered herself back onto the bottom step of the stairs, gathering her skirt under her with her free hand. Suddenly the house alarm began to ring. And ring.

She lowered the book and began to laugh. She didn't know the code to silence it. He had never told her.

The house began to vibrate with the sound, the electronic whooping reaching a screeching crescendo.

She laughed louder.

CHAPTER TWENTY-FOUR

A drunken Jim Quilter punched his hand in triumph at the television in the crowded Conroy's Bar, yelling at the top of his voice. Hickey threw his arm over his shoulder and both of them jumped up and down together like excited football fans.

Big Madge reached wildly across the counter at them, her fleshy hand opening and closing as she attempted to grab him. 'Will you shut up and listen,' she shouted angrily.

They stopped and smiled at each other. Big Madge turned up the volume to a blare.

'Three men have been arrested today in connection with the murder of country businessman

John Burns. The body of John Burns was found two days ago in a river near the village of Dunsheerin. The three men, all with Dublin addresses, are being held at various Garda stations in the city. The first man was arrested in an early-morning raid by detectives backed up by uniformed gardaí.'

'Good man, Jack Hegarty,' shouted an elderly man in the crowd.

'Although gardaí have refused to comment further on the arrests, it is believed that the third man arrested has connections with Dublin's criminal underworld.'

A hush filled the bar. Locals looked at one another but said nothing.

Hickey whispered to Quilter from the side of his mouth. 'Be the Jaysus Jim, aren't ya lucky that you got the all-clear from Hegarty. Or they'd be saying that you were a big crime lad like those fellas. You know, the fellas with the quare nicknames.'

Conversation began in the bar again, hurried and confused.

Quilter laughed and looked down at Hickey. 'I wonder what my nickname would be?'

Hickey picked his pint up from the counter and took a long thoughtful gulp. He replaced the glass on the counter and smacked his lips.

'The Snipe!' he exclaimed and roared with laughter.

Quilter roared with him as they exchanged

ideas. 'The Bollocks ... no ... The Drunk Bollocks.'

They held each other's shoulders and squealed with laughter, Quilter bending in half in front of Hickey and coughing until his face turned crimson.

'The Shitemaster,' Hickey roared through the tears.

Their laughter faded to a series of quiet sighs as they watched Big Madge lift the flap of the counter and trundle towards them, her arms outstretched holding two pudgy fists.

'Did I not tell ye to shut up?' she demanded. 'How many times did I tell ye?'

The locals nodded and smiled at one another as they watched. Free entertainment.

Hickey stepped gingerly behind Quilter, who held his hands up to defend himself. She dropped her fists and moved her face to within an inch if his. '*Did I*?' she roared.

Quilter flinched back. Leering with pleasure he leaned forward again. 'Why, Madge,' he said in a low whisper, and then glanced around the bar. 'That's a lovely perfume that you're wearing this evening.'

Big Madge lifted the collar of her blouse and sniffed at it. 'What perfume?' she asked in a tone of surprise.

Quilter gave her a knowing look. 'Come on now, Madge. You don't mean to tell me that you smell like the wild apple blossom all the time?'

Her angry face softened to a coy smile. She pushed Quilter back gently from her. 'Get away out of that you charmer you.' She raised her eyes to heaven. 'You know very well by now, that I never wear perfume.'

Quilter shook his head in false disbelief. Hickey edged his face around from behind him.

'I'm wondering, could it be the smell of your after-shave then?' he enquired.

There was a short silence before the bar rocked with laughter.

'Ya pair o' tramps, ya,' shouted Madge, as she grabbed the two of them by their jackets and pulled them towards the door. Both of them sang their familiar song as they were escorted outside. 'Oh . . . weeee're on our way, 'cos we just can't stay, and just as the *craic* was good . . .'

Big Madge slammed the door after them and turned back to the hysterical crowd. She looked at a group of local elderly men who sat at a low table in front of the empty fireplace, holding their chests, Flann O'Neill in the middle, his face purple from the exertion.

'There'll be no wake in this house for any of you lot,' she shouted at them, and then smiled to herself as she went behind the bar.

Hickey and Quilter stood outside on the street, their hands on their knees as they sniggered the remainder of the joke to an end.

'You're a hard man on her, Myles,' said Quilter as he stood upright and put his arm around him for support.

He searched his pocket with his free hand and closed his fist around the crumpled banknotes.

The fee which his close friend and 'agent' had demanded from an English tabloid newspaper for the interview and photographs was still in the early stages of being spent.

'Clancy's, I suppose?' asked Quilter, already knowing the answer.

Hickey gave a wide grin and slapped his hands together.

'Why not, James?' he replied. 'The night is still young.'

The small room in Dunsheerin Garda Station looked as if it had been raided by an untidy burglar. Papers were scattered across the large oak desk, piles more lay on the ground beside it. A lone detective sat behind the desk sorting through the questionnaires, giving them one final check before stacking them in order of importance.

Outside in the dayroom, Brosnan sat behind the desk. Hegarty stood at the counter, fidgeting nervously with his cap. Brosnan looked up at him and then back at the two young guards who sat opposite him.

'Are we ready then?' he asked finally.

Costigan and Daly nodded. 'Yes, sir,' they answered in unison.

Brosnan had picked them especially for the task. Not because of their ability as policemen, but because they were local. Men should be seen to sort out their own problems, and not to depend on help from outside. It would also be something of a comfort to the locals to know that their own guards had been instrumental in the arrest.

Brosnan rose to his feet and ushered them out the door before him.

There was a deathly silence in the patrol car as it made its way to the Burns residence. Brosnan prepared the words in his mind. Words he had used many times in the past. Daly and Costigan sat pale-faced in the back seat. It was all new to them. Although their task was merely to stand and listen, the gravity of the situation was unnerving.

Hegarty turned the car off the road and drove across the cattle-grid. His mind was still in turmoil, his head lightened by the three bowls of strong tobacco he had smoked.

The outside lanterns shone brightly down on the parking area outside the house. The four doors of the car slammed together and they made their way up the steps to the front door, led by Brosnan. He straightened up and pressed the doorbell. They looked at each other and listened to the sound of approaching footsteps and laughter.

Claire Burns smiled as she opened the door. Her expression changed when she saw the four solemn policemen on the steps outside. Hegarty winced when she looked at him.

Behind her, Jenny approached along the hall-way. 'Who is it, Claire?' she asked.

Brosnan raised his hand slowly and pushed the front door open wide.

'Jenny Maguire,' he started as he moved towards her. 'I am arresting you for conspiracy in the murder of John Burns.'

The words hung like a ticking bomb over all present.

Claire turned to her and gave a short, nervous laugh. Jenny had stopped in the middle of the hall-way. Although her hands trembled at her sides, her face was a grimace of stone.

Brosnan explained her rights. She did not respond when he asked if she understood, his voice echoing in some remote chamber of her brain. He took her gently by the arm.

Jenny looked at Claire as she passed her in the doorway. Claire looked at her friend in disbelief and then at Hegarty. His face was expressionless, as were the faces of the two young guards who stood behind him.

'What's all this about, Jack?' asked Claire. The tears welled in her eyes.

He moved forward and touched her arm. 'I . . .' he started. 'Will you be all right? I mean, is there anything that we can . . .?' His voice trailed off. 'We have to go, Claire,' he said finally, and turned.

'Is there anybody that you want us to contact, Mrs Maguire?' Brosnan asked in a low voice as he held the back door of the patrol car open for her.

'No, Chief Superintendent,' she replied calmly. 'I have nothing to say.'

Brosnan closed the door and signalled to Costigan to sit in on the other side. He turned to Daly. 'Nice night for a walk, Guard,' he said. Daly nodded in understanding and turned away. He was no longer needed.

'Guard!' Brosnan called after him. Daly turned. 'Good work yesterday,' he nodded, referring to

Daly's questionnaire, which had placed Seanie Hughes and Tony Kearns in Dunsheerin at the time of the murder.

Daly gave a weak smile. 'Thanks, Chief,' he said, and turned to walk away. 'But I think I'll stick to catching the speeders from now on.'

CHAPTER TWENTY-FIVE

Superintendent Eamon Murray stood with folded arms outside divisional headquarters in the town. He looked upwards with a studious expression as he thought about the question. The local newspaper reporter stood in front of him, notebook open, pen at the ready. Murray looked down at him and gave a knowing smile.

'Well,' he started, 'the whole thing was quite obvious to us from the outset. Naturally, due to the sensitive nature of the investigation, we were not in a position to reveal our methods at the time.'

The reporter looked confused. 'What does that *mean* exactly, Superintendent?' he asked.

Murray gave a condescending shake of his head.

'The investigation of serious crime is a task that requires precision and dedication,' he smiled. 'As well as the utmost secrecy.'

'And of course luck,' the reporter added quickly.

Murray shook his head in admonishment. 'My good man, when it comes to solving the crime of murder, as in this case, which *was* murder, luck does not enter into the equation.' He laughed suddenly. 'You fellas seem to think that we all just plod along waiting for the perpetrator to give himself up. Absolutely not the case, I can assure you.'

The reporter looked down and sighed at the empty page. 'You say that you were in charge of the investigation, is that correct, Superintendent?'

'From this end, yes,' replied Murray. A picture of a red-faced, teeth-grinding Pat Brosnan flashed through his mind. 'Well, no, actually,' he corrected himself. 'When I say from this end, what I mean is emm . . .,' He faltered for a moment. 'As you well know, Chief Superintendent Pat Brosnan is the head of the Murder Squad and as such heads up such investigations. He's done a wonderful job. Just wonderful!'

'So what was your function?'

Murray gave a wry smile. 'Well, far be it from me to steal the thunder. But I was in charge of the co-ordination of personnel.'

The reporter scratched his head with his pen. 'What about this mention of a connection between the murder of John Burns, and Dublin's gangland?'

Murray held his hands up quickly to halt the question. 'I'm sorry but I can make no comment on that. It's *sub judice*, you understand.' He gave the reporter a roguish smile and leaned towards him. 'But, strictly off the record, *se non è vero, è ben trovato*,' he added with a confidential whisper.

He paused for a moment, then continued as a perplexed look appeared on the reporter's face. 'That's Italian for, "If it's not true, then it has been well invented,"' he clarified with a smile.

'Jesus Christ,' the reporter muttered under his breath and flapped the cover closed on the empty page. 'Thank you for the interview, Superintendent,' he said hurriedly and turned to go.

The reporter stopped as he saw the heavily laden patrol car enter through the station gates. It pulled up beside them at the front door. Murray moved forward and opened the passenger door.

'Chief Superintendent,' he smiled nervously. 'Welcome back.'

Brosnan eyed the reporter who was looking through the rear window of the patrol car at the woman and young guard. 'Who's that fella?' he asked abruptly. 'Get rid of him or *I* will,' he ordered.

He waited until Murray had taken the reporter to the main gate of the station, then opened the back door.

'Thank you, Pat,' said Jenny as she stepped out.

Hegarty looked at Brosnan as Jenny walked unaccompanied towards the station door and mouthed 'Pat?' across the roof of the car to him.

Brosnan gave a shake of his head as he turned and followed her inside.

Costigan stood beside Hegarty at the car. 'Is that it so?' he asked in a tone of relief.

Hegarty nodded. 'That's it now, lad,' he replied softly, and moved towards the door.

Inside, the station orderly was completing the record of custody.

'Do you require a solicitor?' he asked.

Jenny smiled at him and shrugged. 'Why should I require one?' she said.

He started to explain. 'It is the right of every arrested person to . . .'

'No!' she snapped, cutting him off. 'I don't want a solicitor, thank you.'

When he had filled out the details and completed the formalities he turned to Brosnan. 'Interview room number three,' he said. 'Down the hall, second on the left.'

Brosnan nodded in understanding and held his hand out. 'Are we ready then, Jenny?' he said. She rose to her feet and gave an indifferent glance as she passed him. She smiled at Hegarty in the hallway. 'Second on the left, Jack,' said Brosnan and turned back to the dayroom.

'So what's going to happen now, Jack?' asked Jenny as he held the door open for her. She chose one of the chairs inside the room and sat down, waiting for him to answer.

'Well,' he started. 'You will be interviewed by the chief.'

'Interviewed,' she laughed. 'You make it sound like I'm looking for a job in the guards.'

'Questioned,' he explained. 'Questioned about the murder of John Burns.'

She pursed her lips and frowned at the floor.

Hegarty closed the door and lowered his voice

to a whisper. 'For Christ's sake, Jenny, will you get a solicitor?' he advised.

She looked up at him and smiled. 'You're a good man, Jack Hegarty,' she said, and shook her head slowly. 'I don't need a solicitor. This whole thing is a big mistake.'

Outside in the dayroom, Brosnan shouted instructions down the phone.

'I want a copy of McCann's statement faxed down. How did the forensics go on Seanie Hughes's clothes and runners?'

He listened as the detective outlined the findings and then clenched his fist in delight.

'That must have been from when he hid the bar on the way back from the scene. Is it a match with John Burns's blood? Right then . . . let me know when the results are back. Good work . . . keep it up. How are the lads getting on with Carroll?'

He listened for a few seconds then grimaced with disappointment. 'Tough bastard all right,' he said. 'Tell them to stick with it. And no mention of deals. Got it?'

He replaced the receiver and drummed his fingers on the desk as he contemplated his approach to Jenny Maguire. His thoughts were interrupted by a tapping noise on the glass hatch at the counter. A distressed Claire Burns beckoned to him.

'I want to see Jenny . . . I want to see her now,' she cried, her voice cracking and rising to a squeal. 'Let her go,' she continued in a frenzy. 'You can't do this.'

By now the tears flowed freely from Claire's eyes. Brosnan walked through the side door and out into the hall. He took her gently by the arm.

'Calm yourself, Mrs Burns,' he said. 'Look, all I can tell you at the moment is that there is evidence to suggest that she was involved in some way.'

Claire wrung her hands together and looked down at them. She wiped a tear away with her sleeve and looked up at Brosnan.

'She had nothing to do with it, I tell you. What possible proof could you have of such a thing? She's my best and only friend.'

Brosnan pursed his lips and sighed. He spoke in a low voice, almost a whisper. 'It seems that she may have arranged for someone to kill your husband,' he explained. 'We have arrested three men in Dublin. The connection points back to Jenny.'

'Just let me speak to her for a few minutes,' she pleaded. 'Surely that's not too much to ask? Just a few minutes.'

Brosnan's face relaxed. He motioned with his hand towards the hall.

'Very well, Mrs Burns. You can see her for a short while.'

He accompanied Claire down the long stark hallway. There was nothing to be heard except the tapping of her heels on the grey tiled floor. Brosnan opened the door and stood back.

Jenny rose quickly from her seat and the two women hugged warmly. Nothing was said between them as they cried into each other's arms.

Brosnan looked at Hegarty and beckoned to him to join him outside. They closed the door quietly on the silent women and walked together up the hall.

'They found a sample of dried blood on the inside of Seanie Hughes's jacket,' said Brosnan, glad to have something to say. 'They're going to see if it matches John Burns's.'

Both men had felt uncomfortable witnessing the scene between the two women. They were embarrassed both by the display of grief and the fact that they were party to its making. The information about Seanie had restored a sense of normality.

'What do you make of what's going on in there?' asked Brosnan, nodding back down the hall.

'Just one friend comforting another, I suppose, Pat,' replied Hegarty in a quiet voice.

In the moment's silence that followed between the two men, a loud voice was audible from the room down the hall.

'But *why*, Jenny . . . *why*?'

Brosnan looked at Hegarty.

'Looks like the friendship is being tested, Jack. Give them a few more minutes before I start the interview. I'm going to have a cup of tea, do you want one?'

Hegarty lit his pipe.

'No thanks, Pat. I'll wait here.'

CHAPTER TWENTY-SIX

Nearly half an hour had passed. Brosnan walked down the hall, followed closely by Hegarty.

'They've had a long enough chat by now, Jack,' he said, grasping at the door handle.

The atmosphere in the room had changed. Gone was the air of grief-stricken panic. In its place, a sense of confidence and understanding pervaded. The two women, their eyes now dry, sat opposite each other holding hands, their knees touching.

Claire stood up. 'Thank you for those few minutes, Chief Superintendent,' she said with a wavering smile.

Brosnan nodded to her as she stood up to leave.

'Get Mrs Burns a cup of tea, Jack,' he said. 'Make sure she's okay.'

Hegarty took Claire gently by the arm and Jenny squeezed her hand as she let her go.

The door was closed. Brosnan removed his jacket and threw it on a nearby chair, then sat down opposite Jenny.

'Before you say anything, I must caution you.'

She threw her eyes up, reached into her coat, which Claire had brought for her, and took her cigarettes out of the pocket. Brosnan advised her of her rights. When he had finished, he sat back.

'Is there anything you'd like to tell me before we start the questioning?' he asked. Jenny smiled and took a long pull on her cigarette. 'I'll tell you everything, Pat,' she said calmly.

Brosnan's jaw fell. Almost immediately he corrected himself and resumed the pose of tough question-master. He reached behind to the chair where his jacket hung and removed his copybook.

She tut-tutted gently. 'If you take out that nice pen I won't tell you anything.'

Brosnan rolled the copybook between his hands for a moment then threw it back on the chair behind him. 'Why the change of heart, Jenny?' he asked. She smiled and blew puffs of smoke above her head. She paused for a moment to look at him, her eyes sparkling.

'I can talk about it now because I feel no guilt. My friendship with Claire is still as strong, if not more so. I am not the guilty one any longer. My guilt died with John Burns. *The truth will set you free,* isn't that the saying, Chief Superintendent?'

Brosnan folded his arms and settled himself in the chair. 'Let's hear it then,' he said.

He listened intently to Jenny as she spoke, recounting her story from the very beginning of her life-long friendship with Claire and how she had stood idly by for years while her best friend was beaten by John Burns. How she had visited her daily and tended her injuries, an icepack here, a strip of plaster there. How she had watched her once happy and carefree friend turn slowly into a defeated shell who had lost the will to live.

She continued for some time, pausing occasionally to drag heavily on her cigarette. Brosnan's heart pounded at the mention of Michael Carroll as she recounted the plan which they drew up together to arrange for the killing of John Burns.

'I couldn't take it any more. Not only was he slowly killing her body, her spirit had started to die as well. It couldn't go on . . . I could not allow it.'

She placed another cigarette in her mouth. Brosnan watched as she fidgeted with her cigarette lighter, her hand shaking. Gently, he took it from her and held the flame steady.

'That's quite a story, Mrs Maguire,' he said calmly. 'Unfortunately there are parts of it which have unanswered questions.'

Jenny shrugged and pulled on her cigarette. 'Like?'

'Well,' Brosnan explained. 'Why did you both go to the station the day of the murder and tell Jack Hegarty that John Burns was beating Claire?'

Jenny looked at him in mock disappointment. 'To throw off the scent of the hunt of course,' she replied. 'That was the way it was planned. I had some job trying to convince Claire, I can tell you. I nearly had to drag her there by the heels.'

'So she knew nothing about it?' he asked. His tone smacked of scepticism.

Jenny shook her head. 'Not a clue,' she said calmly.

'You mean to tell me that you arranged for the killing of your best friend's husband, who was beating her, and never mentioned a word!' said Brosnan incredulously.

'Yes.'

'Now Mrs Maguire, you surely don't expect me . . .'

'Chief Superintendent?'

'Yes, Mrs Maguire?'

'Did you ever take the law into your own hands? I mean did you ever do something which might not be to the letter of the law, but you felt that in the situation your action was warranted?'

Brosnan looked across the table at Jenny.

'I have to point out, Mrs Maguire, that this interview is not about me. Now can you get back to the matter in question, please.'

'But this *is* the matter in question. Please . . . it's important to me to know that you understand my motives.'

Brosnan sat forward in the seat and rested his elbows on his knees.

'Mrs Maguire, there's a very great difference between letting the mother of a young family off a first shoplifting offence and arranging to kill a man.'

Jenny lowered her head. It was obvious that he would not understand.

'It's like I told you, it was him or her. I never told her. Why should I? But it was not long before she realised the implications of his being gone. I'd go so far to say that she was happy . . . there's no crime in that, is there?'

Brosnan ignored the question.

'What about Carroll?' he asked eagerly. 'How did your connection with him come about?'

Jenny laughed. 'Connection! Is that what they call it nowadays? They used to call it sex when I was young.'

Brosnan looked at the floor in embarrassment. 'What I mean is,' he said quietly, 'how did you *meet* Michael Carroll?'

Again she gave him a look of surprise. 'You really haven't done your research, have you, Pat?' she scolded. 'What does my husband do for a living?'

Brosnan shook his head. He did not know.

'He's in the same business as Michael Carroll,' she said, putting him out of his misery. 'The same make of cars actually,' she added. 'I met Michael at a convention in Dublin with my husband. We became friends and . . . well . . . we liked each other.'

She slapped her hands on her thighs. 'Well, Pat, I'm sure you can figure out the rest for yourself,' she smiled.

Brosnan gave a short cough of understanding then sat back and folded his arms. 'Which brings me to my next question,' he said, 'Why would a woman like you be prepared to forfeit everything, her marriage, her life of romance and more importantly, her freedom, to involve herself in the murder of John Burns? To set the whole thing in motion in fact.'

Jenny leaned forward on the chair. 'That should be fairly obvious to you at this stage.'

Brosnan looked puzzled.

'Guilt, Chief Superintendent – it gnaws away at me every day.'

Silence followed as Jenny's voice choked. She cleared her throat and continued.

'Do you have a good friend?' She continued before Brosnan could reply: 'Well, Claire is my best friend . . . and for all those years, I let her down. Do you know, Chief Superintendent, that the greatest sin of all is the sin of silence? *Omertà* I think they call it in the gangster movies. My failure to call a halt to the situation aided and abetted John Burns in the very same way as if I had handed him a big stick with which to beat my best friend. Well, this is one gangster's moll who is prepared to pay the price, if not for Claire, then for my own peace of mind.'

Brosnan was lost for words. He felt like a failed contestant in a television game show entitled 'Follow That'. Looking at this woman he felt both a sense of great admiration for her stoicism and at the same time, a great loathing for the fact that she had been instrumental in the taking of a life.

But still, something niggled at him. There was silence as he took a moment to arrange his thoughts. In his many years of service he had heard it all. The understandable, sometimes crazed justifications of crimes, spouted by all from the murderer to the petty thief. But to be party to a murder to atone for the sin of silence, for a sin of omission? That was a new one on him.

Then again, Jenny was a woman, an intelligent woman at that. He would never assume to fully understand the mystery of the female psyche. Everything ran deeper. It was different with men. Black or white. Case open, case closed.

Furthermore, what she said *was* impressive and undoubtedly came from the heart.

But no. Human nature didn't vary that much. There was more to it. He would make one final effort.

'I believe that there is something that you aren't telling me about all of this, Jenny,' he said.

She stared at him with glazed eyes for a moment, her lips parted as if to speak. Brosnan leaned towards her, willing the words to come. As if snapping out of a daydream, she looked directly into his eyes and slowly shook her head.

'No, Pat. I have nothing more to add,' she said with a faint smile.

His instinct told him that he would get no further. It would be a waste of time to continue. He reached back and took the copybook and began to write. When he was finished, he looked up at her.

'Are you prepared to make a written statement outlining what you have told me?' he asked. He held out the copybook. 'Or perhaps sign to acknowledge that these notes are correct?'

Calmly, she reached forward and lit up a cigarette. Her hand was steady now.

'You must be joking me, Pat,' she smiled and turned her back to him. She spoke to the wall. 'You're the only one who will ever hear what I've said. I'm not guilty *any more*.'

'The truth will set you free, eh, Jenny,' he said standing up.

'Something like that.'

'*Something* like that, is right.'

Brosnan's tone was heavy with insinuation. He stared down at her, determined to make eye contact. He wanted her to know that she hadn't beguiled him. It was his small compensation for the lack of a watertight case. She turned slowly as if obeying his silent need. There was no flinching, no nervous eye movement, nothing that suggested that she had been lying.

Could he be mistaken? he wondered. No one could hold the truth so tight.

He nodded in silence and left the room.

Standing in the hall, he leaned against the wall and lowered his head in thought. In the few minutes that he remained there he recalled what Jenny Maguire had said. *The truth will set you free*. She was right. His own evidence of what she had told him, without a signed statement of admission, might not be sufficient. Carroll, he knew, would never give her up. Carroll would remain silent and let the chips fall as they might. McCann's statement as a co-conspirator would serve little purpose in her case. All he had was a name. Still, he was satisfied.

The station-orderly rounded the corner and held out a handful of fax sheets. 'For you, Chief,' he said. 'From Dublin.'

'Thank you,' murmured Brosnan and took them.

He glanced down when the station-orderly was gone. 'Statement of Liam McCann . . .' He smiled to himself as he crushed the paper in a ball and placed it in his pocket.

When he looked up, he became aware of Hegarty and Claire at the end of the corridor. Claire looked frail, sitting there wringing her hands. He walked towards them and stopped to look down at her pale, frightened face. He extended his hand down to her. She took it and stood up.

He squeezed her hand gently and placed his other hand on her shoulder. The tears rolled from her cheeks and landed on the sleeve of her coat. He withdrew his hand gently.

'Everything will be all right now, Mrs Burns,' he said with an understanding nod.

'What will happen to my friend?' she asked, looking up at him.

Brosnan wished that there was another way to answer the question without sounding like an executioner. But there wasn't.

'She will be charged and will appear before a special sitting of the local court. And she will be released on bail pending the date of the trial.'

Claire nodded once in response and moved slowly towards the door.

The wrought iron gate groaned open. She breathed deeply as she stepped inside. The eerie stillness unnerved her, yet the crunching of her heels on the pebbled pathway gave her comfort in the silence of the late summer's evening. She drew her cardigan tightly around her shoulders, glad now that she had brought it to ward off the late chill. She knew where she had to go. Nine rows down, fourth grave on the left. She walked with purpose past the towering Celtic crosses, the names of long forgotten parish priests and canons, by now illegible from moss and harsh winters.

Was it really only six months since, arm in arm with her best friend, she had led the slow procession of black umbrellas that sheltered the mourners from the soft summer rain, up the very same path? It seemed much longer. Then again, so much had happened.

She stopped at the graveside, folded her arms and looked down. The mound of heavy clay had sunk and was by now almost in line with the freshly mown grass around it. An open-plan plot. How John would have hated that. Sharing the services of a ride-on lawnmower with his neighbours, no limestone kerbing or high walls to keep out the riff-raff.

Although she knew that something would be put up in time to mark his passing, his present state of anonymity pleased her.

'Bastard.'

Immediately she admonished herself. That was not the purpose of her coming. He would not bring out the worst in her. In death he was to be denied that power. He had taken so much from her already and now, as he lay in the settling grave, she needed to tell him that.

Jenny clasped her hands in front of her and lowered her head as if in prayer. She winced back the tears as she recalled that night. The rhythmic grunting amidst the rustling of the taffeta dress she had spent so many evenings making with her mother. Her low pleadings ignored. The sounds of music and laughter coming from the open rear door of the hotel function-room. The smell of newly mown grass and the searing pain. Finally the 'gotcha' wink from the young John Burns before he stood up and quickly fastened the fly of his dress suit. 'I needed that,' he had leered. 'The lads were right. You're a real little tease.'

As she watched him making his way back into the hotel, she had remained on the ground, trying desperately to tie up the torn shoulder-strap of her dress. The music had started up again.

'C'mon girls,' shouted the band-leader. 'Don't let the convent down.'

Jenny was engulfed by a sea of guilt and shame after the rape. Now, her pretty debutante's dress seemed cheap and sordid, and she would have gladly ripped it off to rid her of his smell.

She didn't. Instead, she made her way back inside where she was swept up in a frenzied 'Siege of Ennis'.

Jenny opened her eyes and glanced furtively around the graveyard before turning back to the grave.

'I want you to know,' she began in a low voice, 'that I did what I did for Claire, not for myself. I would not be worth such an action. The life I have led is proof of that. But Claire . . . she's different . . . good . . . not like us.'

She swallowed hard, fighting the tears back, determined now to have her say.

'You deserved to die,' she continued in a shaky whisper. 'Because every day you lived, you damaged a good woman. And I could not let it go on. What you did to me when we were young just made the decision to kill you that much easier.'

She stood for a moment staring at the grave in the dusky silence, and noticed a short clump of thistle, its prickly green foliage forcing its way up from between the mouldering wreaths. Without thinking, she bent down and withdrew it gently from the soil. As she stood upright, she was overcome with a sense of calm. She did not understand why, but it seemed that in doing this simple task that a burden had been lifted.

Her trial in the Central Criminal Court was to begin in a week's time. She would be pleading not guilty. Whatever the outcome, she was satisfied that she had done the right thing.

She looked down at the grave and then turned to go. It was getting late. Her husband would be waiting.

CHAPTER TWENTY-SEVEN

Jack Hegarty sat back in the hush of the Monday morning silence in the day room of Dunsheerin station. Seven weeks had passed since the final trial of the case at the Central Criminal Court. He pulled open the table drawer and threw the folder of tabloid cuttings down in front of him. He knew every word of the articles by now, he had scanned the pages so often in the past few weeks.

'Guilty – Crimelord and gang members get life.'

The photographs of a smartly-dressed Carroll being led down the steps. Seanie Hughes and Liam McCann handcuffed to indifferent prison officers. One of Seanie giving the two fingers, standing at the sliding door of the paddy-wagon.

He lifted the page to the separate trial of Jenny Maguire.

'Widow's friend not guilty – Jury unanimous.'

A photograph of Jenny and her husband smiling beside the tall pillars of the court, arms locked together.

The clippings underneath were beginning to yellow with age.

'A Community Mourns.'

The black and white photograph of John Burn's coffin being carried out of the local church by a few locals, followed by Jenny and Claire dressed in black, Bill Jennings with a paternal arm on the widow's shoulder.

Hegarty sat back and pensively filled his pipe.

The trials had gone on for almost three months in total. The only light moment came when eleven-year-old Healy had pointed a confident and accusing finger at Hughes and declared, 'That's him . . . that's the fella who called me a little bollocks!'

His evidence was merely to prove that Seanie had been in the area at the time, but young Healy had needed no encouragement.

The jury had taken just two hours to decide their fate.

Jenny's trial had lasted six days. The jury had taken just forty-five minutes to agree with her plea of not guilty. Hegarty, who had sat beside Brosnan for both trials, sensed the chief nodding to himself in acceptance when the verdict was read out.

'Coming for a drink, Jack?' he asked as he rose to his feet.

After a brandy and a cigar, they had taken a stroll along the city quay towards the railway station. When they reached the bridge, they stopped, leaning over it and looking into the river below.

'Well, you said that she'd be found not guilty and you were right,' said Hegarty.

A moment's silence followed.

'Yes, Jack, I knew,' said Brosnan. 'It came as no surprise. Sometimes, motive and unsigned admissions just aren't enough to convince a jury. I gave them the full account of what she told me, but we just didn't have enough evidence of the connection.' He snorted a laugh and shook his head. 'I never thought I'd hear myself say this, but you have to hand it to Carroll. When he said, "I've never seen this woman before in my life," I knew we were shagged. Did you see the way the jury looked at one another?'

Hegarty nodded his head and said nothing for a moment. Then he pushed himself back from the wall and extended his hand to Brosnan.

'Good luck to you, Pat, and enjoy the retirement. My only wish is that you draw at least thirty years off them.'

Brosnan laughed as he took the other man's hand and shook it firmly.

'You're no spring chicken yourself, Jack. I wouldn't wait too long to dust off the golf clubs if I were you.'

'Not yet, boyo. There's life in the old dog yet.' Hegarty smiled. 'Well, I better get going. Time to leave the big smoke and get back to roaming cattle and broken bicycle lamps. Be sure and give me a call now.'

Brosnan watched his old friend turn and walk across the bridge in the direction of the railway station. He promised himself he'd visit Hegarty the following summer. He would miss his company.

Hegarty closed the folder and threw it back in the drawer. He stood up, stretched himself and made his way slowly towards the front door and out to the gate of the station. Sitting down on the low wall, he glanced up and down the quiet street. The murder and all the events surrounding it seemed a distant memory to him. Indeed the whole thing had an unreal quality about it, so peaceful was the village now.

His thoughts were interrupted by the sound of a blowing car-horn and he looked up to see the green post office van approach. It swerved over towards the path and pulled in beside him. The young postman wound down the window and smiled out at him.

'Well, Guard Hegarty, how's the body?' he said.

'You'll be a *body* if you keep driving like that,' Hegarty grinned back. 'Well, what have you for me?'

The postman rummaged in the passenger seat for a moment, then handed out a bundle tied with white string. 'More top secret stuff, Jack,' he joked. 'By the way,' he continued. 'There's a shocking amount of cattle on the road at the foot of the hill. I'd say they're ould Dan's, 'cos they look like they haven't seen grass in months.'

Hegarty struggled with the knot on the post as

he replied. 'I'll let them have a feed from the long acre for a while so, before I hunt them back in.'

'Only right too,' agreed the young man, and drove away.

Hegarty placed the string in his pocket and flicked through the envelopes. He paused at the election leaflet and smiled. 'Bill Jennings – Man on a Mission' was the caption. Underneath this promise, a photograph of the councillor with an expression of impending doom, pointing to a huge pothole with one hand, the other hand resting on the shoulder of a small child on a bike.

'Eejit', muttered Hegarty, as he balled the leaflet in his fist and dropped it inside the low wall.

He held up the tightly bound, small parcel which was addressed to him, and placed the remainder of the post on the capping of the wall. He removed the wrapping and peeled off the greeting card that had been sellotaped to the front of the small notebook. The message simply read:

Dear Jack,

I found this in my pocket the other day. It must have fallen in there when I was in the hospital for the identification of John Burns. As your Super told me that there was nothing of evidential value in it anyway, I think that you should have it as a souvenir.

Keep in touch.
Your friend always,
Pat

Hegarty thumbed through the pages of the notebook. There was nothing but weights and dates.

He flicked to the last couple of pages which had been written crudely in pencil, and read through them. 'June 6th – 12lbs 3oz.' 'June 7th – 8lbs 6oz.' 'June 12th 10lbs 7oz.'

His eyes widened as they fixed on the final entry. 'June 12th – threatened with violence by Garda Jack Hegarty.'

He closed the notebook and held it between his two palms.

'You may lose touch, but you never forget,' he thought to himself.

His thoughts were interrupted by a shout from Big Madge, who was struggling towards him, her hand held aloft as if demanding that he stay where he was.

He quickly placed the notebook in the top pocket of his shirt.

'Jack Hegarty, the very man!' she puffed as she neared him. 'Is there any chance that we can stay open a bit later tonight? For an extra hour, say?'

She stood in front of him and folded her arms, panting as she waited for an answer.

Hegarty eyed her with suspicion.

'Why, Madge? What occasion could be so important that it requires porter during prohibited hours?'

Big Madge looked down at the ground, then threw her eyes up to heaven and spoke in an embarrassed whisper.

'It's Quilter's birthday,' she sighed. 'I always put up a pint and a few sandwiches for himself and Myles Hickey. They're my best customers, you know.'

Hegarty looked down at his shoes and rubbed them in turn on the calves of his trousers.

'You don't have to tell me that, Madge,' he said sternly.

Madge was disappointed by his tone.

'And by the way, Madge . . .' continued Hegarty, 'would these sandwiches you're supplying be of the same sell-by-date sandwiches that resulted in a ten per cent decrease in the manpower of An Garda Síochána last year?'

Madge dropped her hands to her side as if preparing for a fight.

He laughed as he continued: 'Daly in the Traffic Corps reckons that one of those ham sandwiches of yours will cause the same weight loss as an internal sworn inquiry.'

'What's that supposed to mean, Jack?' asked Madge, moving closer.

'Well . . . he reckons that after either of them, a man would spend the next two weeks shitting in his trousers.'

He leaned back on the wall and laughed loudly.

Big Madge tried to keep her serious face, but Hegarty's laugh was too contagious. She punched him hard on the shoulder and snorted a laugh.

'You're an awful tramp, Jack Hegarty.'

The laughter died down and she stood, waiting for an answer to her request.

'Fair enough, Madge,' he said. Then he raised a cautionary finger. 'But warn them that I'll be on the lookout for any drunken eejits who might be thinking of a visit to the convent.'

'Thanks, Jack. Right you are. I'll tell them.'

Her business done, Madge turned on her heels and made her way hurriedly down to the pub.

Hegarty stood up from the wall and rubbed the flakes of loose whitewash from the seat of his trousers. He glanced up and down, giving the village street a final check, then took the remaining envelopes from the wall and patted gently at his shirt pocket.

He smiled to himself as he made his way inside. 'A birthday party for Quilter,' he laughed, and closed the door behind him.

Literary Fiction from Town House

Fergus Linehan

Under the Durian Tree
'Poignantly engaging and expertly executed' *Books Ireland*
Paperback IR£5.95

The Safest Place
'Gripping and well paced' *Sunday Tribune*
'A sure if quiet triumph' *Books Ireland*
'Absorbing' *The Irish Times*
Paperback IR£7.99

Marian O'Neill

Miss Harrie Elliot
'... hugely accomplished ... this novel has [high]
aspirations and it fulfils them' *Sunday Tribune*
'... a fascinating first novel ... Irish fiction has gained
a distinctive new voice that may well transcend
fashion' *The Irish Times*
'... beautifully written ... as first novels go [it]
beggars belief' *Irish Independent*
Paperback IR£7.99

Fiction from Town House

☐	A PLACE OF STONES	Deirdre Purcell	IR£6.99
☐	THAT CHILDHOOD COUNTRY	Deirdre Purcell	IR£6.99
☐	SKY	Deirdre Purcell	IR£5.99
☐	FRANCEY	Deirdre Purcell	IR£6.99
☐	FALLING FOR A DANCER	Deirdre Purcell	IR£6.99
☐	LOVE LIKE HATE ADORE	Deirdre Purcell	IR£6.99
☐	KIMBAY	Rose Doyle	IR£4.99
☐	ALVA	Rose Doyle	IR£5.99
☐	PERFECTLY NATURAL	Rose Doyle	IR£5.99
☐	THE SHADOW PLAYER	Rose Doyle	IR£6.99
☐	MARY, MARY	Julie Parsons	IR£6.99
☐	THE COURTSHIP GIFT	Julie Parsons	IR£6.99
☐	UNDER THE DURIAN TREE	Fergus Linehan	IR£5.95
☐	THE SAFEST PLACE	Fergus Linehan	IR£7.99
☐	MISS HARRIE ELLIOT	Marian O'Neill	IR£7.99
☐	HUSH, HUSH	Gabrielle Mullarkey	IR£6.99

- All Town House books are available through mail order or from your local bookshop.
- For a full list of Town House titles please send away for our catalogue at the address below.
- To order any of the above, please make your cheque/banker's.draft payable to THCH LTD.
- Visa/Mastercard also accepted.

☐☐☐☐☐☐☐☐☐☐☐☐☐☐☐☐

Expiry Date:_____ Signature:_____

Please allow 70 pence/book for post & packing Ireland. Overseas customers please allow £1.00 per copy for post & packing.

ALL ORDERS TO:
Town House and Country House, Books by Post, Trinity House, Charleston Road, Ranelagh, Dublin 6.

NAME: _____

ADDRESS _____

_____

_____

Please allow 28 days for delivery. Prices and availability subject to change without notice. You may also order at *books@townhouse.ie* (T)+353 1 4972399; (F) +353 1 4970927.